I0598042

The Cursed

A WITCH IN TIME

L.A. KENNEDY

A WITCH IN TIME

Dedication

To Jamie Rose. You're more than an editor.
Thank you for helping me bring this world together.

"The devil's finest trick is to persuade you that he does not exist."
— Charles Baudelaire

Chapter One

Nothing lights a fire and warms the soul quite like the need for revenge. Both bitter and sweet, it powered man and monster alike. It raised nations and crumbled entire cities in one gulp. And a witch hellbent on getting justice, no matter the cost, was something entire civilizations had feared throughout history. It was no wonder witches were hunted to the ends of the earth some three hundred years ago. An angry, vengeful witch always left a trail of dead bodies and beheaded chickens in their wake, and I was devilishly enraged, looking up bulk chicken purchases. My soul twisted with regret, retribution and reasons hell would be worth the trip, sooner rather than later. Cisco, my friend, dead and dumped without a head, would be worth sitting in a cage in the pits. Innocents being tied down for the slaughter would be worth flaying my soul over and over. I'd done it once already. I could do it again. What better way to slide into hell than covered in the blood of my enemies? Justice, revenge...same difference, same outcome. But this time, I wouldn't go to hell alone. I'd drag those evil and deserving bitches with me.

Shakespeare got it right. Hell was empty, and all the devils were here. I'd met the worst of them since stepping foot off the plane in Mexico. The lowest, most vile monsters of them all...humans. Hell — the original social experiment, the creator of Stockholm Syndrome, the maker of gambling and addiction, the reason mothers drowned their children with a smile, the patient holder of nightmares — had nothing on the dark side of humanity, and I got a front row ticket to the dark underbelly in Mexico. Every single day since leaving Van had been one ongoing nightmare that only I had the power to stop, if I were willing to pay the price of ending it. When the total at the bottom of the bill was one soul, it tended to make a witch take pause and make sure it was worth it. There were no refunds. I couldn't change my mind later. Hell didn't work that way. *Nothing* really worked that way.

My vacation had gone from painful to bad, to worse and finally turned into another trip through hell, only this one took parts of my soul that I'd never get back — pieces that kept my mind from thinking up ways to kill those responsible for the deaths of many and the torture of my friend in the worst possible of ways. But those parts were gone now, and I was an awfully creative witch when I was pissed off. At least my first stint in the pit only left me with a broken soul, not chunks pissed down the drain. Sure, it was smashed to bits, but all the pieces were still there, last I looked. They just needed to be reglued every now and again. Mexico, on the other hand, stole from me, and I'd never see those shards of my soul again. Soon, there'd be nothing left to keep me from knocking on the door of those to blame, reminding them of why they *never* should have taken someone I cared about. They *never* should have pinched from a witch. There was a reason not many sane people meddled with full-blooded witches. Our vengeance was long-lasting and cursed the line of those who scorned us. Generations would feel the mistake of one fool, long dead, in an unmarked grave. Just ask any parent of a ginger child. That curse was still alive and well...and a bright red beacon that told the rest of the world that one of their ancestors had pissed off the wrong person.

After owing a favor and getting on a plane to pay it off, things had gone downhill faster than the fall from grace that had opened the pit, and each day passing had got worse and worse. My grandmother had once said I was a magnet for trouble. I couldn't argue that point, not with scabs on my arms, dried tears on my face and a death sentence with my name on it. I wasn't just a magnet. I called it from the rooftops into my waiting arms every chance I got. I danced with the devils, then cried when my feet hurt and my soul was a few ounces lighter. I learned nothing the easy way, and coming to Mexico was a lesson I'd likely die before learning.

Discovering the lie of a lifetime, being attacked by what I had once thought was folklore and signing up for the 'you-might-die-on-the-next-full-moon' club was all just the tip of the iceberg, the start of a very deep fall into misery. Because those twenty-four hours weren't rough enough, I tempted fate by thinking it couldn't get any worse. *Foolish little witch. Things can always get worse, with or without a pulse.* I had been eating dinner in a five-diamond resort in sunny Mexico, after having been mauled by a Lycan when my point was proven. It was the first real meal since landing, and with fresh bandages covering claw marks on my arm, I had watched my friend Cisco suffer a cruel death because I was too scared to leave with two witches. Leaving would have meant that he and I would have both died together. I hadn't even tried to save his life. I hadn't asked. I hadn't bargained. I hadn't begged. I'd sat back and watched his ending play over the screen of a small black tablet. A Lycan, a man, an officer of the law, a son, a soon-to-be marine biologist, had been gone in an instant. His life had flashed across a screen, and the fate of two witches had been sealed in a five-minute livestream. They were dead witches walking. I just hadn't kicked the dirt over their bodies yet.

The two witches had taken a seat at my table and slid a tablet toward me, one witch bleeding because of it. For however short the witch's life would be, I hoped every time she flexed her hand, she remembered the moment I'd stabbed her. On the screen, Cisco had sat tied to a chair, swollen and bloodied. His smile would stay with me forever. His cut lips and broken teeth had been something made of nightmares, but somehow, it made him look braver. The stone room he had been held in was built for torture and looked like it had seen the end of many lives before Cisco's had come to a sudden halt.

His last words were a warning. As he looked his death in the eyes, he still tried to save me. "You were right all along. Don't come. These bloodsuckers…"

And with that final warning, his life had been taken. He had been calm and hadn't fought the knife at his throat. I had been his witness. I had been the last friend to see him alive, and as awful as it had been, I was thankful he had someone who cared about him with him in those final moments. I'd remember every detail with perfect clarity, whether I wanted to or not. The brain never lets go of such things. It would stain my soul until I brought those responsible to their shallow and unmarked graves. Nothing I would ever see or hear would compare to the moment Cisco had died. I'd closed my eyes for the finality of it. Watching someone have their head removed would have destroyed my mind and soul, and I was barely holding onto my tattered soul as it was. To have watched would have meant I'd lose my death grip on my morality. It would have been the final nail in my coffin and theirs. I'd have done things that would send me to hell faster than I was already chugging along.

I'd warned the witches as they'd sat across from me. I'd told them to kill me then or risk looking over their shoulders for the rest of their short lives. I would kill them both, sooner or later. My threats weren't idle. Like demons, I had a lasting memory and would wait it out until the opportunity arose. I'd do everything in my power to end them and their reign of terror. If I had to pry open hell to get my revenge, so be it. What they had done to innocents and my friend would not go unpunished. Hanging, drowning or burning, I didn't care how they chose to die, but they'd taste death before I returned home—on that I promised. I was pretty sure I'd taste my own death as well, but the price for revenge was steep, and I was prepared to pay. I might as well get something good out of this vacation.

Instead of listening to me, they'd threatened to take more innocents. Others would die in my place until I willingly helped them. They'd left me to my dinner and the misery of what I had just seen. Once the rage had settled, I had to tell Miguel about Cisco, and that hurt almost as much as why I had to make the call. Hearing the pain in Miguel's voice crushed me. Cisco had been Miguel's to protect, a member of his Pack, and had been mine to befriend. The pain of it all had rolled from my heart and soul, ending with me in the arms of the only person I had ever loved...Miguel. He had come, as he always did when my soul was torn apart. Like the first time he'd shown up, he'd done his best to put the pieces back together and held me until I could help hold myself up on my own. He had never been my knight in shining armor. He was my wolf with claws and teeth, and I would never doubt again what he would do to protect me.

Two bodies had been found dumped at a local clinic. Although their tags had been pinned to their chests — Cisco and his patrol partner for the day, Martins — the news had reported two unnamed officers dead at the hands of the cartels. They were just another statistic in the war on drugs. They were withholding Cisco and Martin's names until notification could be given to the families. The general public would never know who killed them or why. Cisco deserved better than that. He had earned the truth with his own blood, but the truth would never be told. If I were to tell the world of his bravery, it would end my life faster than this nightmare could play out. The Lycan secret would remain as such, even if it meant Cisco would be just another dead cop.

Even though I knew some secrets were worth keeping, it still bothered me to watch the reporter talk about Cisco as though he were nothing more than a number on someone's scorecard. He was a decorated officer, a protective Lycan. He'd fought for the lives of those who would never know his name. He had been worth more than being a pawn in the witch's game. He was supposed to spend his life in the water, saving the parts of the world he loved. Cisco was a friend, someone who protected others to his very death. He wasn't just another number. His body had been found dumped on the roadside of a clinic like garbage. I didn't know what angered me more — his body thrown away, his life reduced to a five-minute news report or that no one would ever know of his sacrifices and his utter devotion to mankind.

All of it made me dig my heels in deeper. The bad guys would pay. They had to. That's how things were supposed to work. Good guys win, and bad guys get punished. If I didn't believe that, what was the point of any of this? If I didn't want justice for those who died, wouldn't I be one of the bad guys myself? Or was that what made me just another vindictive monster? Did I really care one way or the other? If my revenge killed them all and I damned myself in return, it didn't really change the outcome of my life. I was going to hell, no matter what. When I left the first time, they'd marked me with a return order. A counted soul is a counted soul, so no, I guess I didn't care — at least, not as much as I once had and not as much as I probably should. *Shoulda, coulda, woulda.* I'll save the worrying for my damned soul for when I was back home, safe and still had a life to worry about. If I didn't make it home, the worrying wasn't going to help me get out of where I was going, so why waste time on it?

Of everything Mexico has taught me, the one thing I was absolutely certain of was that I'd never be whole again, not after coming here. I'm changed, stained and tarnished by too much pain and heartache. Could a person lose their humanity in a single moment? Could you get it back once it was gone? Was my humanity, what made me the human I claimed to be, lost for good, dumped on the side of the road like trash with Cisco? I didn't feel particularly human right now. I think I craved payback far too much to feel anything else, and that included my soul, my mortality, the little voice inside of me that told me killing was bad. If I could ignore a monster in the corner of a room, I could ignore my wildly spinning moral compass for a few more days, couldn't I?

The only thing that kept me on this side of the crust for this long was my grip on my humanity. What a waste it would be if I let go. All that suffering for nothing, for it to be taken from me by second-rate kitchen witches. I had fought to be called human my entire life, that being a witch didn't make me one of the bad guys. But I couldn't fully hold onto that argument for much longer. I wouldn't be human once I lost what made me one, when I crossed the line to punish those deserving of it. It should have bothered me more. But right now, I needed to be the bigger monster — bigger and badder. I couldn't be weighed down by any emotion that could break me. Monsters didn't have room for love of anything other than wicked things, and I was about to unleash the beast within that hungered for vengeance. Revenge, something I considered to be a much-belied concept, made sense now. It felt right, and it gnawed on me like a starved rat. This time, I would feed it. I would let it gorge until it puked. It was the only way to win. I understood perfectly how an otherwise kind and loving person could become a monster and need to be hunted down. A soul could only take so much, and mine was done fucking around.

I sat on my bed in a hotel I hadn't seen much of and picked through a file from the local Pack Leader, Caser, and the police reports from Miguel with a determined eye. No detail was too small. Ordinarily, I came into the game late. The bodies were gone and picked apart for the second time by the medical examiner. This time, I was on the scene before the bodies grew colder than the stones they were found on. Although I wasn't a detective or a crime scene analyst, I knew evil. I knew monsters. I knew them better than most. We can't be good at everything, but the one thing I was good at made me more valuable than I wanted to be. Going to hell for two long minutes, lifetimes for a soul, had left me tainted and allowed me to see the world for what it truly was—a sunnier version of hell with parking tickets and taxes.

I flicked through the pages and photos of horror and death, last moments frozen in time. I couldn't shake the feeling in my gut that I had missed something, but I couldn't quite figure it out. But that was the thing about looking at evil. The devil was in the details. I kept going back to the same group of photos. I compared them to each other. Each victim was roughly the same height and size as the other, but they were too different in appearance to think there was a preferred brand of victim. Most serial killers had a specific type of victim—twenty-eight, blonde with blue eyes, size thirty-two hips. They were particular with who they selected, down to the details no one else would notice but them. But with these victims, aside from Lycan blood and living a somewhat humble life, they shared nothing more. Like most of their community, they went to church, were unmarried virgins, led normal lives outside of turning furry and shopped at various local markets. Like the tune of a favorite song that I couldn't remember the lyrics to, it sat on the tip of my tongue. I just couldn't put my finger on it.

I went back to the notes I had made on my laptop, reading and rereading every detail about where they'd gone missing, when they'd last been seen, who'd last seen them, every physical attribute, right down to the size of their shoes. I made myself another coffee and rubbed my eyes. There was something. There was *always* something. But I was missing it. I was either too tired to see it, too emotionally invested or my mind had seen enough and simply refused to help me traumatize myself more. But I wasn't a 'call-it-quits' kind of witch.

Rather than give up, I called Samuel. A live video feed on my laptop filled my screen. Sure, it was against the rules to share information, but if it got the job done, I'd break more than a few rules. I'd go for kneecaps. It wouldn't be the first time Samuel had helped me pick through a case. He'd seen worse. Even if he had virgin eyes, I'd have scarred him willingly. A few bad dreams were worth saving a life. The moment he answered, I went straight to it. Time wasn't a luxury I had. And just as he did, every other time I consulted with him, he pulled out a pad and pen to take notes while I showed him every scrap of paper in the file. I didn't hold anything back. From the lack of surprise and questions, he knew about the unmentionable Lycan. I was thankful there wasn't a need to keep Pack's secret a secret from him. It would have limited our conversation and the ability to find what I couldn't see or think of.

I wondered for a moment while Samuel took notes. If he didn't know, would I have risked his life with the knowledge of Pack to save more lives? It was Samuel, the closest friend I've ever had. He was like family to me, and the only family I had left. If I were being honest, I'd have watched more die before I willingly served him up on a silver platter. But from his nods and murmurs, I wasn't telling him anything he didn't already know.

Showing Samuel each page didn't stir so much as a flinch in me. The photos and reports didn't bother me as much anymore. I had gone through the files enough times that the blood didn't look as brilliant. The bodies were just bodies. They weren't people. They were nothing more than a book read too many times. It didn't carry the same weight as the first few glances and would never be as bad as seeing it all firsthand. Samuel didn't recoil a single time. It made me sad for him to know he had seen so much over his lifetimes that horror like this didn't faze him.

"What's going on, Ailis?" Samuel stopped the show. "Something, not just this, is bothering you. Spit it out. I can't focus on your crime scene when I'm worried about you. You're off—and don't tell me it's these crimes."

I groaned. "I think you already know. It's Miguel. It's always Miguel."

"What did he do this time?" Samuel asked, making me smile at how protective he was of me. Whenever I felt completely alone in the world, one call to Samuel changed my mind. "I'm guessing it isn't as bad as what he did to drive you away, since you're still there."

"Oh, it's bad...life or death kind of bad. Miguel and I are going to have some serious words when this nightmare is over. He held back a secret that kills," I replied, and Samuel nodded, fully understanding the secret I was referring to. "But that's oddly not why I'm upset. I mean, it pisses me off, but that's not what's bugging me." I released a deep breath, knowing I had to say something or Samuel would never drop it. "Miguel was here, and things got pretty heated, as they always do between us—not the usual hot-headed tempers flaring, but...the touchy-feely kind of heat."

"And?" He raised his one eyebrow.

"And? And, Samuel, it's complicated," I answered. I felt awkward talking to him about my love life. Another glance from Samuel and I groaned. "At first, he was a good distraction. And now it's more."

"What's wrong with more?" he asked.

"For starters, *more* comes with fur and claws and an entire group of people who are calling for me to head for the hills and not look back," I replied. "If I don't back down, I don't have a good feeling about my next little chat with them."

"You two are foolish in love. The sooner you both realize this, the easier your lives will be." Samuel smiled.

"I don't think that's an option," I replied. "They're pretty keen on him finding a nice little furry lady and settling down, spitting out a pack of pups of their own. How the hell do I go up against that? Love or no love, I don't want to die to keep sleeping with a guy."

"I doubt his people will knock on your door if you choose to be with him. They'd have come for you a decade ago if you were easy to pick off. But you're not, and neither is Miguel. Together, you are not worth the devastation you both would bring if one of you was under threat," he answered. He looked more confident than I felt. "That isn't the kind of love you just throw away."

"I never said I didn't love him. But it takes more than love for a relationship to work, Samuel." I countered.

"No, it doesn't. Sometimes love is all you have and all you need. In a world like ours, love is mighty precious."

"I don't want to die for a date," I answered and squirmed a little. Samuel was a brilliant man, but sometimes I think he forgets what dating and relationships are like. "It's complicated, and those complications aren't in this file tonight. When this is over, I'm all ears." I lied. I wouldn't be.

"Be a fool, then...a lonely fool in love. If you both want it badly enough, you will find a way around the oath of silence and demands of a leader with an ego. Caser will either bend to the will of Miguel or will die at Miguel's hands when he protects you. Miguel has never killed easily, but any threat toward you and he wouldn't second guess what he had to do. It would come as naturally to him as the sun to the sky. The Pack would stand with Miguel, and through him, they will protect you," he answered. I huffed a laugh. Samuel knew much more than I thought he did. It didn't surprise me. He seemed to know a bit about everything. I would, too, if I had a few centuries on him. "If you don't find a way, it will hurt you for all your days. Your emotional pain makes you weaker and a bigger target. But, if this is what you want, you'll learn the hard way. But don't say I didn't warn you."

"It's the only way a person truly learns, isn't it? The hard way? Whatever the case, it's mine to learn and yours to keep your nose out of." I was firm on that, and he nodded. "I have too much on my plate at the moment. My love life takes the bottom of the list. I'll circle back when I'm not shoveling shit."

"Eloquent as always, Ailis. Very well. Should I bother asking you about the fresh bandages covering your arms?" Samuel asked, and I cringed. "Was that how your last conversation with Caser and his people went?"

"I wasn't kidding when I said I wasn't looking forward to another talk with them," I replied.

"When?"

I looked at the clock. "About twenty or so hours ago."

"Let me see the damage," he said. I pulled off one of the bandages and turned my arm for Samuel to see. "I've seen much worse, where meat hung in strips. Do you have holy water?"

"Never travel without it," I answered. "I have five bottles."

"Clean it with holy water, every drop you brought. It's going to hurt like hell, but it'll help flush the curse from your system," he answered. "Save a bottle to drink. If it doesn't feel like you're being boiled alive, you will need to find holy ground and take a nice long bath in holy water."

"Curse? An infection or virus isn't a curse."

He shook his head. "Let's not pretend we both don't know what attacked you, Ailis. Let's skip the parts where we both deny knowledge of what clawed you up. It'll save us time. Open the wounds and pour holy water into them. I've seen a man ripped to shreds and bathed in a tub of holy water. It was a painful experience for the young lad. He lost consciousness twice, but he never met his cursed fate."

"Maybe he didn't have the virus, and you tortured him for no reason," I said with raised eyebrows and a dash of judgment in my voice.

"If he had no virus, as you call it, it would not have hurt him so. Holy water doesn't burn like bathing in the pits of hell if you don't have any hell in your system to cleanse. The pain comes from cleaning the curse from your soul. Purifying a soul is painful business," Samuel countered. "It is the same with a vampire's bite. It must be cleaned within twenty-four hours to wash the curse from the victim's body. If it doesn't hurt at all, it is too late."

"Are you speaking from experience?" I asked.

He nodded. "I will say no more on the subject. Some secrets are not yours to have, and some memories I do not wish to speak of."

"For once, I'm not going to push. The last secret I learned landed me in the middle of a species I didn't even know about," I replied and glanced at my arms. "Are you sure about the holy water? It sounds like a lot of pain that could be for nothing."

"You will do what you want to you, but don't let your stubbornness seal your fate. I'd hate to stand over your grave and know you could have been saved with something as simple as water and a bit of pain."

"I won't have a grave, Samuel. You'll never find my body," I answered and finally grumbled in agreement. "Okay, I'll do it. This is going to hurt so bad."

"Deliverance is never pleasant. Everything has a price. Shall we continue?" he asked and dropped it.

We went back to the case. He knew when I had heard enough. If he pushed again, I would argue instead of listening, and it would be for nothing. I hated being told what to do, more so when what I was told was something I didn't want to do. Pain is funny like that. We could be given the best advice on this side of God's door, and we'd ignore it because it was going to hurt. Needling me on it wasn't going to move me toward what I should do. It would do the opposite. Those who knew me knew when to leave it alone and let it sink in.

"Thanks, Samuel. I do appreciate your insights. It's just hard to swallow sometimes," I replied. I turned back to the case. "Okay, back to the current nightmare. Why these women?"

"If we take out their commonalities, size, jobs and personality, what do we have left?" he asked, and I shrugged. "The question isn't so much why these women. It's too late for them. They're already dead. We need to ask who the next victims will be. We can talk for hours about why the previous victims were selected and come up with little to no useful information we don't already know. But you'll have a better chance at catching those responsible or saving others if you know who will be next and why."

"Well, they're all Pack. It makes sense that'll be who the next victims are," I answered and skipped the secrecy. I doubted anyone would knock on Samuel's door, not unless they had already made peace with their deaths. He hasn't lived this long with the secrets of the darkness and not be one scary man to mess with. "How the hell do we narrow down which ones are the targets?"

"The previous victims wouldn't be missed by anyone important, Ailis. They weren't really a loss. That's what they all have in common. The weaker are being taken, and that's who will go next. They're the easiest to pick off. Compared to the Alphas, lowly wolves are untrained. They lack control and skill. If I were hunting Lycan, that's who I'd take out first," Samuel said after ten minutes of silence to review his notes. "Think about it. Sure, those who have gone missing, their disappearances were noticed. Their crime scenes weren't lost or brushed off as another gang causality. But what loss would they really be? They weren't anyone special in terms of Pack community. If an Alpha or leader were to die a grizzly death, their ending would bring the attention of every Pack within Mexico. The hills would be crawling with outside Pack. Not the best way to go about business if your business is to keep killing Lycan."

"Their deaths weren't a direct hit to the group. Them gone does nothing to the overall power structure," I added.

"Their contributions to the Pack community were almost nil. One was a server at a coffee shop, one worked at a bar and one was a teacher. A few of the missing haven't even raised flags with their friends outside of Pack. There are no missing person reports on the news for any of them. There's no chatter among my circle of any happenings in Mexico. People don't just go missing, and no one notices unless they are unimportant loners. Yet, they still had something unique to offer."

"They're innocents, virginal and dedicated to the calling of God. Only virgins have died so far, aside from one of Miguel's men, who I think just got in the way," I answered. My heart skipped a beat at the thought of Cisco. Another piece of the puzzle clicked into place. "If you were trying to raise a demon or devil, why wouldn't you take the strongest in power? You can't knock on the door of the pit with a pocketful of hope. It takes real power to get those doors open."

"Just because you're weaker than those around you doesn't mean you're weak of soul. It just means those around you are far more powerful. Their souls are as good as any other." Samuel shuffled through his notes, nodding to himself. "As you said, they're virgins who believed in a higher power, went to church, volunteered, did community service and stood for a righteous calling through their blood oaths to God. They quite literally are the perfect sacrifice. They may be weaker within the Pack, but the power within their souls would be a dish fit for the gods." Samuel flipped through his notes again. "Go back to the candles. Get as close as you can."

I lifted each picture and zoomed into the candles. "What did you see?"

"There, Ailis," he spoke up, and I looked at the candle. "There are small symbols near the base of the candle. It's almost too small to notice. The wax covers it on the other candles, but this one still has a few of them."

I leaned in and could barely see what he saw. It was a squared face with fangs, large round eyes and a proboscis-like nose. Around his head were what looked like clouds, a lightning bolt and a drop of water. I hadn't seen the symbol before, but I had seen pieces of it in various texts. "What the hell is that?"

"Hell. It is always hell. It's an old symbol. Aztec, maybe? Hold on." He stood and pulled a few books from the shelves that took up all the walls in his study. His house was a small library with one bedroom, a bathroom and a main floor turned into one massive study. He kept his important books there, along with journals that were blank to everyone's but his eyes. Thumbing through a book, he finally found what he was looking for. "Those are the symbols for rain, thunder and lightning. In Maya mythology, Chac is the Maya rain deity, god of rain, thunder and lightning. The head symbolizes the god, Chac. Equipped with his lightning ax, he strikes the clouds and makes thunder and rain."

"Isn't Chac the name of the four priests who would hold down each limb for the sacrifices in Maya religious ceremonies?" I asked.

"Yes. Chac was an important part of the religious and sacrificial ceremonies," he answered, "with sharp teeth, huge eyes that shed tears of rain, a snout-like nose and the body of a reptilian. He carried a serpent ax, which is said to represent lightning bolts. Unlike the other Maya gods, Chac possessed four personalities, each associated with the four points of a compass, called the Chacs. And, like you mentioned, that was also the name given to the priests who held down each limb of the person to be sacrificed. He was highly respected and a god among his people."

"A god? The witches believe they can summon a god with black arts?" I asked. I almost laughed at the absurdity. "No one still above dirt has an ego that big."

"They may believe they can, but they won't. Not even with the combined power of all hell could they summon an angel, let alone a god. But this isn't the real deal, Ailis," he answered. "Whoever they're trying to raise may be calling himself a god, but calling yourself a god doesn't make you one. Unfortunately, they're just as dangerous as a deity, if not more. They have a few more screws loose than the average demon. Just the same. Whatever they're unleashing is not a god. If it's taken them this long, feeding it soul after soul, and the demon is still not free, it is something beyond your imagination. Devils jail what is beyond our capability of understanding. They are too insane to be allowed to come up. Anything this powerful will be the doom of you all."

"Doom and death...naturally." I sighed. I was hoping the bad guys were wasting their energy on a hopeless pursuit, either something impossible or something manageable. This wasn't something controllable. "How do I kill it?"

"Ailis, can you really kill a devil or demon? Do they truly die or just go back to hell where they try again?" Samuel asked.

"I can try," I replied. "Death or a ticket back, I'm not that picky."

"No, don't try, Ailis. If it is a demon jailed, it is far too powerful. That is why it is locked up. If the devils don't want it out, you're not going to be able to kill it. Stay away from this one. You're going to touch your own death the closer you get to it."

"How did hell even get him in there if he's that powerful?" I asked.

"Hellhounds. And before you ask, you can't call a hellhound to help you stuff the damn thing back in once it's loose."

"Why not? In everything I've read on the matter, I've never actually learned of the reason hellhounds can't be summoned. Am I looking at being maimed and scarred for life or a horrible death and dragged to hell by hellhounds?"

"Hell. It's always hell. To call on a hound is to be dragged to hell. They do not answer to anything short of their god — and you, Ailis, are very much *not* their god," he replied. "I don't often tell you not to mess with something, but this one, you need to get on a plane and come home. Until this thing is contained, I'll keep you here. You'll be safe here." Samuel's eyes were tight, concerned. I knew that look. He was right one hundred percent of the time when it came to things dark and deadly. The last time I didn't listen, I skidded into his apartment with two demons on my back, literally. They sizzled off, but I needed stitches and was out of commission for weeks so my soul could heal. I didn't listen then, and from the look on his face now, he knew I wasn't going to listen now.

"Who the hell is going to contain this, Samuel? Do you know anyone in the area who can help these people the same way I can?" I asked. He didn't have an answer. I didn't think he would. He'd have sent them here by now if he had. "That's what I thought. I can't just leave them. If this wannabe god, Chac, is loosed on the world, a lot of people will die while we're sipping tea in your library. It isn't going to hunker down and remain a local problem. Eventually, it's going to hit home."

"But we'll be alive," he answered matter-of-factly. It was hard to argue his point. "You can't save everyone, Ailis, but you can save yourself."

"I'm well aware I can't save everyone, Samuel," I answered, my voice a little sadder than moments ago. In the last twenty-four hours, I had stood over two dead bodies, each death tied to me. "Thanks for the info. I really appreciate it. I've got to go. I need to talk to Miguel." I lifted the laptop to hang up and paused. "Samuel, would vampires ever work with witches or hell to kill Pack members?"

"Vampires will work with anyone to kill those we should not idly mention. It's hate so deep and old that none of us know why the hate is there. They've always been on the verge of war since I can remember, and I have a lot of years to remember."

"Miguel said the vampires are hunted for their crimes against humanity," I replied. "There, something you've learned from me."

"What crimes? That is the important question. They, like your Miguel, do not kill indiscriminately. How many bodies do you find lying around, drained of blood? Very few. They feed from willing donors, which are aplenty. They bring over those they can, but only the willing and those who have been around for eons bring over the strongest. To not be willing is to create a revenant, and those are just as rare. Their own Elders take care of their messes long before it bleeds out onto the streets. They, like Pack, hunt their own who step out of line." Samuel shook his head. "Ailis, your hate for the darkness is what keeps you in that same darkness. You need to learn about those you're hunting, or you'll never make it to old age."

"We can debate how long I'll live after I live through this." I often felt like a scorned child when I talked to Samuel. He cared. It was the only reason he took the time to teach me, but the learning curve was usually rough. "One of Miguel's men, Cisco, was killed last night. He had mentioned a vampire before they took his head. Who would be working to kill the Lycans? A rogue? A Master?"

"Your guess is as good as mine. This could be a matter of hate or a deep-seated vendetta," he replied. "Whoever it is is working with a traitor within Pack, witches and hell. There aren't many vampires powerful enough to not be fearful of the situation this would put them in. They are standing between three great powers, not to mention the wrath of their Elders. A Master would not risk his entire flock for this type of revenge. Look at someone who is powerful but not enough to claim territory and his own ilk. It'll be someone trying to prove himself as worthy, gain the power needed to become a Master."

"Inviting the coffin club into anything is asking for trouble," I replied. "Why would they risk dancing with demons?"

"Some would say that they *are* demons, Ailis," he answered, and I found myself nodding. "You need to use all your resources. Your friend, Mannix, may have a few leads you may want to look into. I heard he has a friend who has written a book on hell. From what I've been told, it's a book worth thumbing around in."

"What's so special about this book?" I asked.

"That's all I'm saying on the matter. Use your resources, Ailis, and stop trying to browbeat your way through this mess. You won't live if all you're using is sheer will and stubbornness."

"It's gotten me this far, but thanks for the information, Samuel. I got to run," I said and clicked the live stream off before he started to beg me to come home or guilt me into survival. I was young, but in my field, I was middle-aged. No better time to go out than in your prime. Not even I believed the bullshit I was spewing.

Chapter Two

I had two calls to make, and I'd save the one that would hurt for last—Miguel. The mere sound of his voice settled my soul and sent warning flags sailing. To have him was to dig my own grave. My soul would always want him, but I feared his Pack and what they would do to us if I didn't heed the only warning I was sure to get from them. If I threw myself at Miguel again and went against Pack's orders, I'd likely be dead before the next full moon. Caser wanted me gone, and I had wormed my way in a little deeper instead. The closer I got, the more scared I was that Caser's following demands would be placed on Miguel. I could gamble with my own life but never with his. But my uncertainty and reservations would have to wait. I'd burn that bridge when I got to it, and I'd probably be standing on it when I lit the match. For right now, I had other fires to set and flames to stand in.

"Hello, my fourth favorite witch," Philip said when he answered on the third ring. I rolled my eyes at his comment. He sounded fresh as a daisy, but he always did. I could call him at any time of day, and he always answered as if he were smiling. I swear I could tell, just by the tone in someone's voice, if they were smiling or not—and Philip was always smiling when I called. "You've been gone under a week. I'm surprised you waited this long to check up on me."

I laughed softly. "It feels like I've been gone a lot longer than a week."

"Lecture go that bad?" he asked.

"Same as usual. Trying to teach nonbelievers that there is, in fact, a hell down there, is next to impossible. They all believe in heaven. Why the hell not the other side of the coin?"

"Hopefully, they'll never have to find out," he replied.

"Demons always knock on the homes of the foolish first."

"If it weren't for fools, we wouldn't have a job," he replied, laughing. I couldn't really argue that point. Demons kept me in business. "What's up? How's your vacation going?"

"Pretty great, so far." I flat-out lied to him. I couldn't even skirt the truth with a nice, sugar-coated story. It had been hell on earth, and how could I spin that without causing panic? *It's all good. Just some dead bodies, gutted, missing organs, and slowly consumed souls. A demon as strong as a god might be knocking on your door any day. Oh, yeah, and Lycans and werewolves are real.* A lie was a mercy, in my opinion. "From what I've managed to see so far, it's beautiful and hot as hell."

"Your hair must look like one of your cat's hairballs," he joked but nailed it. My hair was a mess of curls and kinks from the humidity. "Did you get a chance to check out the Tulum ruins in Playa del

Carmen? Between the sights and the history, I hear they're breathtaking."

"Breathtaking… That's one way to put it. I took a look, but it wasn't as amazing as I thought it would be." I cringed. I had seen them, along with a dead woman, staked to the stone at the entrance to the Temple of the Wind God. The old buildings were worn, crumbling, their wards falling down with the walls, leaving behind an echo of torture. "I don't think I'd put it on my list if I ever came back. The place holds a lot of death and unease, Philip. I could feel it. Hell, I could hear it. One stroll through social media, and you get the gist of it, without the stain and nightmares."

"If all it did was give you nightmares, I'll scratch it off my list. I don't need to be bumping up against ghosts or bad juju," he replied. Philip was one of the most superstitious people I knew. He once took a week off from work because he had broken his coffee machine and slipped in the shower, and bad things come in threes. He said he didn't want to be run over on his way and waited it out at home until he broke his toe. "I'm going to Mexico with a few friends for spring break. We already have a scuba dive scheduled and a tour of the cenotes. I hear the ocean there is brimming with life so brilliant all other waters look dull. I had a friend who was a hardcore diver and used to post pictures on his socials."

I thought of Cisco immediately. My eyes prickled with unshed tears. It took a few breaths for me to talk again. "I heard the same thing. Try free diving. I was told it was the best way to experience the water."

"So, what's up, Ailis? Did you call to rub it in that you're sitting poolside, and I'm ears deep in grading?"

That was Philip — polite to a fault and straight to the point, but so delicately balanced that it still came out smooth as a professional handshake. It was why we got along so well. He didn't waste my time and didn't care for small talk any more than I did. Unfortunately for me, any time I tried to pull off getting to the point, I was blunt and hostile and hurt people's feelings. Then again, I was blunt and hostile regardless of how hard I tried. Some of us were meant to be social, and some of us were meant to be the reason others regretted trying it. I was somewhere in the middle. I could be social, but you'd regret striking up a conversation with me.

I already had my lie ready. "I'm writing a lecture for a class based on the mythology of Mexico."

"My professor went to Mexico, and all I got was this lousy lecture." Philip's laugh made me smile. God, I missed his laugh. I missed home. I missed all the little things I used to take for granted—alarm clocks and early morning lectures, traffic, being home alone on a Friday night, not being chased by witches, not looking at dead bodies. "What do you need?"

"Have you ever heard of Chac—the demon, not the god?" I asked.

"Anyone who has studied mythology has heard of the god, Chac," he answered, and I frowned. I had spent half my life studying mythology and demons, yet his name meant nothing to me. Goes to show how much I paid attention in school. "The demon, though, not as much is known about him. Ancient texts didn't focus as heavily on hell as they did their gods. From what I know, he's modeled closely after the god, only all horror, terror and brimstone. He is an evil, with four faces and four names, none of which are written in the texts aside from his last used name. It's said that whoever learned of his original name to summon him met an untimely death to keep it a secret."

"That sounds more like a devil than a demon," I said out loud, more to myself than him. "Most demons want to be called out of the pits. They want the chance to walk above, wreaking havoc."

"His current name probably translates to four powers or curses. My money is on the four reasons he was locked away by the devils. He was powerful, Ailis. Chac was a walking curse during his life, and when he went downstairs, he became more powerful than a higher demon. Devils, I'm talking about the majority upper-level devils, jailed him, in fear Chac would bring about the ruin of the pits."

"Jesus," I mumbled. "To have the kind of power to scare a devil? That's some mighty big clout to have."

"It would take him and a holy war to stop Chac if he got out." Philip clicked his pen in the background. His fidgeting told me he was worried. "Is something going on there that I should know about? It isn't every day you want to dig up information on a demon no one has spoken about, outside of vague mentions, in a decade or two."

I did what I did best. I lied. "No. My lecture will include the stains I felt at each location I've visited."

"I've never heard of Chac, the demon, visiting any site in Mexico."

"He hasn't, but while I was researching the gods of the ruins, I came across Chac's name and thought I'd add him in as a warning. Just because they hold the name of a god doesn't make them one. Hell, even a god is wrathful and not to be messed with. But, in my experience, no bit of information is too small. It may just save a life or two down the road."

"Ain't that the truth? One of your students summoned a fucking tooth fairy two nights ago. He showed up in class with four of his front teeth missing.

He didn't believe the damn things were demons until it held him down and ate four teeth before being sent back by his mother." Philip's laughter was contagious. "He's covered in tiny bite marks and a newfound fear of everything demonic."

"At least it was only a tooth fairy and not something more spiteful," I replied. I knew exactly who had done it...Alex Martins. He was an accident waiting to be sucked into hell. This wasn't the first time he had shown up to class after summoning something stupid, and it wouldn't be the last. The last time was always the deadliest. "Some lessons are best learned the hard way."

"If people stopped digging up graves, opening sealed tombs or reselling massacre houses, we wouldn't need to be teaching them how to keep their souls on this side of the gates. Every time I turn on The History Channel, we're knocking on some demon's door."

I found myself nodding to the comment. We didn't just gaze into the abyss. Oh no, we needled it until something with sharp teeth reared its ugly head. It's the very reason there was a channel dedicated to hauntings, exorcisms and monster hunting. "Mankind has a long history of trying, over and over, to bring us to the brink of extinction."

"We just can't have anything pretty nowadays," Philip added. He rustled some pages and groaned at what he was reading. I knew once I had told him what I needed, he'd have started to poke around while we spoke. If nothing else, Philip was Mr. Dependable. He was one of the few I could count on, day or night. "I found the demon you're looking for in one of your old texts. I'll bookmark the pages for when you're back."

"Give me the condensed version."

"Ailis, something is up. I can feel it. I can hear it in your voice. What's going on?" he asked, and I sighed, long and hard. "Should I be asking if you want to be cremated, buried and salted?"

"Always cremated if you find my body. It's in my will. Burn me to pieces and scatter my ashes. I don't want some necromancer digging me up and forcing me to spill secrets," I replied. "The consulting gig Miguel called me for? It's a little worse than I thought. If you don't hear from me in the next few days, grab my cat and go to Samuel. He's the only one who will be able to keep you alive. That's all I can say, but please listen to my warning."

"Fuck." His one word summed it all up. "All right then. The condensed version. You're not going to like this."

"On a scale of one to Lucifer himself, how bad is it?"

"Bad. Kiss-your-ass-goodbye bad. Like, Chac's coming would signal the final days of most of mankind. His prison is tied to the gate. Open his cell, open the gates to hell."

"Naturally." I groaned. "Good times."

"There aren't many ways to banish him. When he was locked away in hell, it took the collective power of higher devils, hellhounds, and...weird, large dogs?"

My eyebrows raised. "What? Say that again? Dogs?"

"It's in Latin and faded. Lupus, maybe?"

My heart skipped a beat. *Wolf.* Miguel's people, no doubt. "Weird."

"I'll leave it on your desk for when you get back." He didn't say *if* I came back. He wouldn't jinx me with words. I heard him shut the book with a thump. The thing was a solid ten pounds. "Maybe talk to Mannix? He has a better understanding of dead languages and demons so old that we stopped talking about them."

"You're not the first one to mention his name," I answered. I chewed my lip, wondering what information I could dig out of his brilliant mind. Mannix forgot nothing. He didn't have an eidetic memory, nothing nearly as fancy as that, but the man's brain was a vault. He once spelled himself in junior high when studying for a test. The spell never wore off, resulting in an inability to forget. It wasn't the cheat he thought it would be and not a skill I'd want to have — cursed to remember every crime scene in glorious detail, all to get a passing grade on an English exam. And that is precisely why meddling in spells or using magic on a whim is a bad idea. Every spell had a hitch, a cost, and Mannix would never stop paying for it.

"What's next?" Philip asked, pulling my attention back to our call. "What's the plan, Lish?"

"My part in Mexico is almost done. There's not much more help I can give. I'm thinking about meeting with the local witches about what's going on here, but it depends on their schedules," I replied, which wasn't too far from the truth. The witches would be back, and what I'd offer them couldn't be considered help.

"Have you seen Miguel at all?" Philip's voice sounded hopeful. He always liked Miguel, and it broke his heart when I called things quits. I think Philip was more torn up about it than I was. He had cried for days, called in sick with a broken heart.

I huffed a laugh. "You know damn well I have, you little fink."

"You can thank me when you get home. I'll take payment in the form of Mexican tequila...not that crap you buy at the airport. I want the stuff you have to smuggle out of the country."

I smiled. "Would I forget about my favorite assistant? I already had some mailed back to you."

"Witch, please. Your favorite? I'm the only one who isn't scared to death of you," he answered, and it was painfully true. Every other assistant I've had has quit, run away, cried, vomited and one even passed out, knocking her little head on my desk and needing stitches. Philip, on the other hand, was smart as a whip, excited and eager to learn, had the same morbid curiosity as I did and the same healthy fear of things you shouldn't poke at. He was my absolute favorite assistant and person.

"I need to go. I have another call to make." But I didn't want to hang up. Ending the call would pull me back to the reality at hand. Philip was my tether to normalcy.

"Stop working, Ailis. If you're almost wrapped up with the locals, try and take a few days for yourself. You deserve it. Start enjoying your vacation. You take all of zero holidays. Get your ass to the pool and have a few drinks before you regret not doing it."

"Thank you, Philip," I answered, my voice soft and tired. My soul was exhausted. "I mean it...for everything you do."

"Thank me by giving me a raise."

"Bye," I said with a chuckle and hung up.

Although I didn't gain as much information as I had hoped, at least I knew how to send the demon back to hell, should it break out—impossibly. All I needed to accomplish this hopeless task were all the devils, hellhounds, my parents and Miguel's people. Though, if the gates opened, I really doubted Chac would be my biggest worry. Hordes upon hordes of demons and devils above the crust... *Easy-peasy lemon squeezy. Just another day in paradise.*

I called Miguel next. Although I felt homesick for my person and craved the sound of his voice, I squirmed a little as I waited for him to pick up. Between my fear of how things stood between us and the consequences of there being an *us* again, I thought of his Pack leader. Caser's final request and warning whispered through my mind. *"I'm asking you to let him go. Without his protection, you're anyone's meat."* My stomach flopped at the memory of meeting Pack. I had agreed to leave Miguel, and yet, I had only just crawled out from his arms. I gripped my phone a little tighter. Although I was well and truly scared of what Pack could and would do to get their point across, I knew in my heart I wouldn't roll over as Caser had demanded of me. I don't bend for anyone. Sure, it made me a liar, but being a liar was one of my more likable qualities. If push came to shove, a furious and cornered witch is who they would meet.

My call went to voicemail twice. I sent Miguel a text and asked him to call me right away. It was important. I poured myself another coffee and pulled up a few online searches of Chac. I had heard nothing of him while cooking off my soul in hell and hadn't heard much of him during all my studies, more because there was never anything new associated with either the god or the demon. The information highway on old dead gods and wannabe gods was a little dried up. Even with the information from Samuel and Philip, I didn't know as much as I wanted to, as much as I hoped I wouldn't need. Truthfully, I was also thankful I didn't come to find out the guy had pages dedicated to him slaughtering his way through villages. No, mankind did the killing for him, sacrificing the innocent in his name — both for the god and the demon.

The internet was one of the greatest tools invented for people like me, even though it was a dead-end this time. It didn't replace original texts, but sometimes, when I was lucky, one would pop up online for me to print my very own copy. I'm sure it's written somewhere that I wasn't allowed to do that. But how else would I get a translated text of a long-dead language about some vague deity too old for people to remember the lore? The life of a petty criminal was full of splitting hairs and making excuses. In my opinion, I shouldn't have to shell out my hard-earned cash to buy information that would save a life. In a perfect world, they would be giving it to me with a thank-you card. But, in a perfect world, I wouldn't need the damn books or a solid defense for theft.

Miguel called back twenty minutes after my text, and the first words out of his mouth were frantic. "Caser's daughter Anna is missing."

"What does she look like?" I asked. I sent up a prayer that she had done what all teenagers do — sneak out to go necking, to a party, to drink, to stick her middle finger up to authorities with a big 'fuck you'. Anything but what I hoped wasn't coming next.

"Like every other victim, Lish. She's petite, pretty and weaker than the rest of us." His voice hitched like it was an effort on his part to not scream or rage. "She's not Lycan. At least, she's not one yet. We won't know if the gene is active or not until she shifts. Even though she's from Caser's line, if she goes through the change while not with one of us, she could die. The shift can be deadly without a guide. Her heart could stop, or her lungs could fail. We've lost plenty on their first shift, and they were damn powerful to begin with. Jesus, she's just a kid."

I didn't want to point out the obvious, that worrying about her was pointless. She was probably already dead or dying. I may have been as blunt as the dull side of a butter knife, but I wasn't going to put those thoughts into his head. "Why weren't you guarding her? Isn't that kind of what you're all supposed to be doing?" I regretted the question immediately after it came out. It sounded like an accusation, like I pointed a finger at him. "Sorry. That wasn't fair."

"We were. One minute she was here, and the next, she was gone," he replied. He sounded defensive, and I didn't blame him one bit. I'd basically just told him it was his fault.

"Like poof, she was gone?" I asked. "Only a demon has that kind of power."

"No, like no one remembers an hour of time."

"Witches," I whispered.

"It smells of witches," he replied.

"Do all witches smell the same?" I asked. "Or could you track a particular witch?"

"Yeah. You all smell like cast-iron cauldrons and matchsticks."

"What? Really?"

"No, not really." He laughed. "Your power has a smell. Everything on this earth, above and below, has a smell. Each type of witch smells different. Your run-of-the-mill kitchen witch smells of herbs and feels like static on my skin. Your elemental witch smells like campfire and feels like spiders crawling across my face. You, on the other hand, smell of it all. You're not staticky, though. You feel more like an electrical fire threatening to burn down a house, depending on your mood. You feel like the air before lightning strikes."

"And hell. Mustn't forget the brimstone," I added. Although that was a sore spot for me, his answer made me smile. I smelled like my mother just before she did magic. She smelled like lightning in a bottle, charging the air around her, creating ozone as it conducted through the air. Every thunderstorm since my parents had died brought me outside, breathing it in, remembering all the times I stood at her side while she worked.

"To some, yes. But you don't smell like hell to me and my...family, not in the way it smells to you. You smell like home." His voice trailed off. Was it possible that his soul was homesick? Could someone miss hell? I sure as shit didn't miss a damn thing from down there.

Two minutes in hell is not two minutes in heaven. I lived an eternity in a cage of suffering and soul-crushing torture. My life ended in the most horrific of ways, day in and day out, and always more creative than the last. After what felt like decades, I was returned, my soul torn to shreds. Thank God for loopholes. Only now, I was a beacon for every devil and demon with a grudge until I waltzed back in there. Hell wasn't a fan of returning goods and would claim me once again the moment my heart stopped. They had a cage with my name on it, and it would be a welcome-home party that would knock my soul off.

"Could you track the scent of the witches who took Anna?" I asked, bringing us back on track.

"We could, but only to the road. They left in vehicles after that. Seven scents. Four cars. We lost the trail twenty klicks up the main road."

Seven witches. I had dreamed of them after visiting the first crime scene. The soul, who had been trapped in a circle of protection, had touched me on her way out of the cenotes, later returning to my dream. My memories jogged back to that dream, but it felt like ages ago since I had landed in Mexico and stepped into that cenote. It had only been mere days since that first crime scene, but the memories were spotty, as if I was looking back on something from years ago. Evil had a way of aging you the same way hell did. It ate away at you like peeling wallpaper. Little by little, gone unnoticed until you saw the bare wall. Like that wall, my soul was feeling patchy.

"I don't mean to be rude, but you asked me to call you, that it was important?" Miguel asked. "Is it more or less important than Caser's daughter missing?"

"More and less, depending on who you ask. I spoke to Samuel about what's happening here." I told him what Samuel had said about Chac and the symbols on the candles. "I haven't been able to dig up much on him, from heaven or hell or how he factors into any of this. I even called Philip and came up short on answers. From what Philip could find, the demon is powerful and is tied to the very gates. I'm not sure if the demon would hold the same or similar power as the god and if that is why he refers to himself as Chac? Or if there's any significance to his name at all. The text mentioned needing devils, hounds and, I think, your people to imprison him."

"Many powerful demons need the help of hounds and Lycan. When mankind fails to send them back after summoning, Lycan hunt them," he replied.

"Oh, I thought maybe we had found a clue," I answered, feeling defeated. "Is there any meaning behind his name?"

"Chac, the true god, was able to call the wild hunt," Miguel explained, to my surprise. "When they say he called thunder, it was the sound of the hellhounds running. The lightning was their power crackling through the air. The rain came after to clean the blood from the streets. He was the only one to make a righteous call on the hellhounds, and we had to obey. We would hunt down the oath breakers and wrongdoers. We hunted the sinners and dragged their souls to hell. This cannot be the real Chac."

"I don't think it is. But could he, the demon, be powerful enough to call the hounds from hell?"

"Some believe any demon strong enough to open the gates can also call the hunt. I don't know how much truth there is to that. But anything is possible, Ailis. Anyone powerful or righteous enough can call the hounds. The hounds are the ones who decide if they come or not," he answered. "If this demon is imprisoned, it is because he is too powerful to go unchecked or unleashed. If the devils have locked him up, it's for a damned good reason. He may just be that powerful."

"Same thing Samuel said. Say, hypothetically, he can call the hounds. What would happen?"

"*If* he could call the horde from the pits of hell, and they answered his call, the wild hunt begins. Death begins. That is what happens when they come. They come for one reason…to hunt. No one would be safe. The wild hunt would drag anything connected to hell back to hell. But if the call is unrighteous, only the caller would die."

I swallowed a rock called fear in the back of my throat. "Even me? They'd take me during a wild hunt?"

"Yes, Ailis, especially those like you. If you weren't taken and forced to ride in the hunt yourself, you'd be sent back to hell. The hunt doesn't care how many souls you have. You went to hell and walked out. They would put you back. They would see you as property of hell and deserving of it. The hounds don't care about splitting hairs or excuses, not during a hunt. You're a suicide, Lish. You already know where suicides go," he answered, and I groaned. Technically, I'd killed myself the moment I'd got into a vehicle with a drunk driver. "With the wild hunt unleashed on earth, controlled by a demon, every magic out there would fall—every witch, sorcerer, vampire, and everything in between. Magic is seen as dark by the hunt. When you all do magic, you take the stain of that magic upon your aura and soul. That is not a pure soul to the hounds. The only ones who will survive are the pure. There is no escaping it."

"What about you?" I asked.

He sighed. "Because I'm a monster?"

"No, because you're Lycan and tied to the gate. What would happen to you?" I said softly, pangs of guilt twisted in my stomach. I had said too many harsh words, and neither of us was the forgetting type.

"I'd be called with the rest of my people back to hell when the hunt was done. There'd be no need for us up here, with the sinners and evildoers gone in one swoop. We'd go back to guarding the gates, back to how it was when the first hunt was called. I'd become a hound and would ride with the rest until the earth was pure once again."

"Was the earth ever really pure, to begin with?"

"If you knew the hunt would rip you apart and drag you into the pits of hell, would you sin?"

"True, probably not. But everything good and fun is a sin."

"In any of your mythology or history books, even the Bible, did anyone look like they were living their best life, having a heyday? Not even close. People worked, they shared, they raised their babies. Life was simple. Life was hard work. Life was short. Life was boring. But they were alive and on this side of the gates for it."

"That sums it up nicely," I answered. Everything I had thought I knew about hellhounds was shot out of the sky. With my skin crawling at the thought of being dragged into hell by a hellhound, I changed the subject.

Unfortunately, there weren't many topics that didn't make my stomach flop. "I don't know if this helps, but how many virgins, lower in Pack, are there?"

Miguel paused for a moment. "All the younger ones are. Why?"

"Long story short, they are who the witches are targeting—the weaker of Pack, the pure of soul and virginal. They're the perfect sacrifice," I answered. "Keep an eye out for them. If I had to guess, they would be who goes next."

"We have all our Pack under lockdown right now, but I'll start handing out hex bags in case the witches show up again," he replied. "Thank you for the information. I appreciate what you're doing for me and my people."

When the conversation stalled out, I felt uncomfortable with the silence. I was usually okay with not filling space with words, but tonight, it made me feel awkward. "Hey, about earlier, I'm sorry. I feel like I cornered you or guilted you into coming back to see me. You have enough going on. Consoling your ex-girlfriend shouldn't be another thing to add to your list."

"Don't apologize, Lish. You didn't guilt me into anything. I wanted to be with you as much as you wanted me there. When things get dark, we seek out comfort and love. It's natural. Please don't regret it. I don't. If nothing else, it's helped me feel less alone, less scared," he replied. "When this nightmare is over, don't bolt, please. Give us a chance to at least talk without hell hanging over our heads. Don't make any decisions while we're ears deep. The stress of it makes us want to pull back to the moment we felt safest. Let this settle before we decide the rest of our lives."

"Okay, I can do that. Just so you know, Miguel, I don't regret you. I never have and don't think I ever could." I said the words because it was true, and I knew it would chase away the heartache he was feeling. Like Samuel had said, sometimes love was enough. At this moment, I could give Miguel the love he needed because I needed it, too. "I regret what happened between us those years ago, but never ever you."

"Thank you for that. I appreciate hearing those words. I think I needed to hear them, especially now," he sighed. It was long and winded. It was the kind of tired that came from deep within and rattled his bones on the way out. "This shit is wearing on my soul. And now, with Anna missing, things in Mexico are about to boil over. We have to watch Caser like a hawk so he doesn't do anything stupid to need to be hunted for. If he sends out a call to the neighboring Packs, all hell is going to break loose, and those who didn't need to die will never be seen again. We'll have to hunt our own people. Fuck, this has gone from bad to worse to a fucking nightmare."

"I'm sorry, Miguel. I wish there was something I could say or do to help," I replied. I may not have liked Caser, but no one deserved their children under threat.

I shuddered, knowing I'd have burned the city to the ground to find my child. I couldn't imagine being forced to stand down in fear of society finding out about my kind. My people had already been there and done that, and it ended with countless witches being set ablaze, their children drowned and their homes burned to the ground. How there were any of us still kicking and out of the closet was a constant surprise to me. Had I not died for two minutes and come back steaming, to the amazement of a group of first responders, I'd have probably kept my witch blood a secret. It had been nothing but a headache since day one.

"I'm sorry as well. I didn't think I'd be pulling you into something like this. I thought, at worst, a lesser demon," he replied and huffed a laugh. "I never thought I'd hope for a demon problem and have that be the lesser of the evils."

"Demons are easier to deal with than people. People are erratic and crazy. Demons are just evil but predictable."

"Ain't that the truth," Miguel said, his voice growing more tired by the minute. "Did Samuel give you anything else we can use? He usually has a few tricks up his sleeve for you."

"Cisco had mentioned bloodsuckers, and Samuel pointed out a few interesting things to investigate. Do you know of a vampire around here who is almost as strong as the Master Sucker? Like a second-in-command or whatever they call their second banana."

"We'll go with 'the second banana'. It's fitting. I could see a vampire mixed up in this. If we were gone or our numbers were next to nothing, there wouldn't be anyone left to keep them in line. We keep the balance between powers, and without us, they'd grow their ilk at a higher rate. They'd have the freedom to grow faster than we allow," he answered. "If it worked, whichever vampire pulled off a take like this would probably be given the country, if not an ear of their grand table, reserved for the most powerful Elders. Having the favor of the Elders is like having the keys to the gates of hell," Miguel answered. "But Mexico doesn't have a huge vampire population. I don't know who it would be."

"Why is the population so low here?" I asked.

"Would you want to basically live on the sun if the daylight fried you to a crisp? Mexico bakes all year long."

"I suppose not," I answered. "I'm not even a vampire, and I have a hard enough time here."

"Our last count, a couple of months ago, said there is just over four hundred in the entire country, give or take a few dozen. It's separated into regions for them, like provinces or states. Each area has its own Master. Mexico has thirty-two states. Vampires occupy eighteen of them. That's eighteen Masters and eighteen second bananas, and God knows how many who want to prove a point or rise faster than they should. Whatever the case, I don't think we'll figure it out in time, Ailis."

"I was scared you'd say that." I sighed. One more road I couldn't go down. It felt like there were too many possibilities and all of them with dead ends. Time was the biggest monster in this mess.

"I'll send word to all states," he added. "I'll let them know we're looking for a bloodsucker with a larger than usual hate-on for Lycan. Maybe something will pop up. The vamps are pretty good at covering their tracks, but if there's an inner squabble or reaching too high, spouting more hate than usual, someone might know something. Hate isn't easiest quieted."

"One more thing before you go. I talked to Samuel, and he told me to pour holy water into the wounds. Will that work?" I asked.

"Sweet Christ on a bicycle, Lish, that's going to hurt like hellfire," Miguel answered. I could almost hear the pain in his voice as he thought about it. "Pouring holy water on a supernatural wound will hurt like nothing you've ever felt. I've seen it done on vampire bites and wounds given by the possessed. I was the unlucky fool to be bitten by a demon when I was eighteen. I remember that holy water like it was done five minutes ago. It felt like my skin was being cooked off."

"I know it'll hurt. Everything that keeps us alive hurts. The question is, will it work?"

"I don't know. I've never tried it on a Lycan wound. More often than not, by the time we know someone has been infected, they've shifted, and it's too late," he answered. "It might — or you may just torment yourself for no reason. Honestly, I'd try it. If it were me, I'd do it. I'm Lycan and can't catch viruses, but when a demon bit me, I wasn't willing to risk a cursed infection."

"I was hoping you wouldn't say that." I groaned. "If it works, what does that mean about your people? If it's not a virus but a curse, I mean."

"Nothing. The virus *is* a curse from hell. It doesn't make us evil. It makes hell evil," he answered. Nothing rattled his faith. It was both endearing and irritating at times. "Do you need help? It took four of my people to hold me down for my introduction to the worst pain I've ever felt, and I've broken both of my femurs."

"Yes. No. Shit. No, I'm pretty sure I can do it myself. If I can't, I'll call you back and get you to hold me down." I groaned out my answer. "Keep me posted on Anna, and be careful." I heard Caser in the background, barking orders. "You should go, Miguel. Caser needs a friend more than I need encouragement to boil my skin off. I'd be losing my bloody mind if I were in his shoes."

"So would I," he replied. "I'll call you later. Stay inside. Salt your doors. And enjoy your holy bath." He hung up. Neither of us said goodbye. It was too final.

"I love you," I whispered to an empty line. I said it because I did. I didn't say it to him because I was scared it would be my last time.

With five bottles of holy water and rolled-up socks to sink my teeth into, I made my way to the bathroom. I turned on some music to drown out my screams. The bathroom was one large open room that looked out into the bedroom. The toilet was in a small room at the far end. The shower had its own enclosure at the front of the bathroom. I stripped down, took a seat on the floor of the shower and closed the glass door. I doubted the door or the music would make much difference. The sounds of pain carried. And the torment I was about to endure would echo into the pits of hell.

The tiles were cold against my hot skin, and after the shock of them on bare skin, the chill felt good. I stared at the small glass bottles and tried to convince myself not to bother. There was no point to it. My fear always had the best arguments. But my unwillingness to become a furry beast had a better argument and won out against my yellow belly. Here's to feeling like I was being boiled alive.

With the bandages off, the wounds open and bleeding, I started the baptism of fire. As soon as I had started, I regretted not asking for help. This would have been easier if someone had been with me to hold me down. Forcing myself to endure the pain would be a battle between my need to protect myself and my need to not be a furry lunatic. The first drop stung like any wound exposed to water would. The second and third drop felt like I had reopened the gashes with a hot knife and dug around with a salted fork. I put the socks in my mouth and poured the liquid fire over my injuries. It reminded me of bleeding in hell, the blistering heat of blood and cooked meat. The thought made me gag. I could almost taste the memory. I gritted my teeth and poured a little more, sobbing into my makeshift gag.

If I could have told someone about this moment, it would have seriously upped my street cred. I jerked and twisted and heaved. I wanted to scream, run, bang my fists. Willing myself to remain still while I dripped acid on my skin was next-level stubbornness. But I'd hate to turn into a creature to be hunted because I couldn't sit still. Though I'd be dead in the next week or two and wouldn't have to live for too long in shame for being a chicken. I shook the temptation from my mind and moved on to my other arm.

My pulse hammered hard enough for me to see my clammy skin flutter at my wrists. Even my pulse couldn't take it and wanted the hell out of here. I was perilously close to passing out. Each moment took more and more effort to focus on. I pulled a towel from the rack and rolled it up for my head. On my back, I dosed the cuts on my chest in one quick pour. They were shallow and barely broke the skin but had hurt as though they were bone-deep. I couldn't risk it, though, leaving even the smallest cut uncleaned. My back arched from slamming into the floor as I twisted in pain. I rolled to my side and was sick. I uncorked another bottle and continued. It felt like hours, days had passed. All four bottles had soaked my skin until it dripped off me. The fifth, for good measure, I drank. Most of it came back up, but I was confident that enough of it had stayed down to work its way through my innards. I'd kill it from the inside, or it would kill me. Lying on the floor in a shower in Mexico, sobbing, it felt like I had just burned off the first few layers of skin. I was fine with either outcome. It took almost an hour before the shaking stopped, and I was able to use my limbs without shooting pain. This was now my new measurement of pain, replacing dying in a car accident, on a scale of stubbing my toe to dousing myself in holy water after a Lycan attack.

I stayed on the ground until the room stopped its dance, and my body no longer felt like it had been dipped in boiling water. Neither Miguel nor Samuel had undersold the pain of it. I couldn't imagine being held down in a tub full of it. No wonder the poor guy had passed out. I was pretty sure Samuel was the poor guy. He wasn't one to recommend something he wouldn't do himself or hadn't already done before. Samuel talked about his scars like battle wounds, proud he came out the other side. But there were some he wouldn't mention. A few of them looked like a devil had ripped its claws down his flesh. I didn't press him on those. I never liked talking about hell, either. But now that I knew it wasn't hell that had sliced him up, I'd ask him again — *if* I made it out of here alive.

When the nausea faded and my vision wasn't doubled, I crawled from the shower and pulled myself to my feet. I grabbed my first-aid kit and began the process of closing the wounds once again. Wrapped in fresh bandages and dressed in loose-fitting clothes, I nibbled on a banana. I drank enough water to help my throat if I puked again. I was tired. I was sore. And I cried until the fear left with the tears. I doubted my body had enough endorphins to help sooth what I had just done to myself, but the emotional flood did help settle me enough for me to stop shaking. The fear of more pain still sat in the back of my mind and kept its eyes peeled for another round. Every noise jerked my attention and watered my eyes. I'd remember tonight for the rest of my life, and if anyone ever mentioned holy water to cleanse a wound, I'd echo what Miguel and Samuel had both said. It would hurt like hell — the *real* hell.

I didn't have time to curl into a ball and waste the rest of the night on my pain and fear, however badly I wanted to. I gave myself thirty minutes and not a second more to wallow in self-pity. My full-on breakdown could wait until I had time for it. When the case was over, I'd schedule another holiday to recover from this one. I'd choose a secluded island, far from people and problems and blistering heat. *Yeah, I'll have a meltdown there, where no one can see the crazy witch screaming and cursing about unmentionable creatures.*

When the timer on my phone went off, my pity party was over. I got dressed and began my research. I would spend the rest of the night on the phone calling in favors for information and fancy room service. Might as well spend it while I got it. I may not have the chance to eat room service again without blood crusted under my nails or a pulse in my body. And with my stomach finally settled enough for food, I had the damn ice cream I had planned to eat from day one. I was exhausted and needed energy, and a banana split hit the spot and hugged me from the inside.

Food, coffee, sugar, revenge…all fuel for the night. I had to figure out where Anna was, why the witches wanted to raise Chac, who from Pack was the traitor and why they sold out their people, what vampire was willing to burn the world to get rid of Lycan, how I could stop Chac, the demon, and how to keep the hounds from their hunt should Chac waltz out of the door? *No big deal.* It's not like the fate of the Pack and anyone within a five-hundred-mile radius didn't depend on me. If I failed, Mexico would be a once-upon-a-time hotspot for tourists and become a little slice of topside hell. It would make the Darvaza gas crater, the Door to Hell, look like a good place to hide out.

As I picked up my cell phone and flipped through my contacts, I knew this would be another night I wouldn't get more than an hour or two of sleep if I was lucky. I hoped when things got really bad, I wouldn't sleep through it. I should have gone to Costa Rica like I had first planned. I should have sent someone else to consult, like my assistant, Philip, who always jumped at the chance for a free trip somewhere rather than volunteering myself as the sacrificial lamb. Never second-guess yourself. Your second choice is always wrong. In my case, it burned my ass like holy water on Lycan scratches.

Chapter Three

"Ailis, how's the trip going?" Mannix answered his phone before it had even rung on my end. He sounded new and shiny, as only a perfect sleep could do. I was jealous. How a witch practitioner got a full night's sleep was beyond me. He had always been the cheerful type, which I also didn't understand, given the pressure he faced being the son of a High Priest.

"Oh, you know me, just out here living my best life," I answered. "Are you back in Van yet?"

"I'm home in two days. The Coven has two more lectures, then I'm out of here. Two days with my dad feel like a lifetime," he replied. The very mention of his father made him sound as tired as I felt. "How the hell do you get around not attending their annual meeting? It seems like everyone else is here but you."

I chuckled. No one liked going to the mandatory conferences, not even the Coven's Priests or level three High Witches. "I'm only level one. I don't have any voting power within the Coven until I pass my next exams, so it's not a requirement for me. I warned you when you were going for your second level you'd have to participate, and you'd regret it. Plus, your practitioner malpractice insurance almost triples, and mine is already through the bloody roof."

"It's not like I had a choice," he grumbled — and he hadn't.

His father, Torin Ashford, a High Priest, the second council member of the Coven, a royal pain in everyone's ass, gave Mannix few choices in life. Be the best or die trying. That was the Ashford way. Had it not been for his father, Mannix would be a level one witch and still working in a not-for-profit, giving legal advice to witches burning down kitchens with wayward spells. Instead, he was a level two, and everyone found out who his father was. No witch looking for a way out of a fine for a spell gone wrong was going to sit across from the son of the man who could order up a witchy bonfire for one. Mannix was now attached to the local city cops as part of their magical investigative branch as a legal practitioner. He loved it but hated that his father had pushed him into it. We weren't the kind of friends who went to the movies together, but we were close enough to call on each other if we were in a bind. I stood up to his father once, and we'd been chummy ever since. It was a win-win. After my temper tantrum, Torin thought twice about bullying me, and impressed, his son was willing to befriend me. For a kid without friends, I was happy to take what I could get. That it kept for years made me not regret having to scrub the Coven halls for two weeks with my own toothbrush.

"My advice? Man, blow something up while trying to do a spell. That's what I did. Maybe if you look too stupid to do higher magic, they won't push you to level three," I said and heard his chuckle on the other end. He was there the day I blew a hole in the wall. The

Coven didn't ask me to do another spell for fear I'd kill someone. I left with a stern warning to study and perfect my magic, but I never went back for retesting. I was just fine with the status quo. I did what I could to stay under their radar, and they left me alone.

"I'll keep that in mind. So, what's going on that you're calling me while you're on vacation?" Mannix asked, a hint of humor in his voice. "Let me guess… Bodies washing up on the beaches? Hell spewing from some fool's circle? Demons rampaging?"

"That pretty much sums up my life to date, but that's not entirely why I'm calling," I answered. "I'm scheduled to return in a week, but it's going to be hard to pull away from all this excitement. Could you cover my classes until I'm back?"

"Of course. Things really that bad?" he asked, lowering his voice. I could hear his feet shuffling on the ground. I knew he was finding a more private place for us to chat. He may have been a legal practitioner, but he was a witch, through and through. His loyalty would always remain with the underdogs of society, which were usually witches who bit off more than they could chew…like me.

I released a heated and frustrated breath. "You could say that."

"How can I help?"

"I was talking to Samuel earlier. He mentioned you have a friend working on a book about hell? I need his name."

"It's a book about shadows." His silence made me question if I'd need this conversation to shift from friendly to 'I'm going to burn down your house with you inside unless you cough up what I need'. Thankfully, Mannix didn't play those games. Most people, when they realized they had the upper hand, used it against you. "You scratch my back. I'll scratch yours."

"Here I was thinking that you didn't play these games and you'd simply help me out of the kindness of your heart." I laughed out loud.

"Not this time."

"I thought you were above bribery."

"Nope, and you know exactly what I want, Ailis," he replied. An impressed sigh that said he had me finally cornered filled my ear. "I may not be there to see you, but I imagine you're giving me the middle finger."

"I am, and I can't hand over that kind of information, Mannix. You know I'm sworn to secrecy."

"And you think I'm not? A book about shadows is powerful, and this one has the stamp of hell across the front. It's the real deal, witchy woman. How bad do you want his name?"

"Have you read it yet?" I asked.

"Since when would someone let me do that? I've seen the book and have given him information for it but haven't seen so much as a page," he answered. "If Samuel is pointing you this way, it probably has the information you're looking for. But, to be perfectly honest, I've no idea what's in there."

"Fine," I answered, a bitter taste in my mouth. Mannix was right. Samuel wouldn't send me on pointless pursuits. "Deal."

"Wait! Let me get out my paper. I don't want to screw up the ingredients."

I waited for the 'I'm ready' mumble before calling him a bastard and holding true to my end of our deal. "My grandmother used a half-and-half mixture of sugar cane and brown sugar, not that white table sugar crap you've been using. And none of that vanilla extract. She ground vanilla beans by hand. Make sure you grab them from the farmer's market in East Van. Go to the purple stand at the end of the park and ask for Marina. Tell her you're making Grandma Kyteler cookies, and she'll hook you up. The vanilla beans are expensive but worth their weight in gold."

"The witch's market is pricey as hell," he complained.

"If you want to taste heaven, it's gonna cost you."

He groaned but finally agreed. "What type of chocolate chips was she using? What brand?"

"She didn't. She ordered slabs of homemade chocolate from the witch who owns Cursed Cookies down on Hastings and broke up the chocolate into bits."

"And now for the coveted spell." His laugh reminded me of every bad guy in the cartoons I'd watched as a child. "I've been waiting for this recipe for years. Don't hold out on me now."

"And I've told you a dozen times, there is no spell. Homemade means homemade. She mixed them all by hand and baked them without a drop of magic." I laughed at the thought of mixing magic with food. "Your spell would make them taste like your aura."

"No wonder all of mine have tasted handsome and smart as a whip," he replied, making me laugh. "I'm making these as soon as I get home. Dear God, I can almost taste them already. Thanks, Lish."

"My grandmother is probably cursing me from beyond," I replied. Really, she wouldn't have cared, but I had liked the game Mannix and I had played over the years. He was the closest thing to a friend I had since childhood. "Your turn, extortionist."

"The name you're after is Mark Castle. I'll text over his info. I wouldn't announce to anyone that you've been in contact with him. He was a level two but was dissipated from the Coven for black arts suspicion. No one could prove he had his fingers in Hades, but his aura is tainted to all hell."

"What is he suspected of doing?" As if it mattered whether he was guilty or not. Suspicion ruined lives. The Coven took no chances when it came to their image.

"The usual things that get a person shunned by Coven. Hell, and all things related. The rumor is that he found a demon to talk to him, and it only cost him a few pounds of soul."

"Making deals with demons... Not a risk I'd take, but I'm thankful someone did," I replied.

"No problem. Call me if you need help."

"Thanks for the information, Mannix. Hopefully, I won't need you to take my classes until a permanent replacement is found."

"Anytime, Ailis. I'll touch base with Philip and grab your schedule. Good luck out there."

"It stands without saying, but we never had this chat."

"What chat?" he replied and hung up.

Once I received the contact information for a soon-to-be-sorry Mark Castle, I cracked my knuckles and let all my pity drain from my soul. He didn't know me, but he'd soon hate me. I was fine with people not liking me. I was born a witch. Hate wasn't new to me. Today, I'd earn it. Today, I'd be just another bad guy in a sea of reasons we have home security and spells on our front doors. I knew I should have cared, but I didn't. I'd do a lot worse than this before my time in Mexico was up.

"Who is this?" Mark answered his phone the third time I called. "How the hell did you get this number?"

"This is Ailis Kyteler," I replied. "We're going to have a little conversation about spells and hell."

"Fuck," he groaned.

* * * *

The feeling of doom washed over me in waves, bits holding onto my bones and weighing me down. I couldn't shake it. Dread wasn't an invisible force. It could be seen in twitchy movements, heard in stuttered speech, felt in the pounding behind a ribcage and the drip of sweat down the spine. It was panic for the inevitable, a wall clock that ticked like a bomb counting down. It couldn't be stopped or slowed. Today, each second brought me closer to my fate, to the witches and the hell they were about to unleash on mankind. My shoulders felt heavy, as if fate were standing behind me, pressing down until my shoulders were hunched, reminding me of everything I would have to do to keep hell from spilling out and killing most of mankind. Sometimes, when shit hit the fan, you had to get your soul a little dirty. What was a little taint for a witch already destined for hell?

I wasn't helpless, but nothing would help stop this runaway train. It was already in motion. Bodies were already on the ground, with a promise of more to come. Nothing would stop what was coming — pain and horror and death. There could be no other way when touching hell and evil. But I didn't fear pain as much as I did the hellish and horrible things lurking down below. I didn't like being afraid, fearing outcomes not yet written, but there were far worse fates than what stood before me. At best, I'd only die. Worst, I wouldn't and would have to watch my failure blanket humanity, eating away at everything worth dying for. Each time I thought about how I'd stop the witches and my anxiety tried to strangle me, I reminded myself that pain eventually ends. A human can't be kept alive forever. It really was the only guarantee in life. Sooner or later, we are given the mercy of death, and nothing else would matter. We got to leave it all behind, the good and especially the bad. Well, most of us do. I'd be entering hell with more baggage than I'd arrived in Mexico with.

My phone buzzed, jerking my attention away from the memories of hell. Miguel had sent a link to a website showing the top ten places to visit in Mexico, along with a text saying we'd see them all when this was over. I had been messaging him throughout the day, in between my hunt for ways around the coming doom and my pacing. Every time my phone vibrated, it felt like another flicker flared to life inside my soul, the reason I was willing to risk it all. Miguel was why I would be brave, even if I wanted to crawl into bed and pull the covers over my head until this all washed over, or I was eaten up with the rest of mankind. Bravery came in many forms, including shaking like a leaf, vomiting on your shoes, sobbing and showing up instead of cowering under the covers.

This time, rather than a text, I dialed his number, and he picked up on the first ring. "Lish, I was just thinking about calling you. Did you get that link?" His voice was smooth and buttery, the way I remembered it sounding at night when he curled around me. It reached all the way down to my soul and touched places that made me want to take off my clothes.

"I just finished reading through it. You live in a beautiful country."

"We'll make a week of it," he promised.

"Sounds like a plan," I answered with a lie.

I didn't have the heart to tell him I didn't think I'd get to visit those places with him, not unless he carried around my ashes. I smiled as I heard him whispering to someone else that he was on an important call, that he was talking to me. My eyes watered at the sound of his voice and weirdly because I was an important call to him. I didn't realize how badly I needed to talk to him until he said my name. Rather than tell him the truth of my call, that I missed him and wanted to hear his voice, I made something up. I couldn't break down. I couldn't tell him I needed his arms around me. I couldn't risk him showing up to the rescue. My plan was in motion, and him standing in my way would only complicate things. He was far too protective and would have only hindered me.

Miguel cleared his throat. "Sorry, Lish. Things are a little tense here. What's up?"

"I thought I'd check in and see how Caser was doing," I finally said.

"He's doing as well as can be expected. It was touch and go for a bit there, but I've got him calmed down for now. We had to bring in every Alpha to keep watch over the younger Lycan so they don't answer Caser's call to arms. We've got eyes on him around the clock," Miguel answered.

"Any news on Anna?" I asked. I didn't yet know if I was praying for Anna to still be alive or praying that she was already gone and it was a quick death. Life is on a pretty damn dark road if you're leaning toward death as a positive outcome.

"No. Not yet," he answered. He sounded how I felt, unsure if he wanted news of Anna's dead body or not. "We're searching every square inch of the back hills, tracking some of the scents we had picked up while the witches were here. Do you have any idea why we're smelling lavender? It grows wild in Mexico, but it's not common around Caser's property, and he doesn't keep it in his house. He pulls it out anytime he sees it. The smell is too powerful for a Lycan. I thought maybe there was a reason within your world, because there isn't one in mine."

"Historically, witches used it to ward off evil spirits. It was hung over doors to keep the evil away or burned in fires for the same reason. It was seen as a symbol of protection, although it didn't do much for them back then. The only proven purpose it has is in homeopathic remedies and inhalation therapies. Unless the demon knocking on your door has a dislike for lavender, it won't keep your skin out of hell," I answered. I had always wondered who had come up with these ideas and how many people had died over the years because of them.

"I've seen bundles of it hanging over windows and doorways. I always thought there was some sort of craft significance," he replied. He released a sigh coated in disappointment. "I think I was hoping it would be a clue."

"I think it's an issue of old habits die hard more than any real significance. There's a demon in LA who has his own home and garden magazine. He did a full issue on lavender. His entire property is bordered by it. Yet, my grandmother kept a dried bundle of lavender over every bed in her house. Sure, they were tied together with a witch's ladder and symbols, but they were still there. They also kept the bedrooms smelling nice." I smiled softly at the quick memory of waking up to the scent. My grandmother's house always felt exactly like what you needed when you needed it. It smelled like home for some and a place of safety for others. I shook the reminiscing from my mind. I'd save those memories for when I really needed something fond to take my mind off hell.

"Not much of a lead."

"Maybe, maybe not. Keep in mind, the witches we're hunting are using whatever they can find in common textbooks rather than skill and technique. They probably read, in one of their books off the bookstore shelf, lavender would ward off evil or some other nonsense. It would fit with what we've been seeing. Every scene, so far, has been cobbled together with layers of random craft. There are about two dozen types of witches, and I think I've seen a bit of them all at every crime scene. In other words, they're winging it. In my opinion, I'd say to keep tracking the smells. It'll probably lead you to them a lot quicker than anything else we've been doing. If it were me, that's what I'd be doing, anyway."

"I'll let the others know to keep on the trail. I also sent out a few people to track the purchases of the items you emailed me earlier. I didn't think any of those crystals would be so rare or expensive. Hopefully, they're rare enough for something to turn up," he replied.

"It's a stab in the dark, but I'm counting on them to screw up eventually, like buying everything in one go or being overheard while shopping. Last year, a small group of teenagers were overheard talking about summoning a demon. In Canada, it's still illegal to summon without a licensed practitioner. That's how they were caught, by running their mouths. Two people died because they each wanted tickets to some sold-out show. The demon killed the two and took their tickets for the kids."

"It should be illegal everywhere. It's harder to buy a gun than it is to summon the end of the bloody world," he replied, and I couldn't argue with that. Mankind will be their own downfall, and it'll probably be for something stupid, like fitting into smaller jeans or youthful skin. "Speaking of hell, how did the holy water work out?"

I huffed a laugh. "Exactly how you said it would. It hurt like hell. I haven't felt that kind of pain in a long friggin' time. It felt like being boiled alive while having my skin peeled off. I can't see myself signing up for that willingly again."

"Most who have it done needed to be held down. I know I did. I thrashed around and cried until I vomited."

"It just goes to show how much tougher women are," I said, which got a laugh from him. It was music to my soul.

"How are you feeling?" Miguel asked, always concerned about everyone but himself. It was who he was and one of the reasons I had fallen so hard for him. "My shift with Caser is over in three hours. Do you want to grab a bite to eat?"

"I'm not sure how much I can keep down, but I'd like the company," I replied. "I should let you go. Lord knows what that busybody, Caser, is up to with your back turned. If it were me, I'd be digging my way out through the drywall. I just wanted to make sure everyone was okay and tell you…I don't know. I guess I just needed to hear your voice. It's getting dark out, and you know how I am with the night."

"As much as I love hearing your voice, too, you sound upset, not just scared of the dark."

"Take your pick, Miguel. There's a lot going on, and I'm tired, emotionally and physically," I answered and paused. There were so many layers to my mood, I didn't know where to start. The pain I felt was deeper than any other I've endured. "My heart is sad. My soul feels heavy today."

"Do you want me to call in my cover sooner? Those of us with families are allowed to leave," he asked. "My cover won't mind at all, and he owes me a few covered shifts."

I smiled. I was sure everyone in his Pack owed him. Miguel may claim to be ruthless, but he was the biggest bleeding heart around. "No. I'm going to dig into my minibar and take a nice, long soak in the tub." I was glad he couldn't see me and smell my lies. Cisco had once mentioned he could tell I was lying by the sickly-sweet smell scent that filled the room. I pushed the thought of Cisco from my mind as my eyes began to water.

"If you're good on your own, I need to stop and grab Sofia from the Pale Horse after my shift. They're releasing Cisco's body to his next of kin, which is Sofia." His voice hitched, along with my pulse. "She has to sign a few things, and Pack will transport him for his transition to his afterlife."

"Oh, Miguel, I'm so sorry. Is there anything I can do to help?" I asked.

"Me coming to you will help. I'll be over as soon as I drop Sofia off at home. Try to get some rest after your bath. If you're asleep when I get there, I'll order us room service, and we can eat in bed, just like old times," he replied. "I'll see you in a bit."

"Goodbye," I answered and hung up. My ending words were final. I wouldn't be asleep when he got to my room. I wouldn't even be here. There were a dozen different things I wanted to say before I hung up, things he needed to know, but he knew them already. His heart knew how deeply I loved him. Like Samuel had said, sometimes, love was enough. Most people didn't know it would be the last time they talked to a loved one, but the loved one always knew, in their heart, how much they were loved. The words didn't always need to be said for them to be true and understood.

Time wasn't infinite for mankind, and my time was up. The countdown was over, as I knew it would be. I knew the witches would be back with new leverage. It was only a matter of time. They didn't come this far to give up, but neither did I. Someone once said that if desperate times called for desperate measures, then I was free to act as desperately as I wished. I was about to show them what cornering me, taking away all my options, would do. If they wanted to play deadly games, they'd win deadly prizes.

With all the cards drawn, I had no tricks left up my sleeve. It was a scary place to be, out of options, with nothing left to lose. I suppose I could lose my life, but it wasn't looking like I'd walk out of here alive, anyway. What better way to enter hell than stumbling in, half-charred, hair wild and frizzy, with a pack of witches, a Lycan, a demon and a vampire, trailing behind me. If that didn't buy me one night of rest in the cage, I'd be filing a complaint.

The moment Miguel had said the words, 'Anna was missing,' I knew I'd see the dark witches sooner rather than later, and this time I was prepared. I spent the entire night and day in preparation for what was about to unfold. The next time, I'd go with them, but I'd make sure they'd regret it. Though, I was sure I would as well. But no plan was perfect. No amount of homework could ever prepare me for true evil. I knew what was at risk if I went, but I also knew the gamble I'd be making if I stayed. Either way, they weren't going to stop coming. The only decision I had to make was how many lives I would allow them to take before I caved and let them take mine. Whatever the outcome, I couldn't let more people die because I was too afraid of death myself. How could I look myself in the eyes if I knew someone else had suffered in my place and I had done nothing? I already had the guilt of Cisco to live with for however long that life would be. I wouldn't survive another person, let alone most of humanity, if the witches succeeded. I couldn't hide out, sipping tea while the world burned because I was afraid. Once upon a time, I could have watched the world burn. Not anymore. Not when someone I loved was out there, fighting for the future of all mankind. I could do my part and save at least one person—Miguel.

I sat at the foot of my bed with my shoes on, my hair pulled back in a braid, wearing comfortable clothes to be tortured in, and ready for what the night had in store for me. I thought of all the ways I had been beaten and abused during my two minutes in hell. I closed my eyes and allowed myself to relive the parts I'd locked away. I told myself that no matter what the witches did to me, it would never be as bad as hell. Because in hell, you don't pass out. In hell, you're wide awake and feeling it all. In hell, it didn't matter what the torture was. You felt it to the bone. You don't die. You can't suffocate or drown or need air, although they'd make you feel like you did. It didn't matter how many books the witches had or if one of them was a High Priest himself—level three degree in witchcraft—they'd never be as bad as demons. I had learned this for two very long and drawn-out minutes. I had been nothing more than nerve endings on fire, with a burning soul clinging to me. Two minutes of pure pain, whether you're in hell or hospital, feels like an eternity. They could pull out all the bells and whistles, but I remembered what real torture felt like, and tonight would be a walk in the park compared to the cage.

I felt them the moment they stepped onto my floor. I could smell the hell they carried around in their souls. They knocked on my door like they were selling cookies—light and polite and drew no attention. They didn't bother with trying more than a knock. Their energy would be wasted within my wards. They'd have felt them as soon as the elevator opened. I may only be a level one witch, but I was a full-blooded, hereditary witch—level one in title, level three in blood. My very blood gave me power you couldn't find in any spell. There was a reason other witches stayed clear of full-bloods. We didn't need to prepare spells. We were born prepared. We didn't need fancy herbs and crystals. Our blood was more than enough. These witches knocked on the wrong door. Soon, they'd realize it.

"That witch doesn't kill you makes you stronger," I whispered to myself. A pun that hung over my mother's spelling altar. It always made me smile, and tonight, it made me stronger.

I stared up at the ceiling and centered myself. I didn't fully know where souls went when good people died. I didn't know what heaven looked like or if it was anything like how I had imagined it. I had learned firsthand where they could go—downstairs. I often wondered if my parents, wherever they were, knew what was going on down here. I had no doubt they passed go, collected two hundred and didn't take the elevator down. I hope they weren't cursing me out right now from wherever they were for my hair-brained idea. My room echoed with another knock, and this time, when I moved to stand, my charm necklace flared against my flesh, a hot warning not to open the door. I didn't listen. I stood and walked to the door, taking deep breaths as I moved across the room. I turned the handle slowly, trying to calm the shake in my hand. There would be no emotional preparation for what stood on the other side. Nothing I could say to myself would be enough. I was scared, and I had every right to be. If I failed, everyone would die. If I succeeded, only my neck would be on the chopping block. As I said, no plan was perfect.

I left a letter on my desk, and in it I'd said goodbye to Miguel. He wouldn't get to say his goodbye, yet again, but he would get my forgiveness for any wrongdoing, my apologies for my own shortcomings and my pleading for him to forgive himself, no matter what. I kept my word to him. I didn't bolt, but I was leaving. I had signed the note with all my love, because now, staring death in the eyes, I was willing to admit out loud just how deep my love went. It was utterly bottomless. The letter and my love were the least I could do before I stepped into my grave. Miguel shouldn't have to live the rest of his life, however long or short it may be after my demise, with my dark words hanging over his head. That's not how I wanted to leave this world or how I wanted to be remembered — the witch who hated everyone, however close to the truth that might be. But Miguel didn't make that list of people I despised. He never did. Of all the things I'd miss in this world, he made the number one spot. My cat and naps were tied for second. I hoped Samuel was right. My cat would see me in hell. At least I wouldn't be alone.

"Good evening, ladies." I smiled as I opened the door wider. "Won't you come in?"

Witch One shook her head. "Thank you, but no."

"So civil," I smirked.

She smiled. "This does not need to turn into a scene, but that choice is yours to make."

I picked at my nails as if bored. "Smile all you want, hag, but I see the fear in your eyes. It sours the air around you. Your soul smells like rotten fruit and yesterday's garbage. Lucky for you, demons don't care what your soul tastes like. They'll eat any old trash kicking around."

"Enough of this," Witch Two said to her counterpart.

But I wasn't done needling her. Anger made people foolish. They made mistakes they wouldn't normally make. Sure, they'd also beat the hell out of me for it, but physical pain didn't scare me like it would someone who hadn't sat in a cage. Tripping them up was worth whatever bruises they'd inflict. I motioned to the bandages on her hand. "I see your stab wound isn't healed yet. You don't rate high enough for your demon to expel energy to heal you? Oh, what a surprise that is. I don't blame him. I'm not even a demon, and I wouldn't waste a Band-Aid on your shriveled soul."

"He has said he will heal me once he comes," she replied.

"Since you already broke rule one and tinkered with hell, I'll give you this one for free," I said, shaking my head. "Rule two of summoning demons... If you're talking to him without needing to summon him from hell, your soul is already damned. Pack your things, find consecrated ground and prepare to spend the rest of your life there. A demon can whisper into the ear of a soul that is his property without being summoned. Holy ground is the only thing that will help you now."

"Rule one?" she asked. She stood with her hip cocked but leaned in like a curious child.

"Rule one, when summoning demons... Never call something you cannot put down on your own. If it takes more than you to call it, leave the fucking thing alone. If even one member of your group dies, you won't have enough juice to send it back. That's just science, really. If you needed a full cup to call him, you'd need that same cup of juice to send him packing."

Witch Two nudged her friend. "Enough of this nonsense. We're not here for this. We're not here to waste our time."

"I'd agree. It's a waste of time. Your souls are already tagged and bagged," I replied. "Is there a reason you're here? Did you come to see how good my aim is with a knife?"

The curious one flinched, and I smiled. Witch One was scared, and she damn well should be. I was terrified of what was coming, and I wasn't even the one chatting with the blasted thing. She pulled out her trusty tablet, and I cringed at what she was about to show me. If it was anything like the last time, I had no doubt I'd jump her in the hall and paint the sparkling white tiles with her blood. She wasted no time and turned on the screen, turning it to face me. Anna sat in a chair, bloodied and bruised. It looked like she had gone a few rounds with a world-class boxer. I abhor violence against children. I won't even take part in an exorcism that involves a child. I tried once, and I puked all over the demon. I couldn't stomach what the hellspawn was doing to the kid from the inside. It laughed at me. The parents didn't pay me. My ego was destroyed.

I vibrated with rage. "If the demon doesn't kill you, I'll hunt you to the ends of the earth if another finger touches Anna."

"You have two choices. You can come with us, or she will die. We will offer this once," Witch Two spoke. She was cocky. I'd give her that. I probably would have been just as smug had I chosen the burnt side of the toast and hadn't a soul to hold me back.

"Kill her, and you both die in this hallway," I replied. "You won't walk away this time."

"But she will still be dead," she answered. "Make your decision."

"I wouldn't call those choices, exactly," I answered. And they weren't. All they meant was that I could let Anna die or kill myself by going with them. They had given me this choice before, with Cisco. I had refused, and they'd cut off his head. I wouldn't survive seeing a child go through that. No one would survive the hell I'd unleash. "Let her go, and I will come."

"Your word," she demanded.

"My word. If you let Anna go back to her father and never bother her again by you or any of your people, I will leave with you," I answered carefully. Every word carried weight. Although I had every intention of going with them, with or without Anna, I'd still try to save the girl before I willingly walked into a trap. "Give me your word. She comes to no harm, goes back to her father and you and your people will never bother her again."

"I give you my word," Witch Two answered, echoed by the wraith of a witch at her side. Witch One was wasting away fast. I wondered if she was bargaining for a little more on the side. Whatever she was asking for wasn't worth it. One look in the mirror should have told her that.

"I accept your oath," I replied.

Witch One placed a necklace on the floor. It was woven hair with a blue stone attached to it. Jade…for protection and to ward me. She kicked it into the room. The wards on my door didn't react to the charm. It was useless. "Put this on."

"Once Anna is freed, I will put it on. You have my word," I replied.

I waited for what felt like hours until the witch's phone beeped. She read her text and smiled. "Your little wolf is outside The Pale Horse. I gave you my word. She was returned. It is your turn to fulfill your end of the bargain."

"And I believe everything I'm told." I rolled my eyes. "Prove it."

She swiped her phone and turned the screen to me. It showed a live feed of Anna on the curb in front of The Pale Horse, in the middle of witnesses and with a lineup around the block. I felt a little more confident Anna would survive the night. And if not, the witches broke their word and would pay three-fold for it. An oath breaker wasn't popular in hell. I picked the necklace off the floor and fought not to cringe. It was made of their hair and other things. I wanted to puke at the thought of it touching my skin, for no other reason than it was gross. Still, I put the charm on because I said I would and stepped out of my room. I closed the door and my eyes. I wasn't foolish enough to think I'd walk out of the hotel on my own accord. The first fist landed, and my legs buckled. I didn't fight back or brace myself from the fall. I was out cold before my cheek touched the tile floor. Thank God for small miracles. I'd rather be unconscious than deal with them as we went to wherever bad witches stored their live victims.

I was in that place between full blackout and awake and rode that edge back and forth. I could still feel them lift me from the floor and carry me. If they wanted me, I wasn't about to help them get me to the place of my death. I was in and out but stayed perfectly still, nothing but dead weight for two women who had the physical strength of an emaciated street dog on its last days. They were weak of mind, body and soul, the cost trifecta of meddling with hell. It ate all of who you were from the inside out. Demons were parasites. They fed off your life force, taking sips here and there until it was too late, and they swallowed you whole — bones, skin and all. My soul smiled, knowing that no matter what, those bitches would rot in hell. Either way, justice would come for them, and it smelled like matchsticks and brimstone.

Chapter Four

As I came around, fragments of the night came into slow focus. At first, all I could think about was the throb between my temples and the confusion as to why my head would feel like a used-up basketball. Little by little, as the waves of nausea faded, the nightmare I had rested in became my reality. I remembered being in a vehicle, the smell of lavender and rosemary, voices and laughter, after being hit hard enough for the world to tilt and my body hit the floor like a sack of potatoes. In the back of my mind, as I curled in the back of a vehicle, hands bound behind my back, I could hear purring. It was a comfortable sound. It kept me calm and relaxed. While being driven to my fate, I was wrapped up in the faint music of home and safety. It didn't matter if the world was burning around me. If I was tucked safely behind the walls of home, it felt like the flames couldn't touch me. Home meant we were protected from the monsters. Now that I was waking up, home felt like a world away. I would have given everything of value to have my cat with me now, even just for the false sense of security.

I came fully alert on the floor, chained and bound with cold iron. I cursed at the loss of my memories of home. My eyes watered when I couldn't hear my cat's music. I blinked away the threat of crying, breathed in and out until the inner shaking of fear calmed and centered my mind. Panic and tears would do nothing for me here. I would only make mistakes if I allowed it to take root. I hummed the tune of my father's favorite blues song while I grounded myself. I made a mental note to send my therapist a thank you basket for this technique.

I took a quick assessment of my body. I was sore, throbbing and thankfully fully dressed. For some reason, I had expected to wake up naked. Being nude was the most vulnerable position to be in. I still wouldn't have caved to the demands of two deranged witches, but I'd likely be less mouthy and violent. I didn't like the idea of fist-fighting with all my bits on display for the world. The thought made my skin crawl. Thank God for small favors. With my clothes on and my limbs still attached, things were looking up for now, but the party had only just begun.

I jiggled my wrists just enough to feel how much wiggle room I had, which was just enough to slide around and pinch the skin. I huffed a laugh at the attempts to extinguish my source of energy. Like them, I had read the same books about containing witches. But I wasn't that kind of witch, where I could be cut off from power through trinkets and locks. My magic came from my blood. It was a curse bound to my soul, passed down from generation to generation. They'd have to drain every ounce of my life force for me to be incapable of using my power. I didn't call on the elements of the earth, where I could be walled off from the energy. But I wouldn't be mentioning that little fact to them. It wasn't my fault they didn't do their homework. It's staggering how few folks read up on what they were trying to kill. More times than not, I was the only one who did. But I wouldn't complain today. Their ignorance would be to my advantage...I hoped. Sometimes it didn't matter how much I prepared. Everyone got lucky once, and that's all it would take to end my life.

I inched my way up from my back to my knees. I didn't like the idea of lying down with bad guys roaming around. On my back, I felt as helpless as going to the bathroom naked. The thought of being caught with my pants down was a very real fear I had since actually being attacked by a demon with my pants down. I stretched out my back as much as I could with my arms tied behind me. Small cracks and pops reminded me that even in my mid-twenties, I was getting too old for this shit. Being passed out on the cold ground didn't help me feel any younger. I'd kill for a holiday right about now — one that didn't involve crime scenes, demons, blood and gore, or being bound and waiting for death. You know, the usual kind of vacation ordinary people got to have. I laughed at myself. *As if... I'm not normal, and I'm a beacon for trouble. Case in point, my current situation.*

I sat in an eight-by-eight stone cell, give or take an inch. It was slightly bigger than the average prison but not nearly as pleasant as one. I had spent enough nights behind bars for being a witch, more than I'd care to admit, to know the ins and outs of holding cells, and my current one was a dump. I doubted this room came with a call to my attorney, scratchy bedding or three squares a day. Hopefully, I'd live long enough to complain about being hungry. In the earlier days, before the Coven stepped in to protect us from blatant discrimination, any time something went bump in the night or a body was found without an organ, cops knocked on the witch's door first. Given I was the only full witch in town, my door was revolving. Even with the Coven's protection, I still made sure I kept clear notes of my schedule, since it seemed witches usually needed an alibi. Some things never changed, no matter how advanced mankind claimed to be. It's the same reason every witch kept their locations active on their phones. Sometimes it's hard to remember what we were doing three weeks ago, on a Thursday, at a quarter after six. Old habits died hard, and witches were still as flammable today as they were three hundred years ago. I was not the only one with the mentality of shooting monsters first and asking questions later. The general public still saw witches as part of the problem.

My newest holiday destination was dank and dingy, a huge step down compared to my last room. I don't know what pissed me off more, that I was sitting in a shithole or that the room I'd paid a fortune to stay in was empty. One glance around the stone suite said I felt a little of both. A sliver of light shined into the room from under an old wooden door. It wasn't bright enough to read by, but it cast enough light for me to see the predicament I was in. I groaned as I took in the sights of my little slice of hell above the crust. Surrounded by aged rock and earth, there was nothing else to do but stare at my windowless room and imagine the horrors that stained the soul of the place. I could feel it dance across my skin like ants on the march. These four walls had once held prisoners, souls who should have never seen the inside of a place like this. Faintly, I could hear the cries of those who had come before me in the back of my mind like the tune of a song I couldn't forget. The stones had scratches, gouged by someone desperate enough to try to dig their way out. I knew they had held the other victims right where I now knelt. The marks on the walls were too fresh to have been done at a time when the stone was new. Time fades everything, including signs of a desperate soul. My heart hurt to see each fresh chip in the stone. It reminded me of my cage in hell, clawed up from the inside, my pitiful attempts at an escape that would never happen. In all my years and research, not a single soul had ever fled from hell. Some were released, but no one broke out. And, like my time in the pits, not a single victim had escaped the clutches of these lunatics, either. I didn't think I stood a chance at escape, but I was hopeful I'd take them with me when my lights went out.

My room was a hollow cube, one way in and one way out. They were not the best odds I had faced, but thankfully not the worst. I could make out glyphs on the ceiling and walls. The floor had smaller ones carved right into the stone. The wooden door was marred with blood, smeared into symbols. I knew the marks by heart. I had drawn them myself at home. These weren't to keep something out like mine at home did. These were on the wrong side of the door for that. They were used to keep evil contained. Was I the evil they were trying to confine to the stone casket? *How rude.* I wasn't evil. Not yet, anyway. Give me a few hours, and I'd show them why they shouldn't meddle with what they couldn't control or put down on their own.

The lack of light and windows made it impossible to know how much time had passed. My internal clock was beaten up by the time zone difference and the perpetual lack of sleep. In any other situation, I knew where the sun was in the sky or when the moon had lost its fight and set until it could try again. I hated the dark enough to know precisely when the sun would rise again. But here, now, I didn't know if the sun was up or down or if it had risen more than once since I'd left my hotel room. Given enough time, I'd bet a person would lose not only time in here but also their own name. The utter isolation made it worse. Maybe it was the dark, or perhaps it was the lack of stimuli from the outside world, but my skin crawled. Whatever it was, I understood why the last person had tried to claw their way out with their own fingernails.

The room reminded me of a blood den I had once been in, from the spiders dancing across my brain to the scent that clung to every inch of the place. Even after the bodies had been removed, the smell hung in the air like fresh paint. A rogue vampire had a little love nest on the outskirts of town, complete with a dungeon and chains. It looked like a BDSM scene meets Freddy Krueger. The vampire had tied up, tortured and slowly bled half a dozen women to death before he had been caught and saw the sun. The stench of blood, death and other things was imprinted on my soul, and this room was every bit as putrid as that basement had been. My stomach flopped at the déjà vu to my senses. I didn't do my usual deep breathing exercises to ground myself and focus. I didn't want to suck in any more of the odor than I had to. The air stank of bodily waste, vomit, blood and death. The rotten stench of sewage rolled my stomach into a knot of disgust. I'd get used to it. But until then, I breathed out of my mouth. I didn't know what was worse, breathing it in or tasting it. I cleared my throat a few times and swallowed my urge to be sick. I didn't need to add fresh vomit to the list of jailhouse aromas I sat in. Although, smelling my own wouldn't be nearly as bad as inhaling someone else's.

"*I need a favor,*" I muttered to myself, thinking back to the conversation with Miguel that had brought me to Mexico. The last time I helped him, I'd ended up in a prison cell, handcuffed. Some things never changed. "Some favor this turned out to be, Miguel."

I wondered how long it would take for Miguel to realize I was missing and if he'd come for me. I told myself he would, since I'd do the same for him. Me being chained in a hellhole proved just how far I'd go to help him. But would he leave his Pack to find me? I had basically told him to side with his people, to always choose them over me. Right about now, a small part of me regretted those words. The rest of me was hoping Miguel would stay away long enough not to be another hostage that I'd have to bury later. *Love bites.*

A wave of shivers rolled through me, from my nose to my toes. It wasn't fear. I was cold to the bone. The stones were chilled, and the room felt like an icebox. It had to be nighttime for me to tremble as I did, unless I was deep underground, which wasn't likely. I doubted the witches were smart enough, or brave enough, to go deep underground. When a person was touching hell, they tended to be afraid of the dark. It was too damn hot during the day in Mexico for me to be this cold, but the nights were cool this time of year. I was betting it was sometime after midnight. At least I'd freeze to death before being tortured. What I wouldn't have given for a little of that sun now, after days of constant grumbling at the heat. I didn't say I was consistent in my complaints.

I cringed at the thought of being underground. It had nothing to do with being a few feet closer to hell and everything to do with logistics. It was simply easier to find people above the dirt. If I were below, I'd be lost down here until my body was found, stumbled upon by a fluke. The smell of my body would attract the monsters and the critters and leave no trace of my even being here. If I was in a cave or whatever they called the place I knelt in, I questioned a rescue party's ability to find me at all. The statistics were against me. Since the war on drugs had begun in Mexico, people had been dropping like flies in these parts. Around forty people were reported as missing daily, which left me wondering what the actual numbers were. Between drugs, gangs and the new wave of practitioners, people weren't just missing. They disappeared indefinitely.

Here I was, in a city I didn't belong in, with people I didn't really know, and those who did weren't my biggest fans and had some odd expectation that they'd even look for me. I'd have better luck getting a genie to pop out of my pocket and grant me the wish of freedom. I was more scared of a run-in with a genie and would sooner take my chances with the witches. Although it was looking like a clandestine grave, my go-to threat was where I'd end up. Less than a decade ago, over two thousand unmarked graves were found, which really freed up some space for foreign witches like me to be dumped into. If only I had gone to Iceland, with its lowest crime rates and highest control over all things demon-related. I could be sipping a Pina Colada poolside right now, instead of sitting in a cell, waiting to die.

I grinned in amusement. My fear made me giddy. It was either make jokes or start screaming for help, and I wasn't a screamer. I shook my morbid thoughts away and brought myself back to the unfortunate turn of events. How long would it take until someone noticed I was gone? Samuel would notice, but I'd be dead and buried long before he was able to come to look for me. Miguel would, when he came to my room for dinner, and he'd likely come for me. But one person didn't make a strong search party, no matter how furry one was. Was it even a 'party' if it was only one person? I didn't doubt Caser would let me die, solving his problem with me meddling with Miguel, but would he keep the rest of their people from helping? They were all in lockdown. Would they risk it to help? I doubted it. I didn't exactly win friends the last time I was there. One of their own ended up dead, and I got clawed up. That was bound to sour a few grapes on the ol' wolf wine. It had certainly left a sour taste in my mouth.

"Who will feed my cat?" I mumbled to myself. I smiled at the silliness of my worry. I was chained down in a room built for death, and my concern was of a cat that was probably a better hunter-gatherer than I was. I could almost see the judgment on my cat's face as I sat in what would become my casket. The blasted thing came into my bedroom every morning to make sure I didn't die in my sleep. The beast had very low expectations of me or my ability to keep myself out of an early grave. To be fair, there were many times I shouldn't have woken up throughout my life. If I opened my eyes tomorrow, I'd be as surprised as my cat was most days.

Whatever my worries — and I had many — I kept myself grounded. Full-out panic wouldn't help, and I'd drain whatever energy I had on a pointless freakout. But even focused, the fear of knowing I had come into the witch's den alone, gnawed at my bravery with each passing minute. Although courage came in many forms, it wasn't endless. To keep myself settled in my decision, I pictured the faces of everyone I had ever met and those I had loved. Knowing they would live kept me centered. Knowing they wouldn't need to be brave in the face of death kept me calm.

"One death over many," I whispered, a reminder to myself. "You can do this, Ailis. Miguel would do it for you. You can do it for him."

Every so often, my ears would twitch from a piercing, pain-filled shriek that penetrated the suffocating silence. It would seem I wasn't the only guest at Hotel Hostage. It changed nothing. Bad guys always had and always will have prisoners, leverage, fodder, souls to torture. It was in their job description. They wouldn't be a bad guy if they weren't out doing bad-guy things, would they? I closed my eyes and waited for my turn. The cries didn't bother me. I could tune them out. A lifetime in hell made me immune to it. I've heard it all before, one hundred times over, only worse. In the real world, being skinned alive wasn't something you screamed through. You passed out and died. In hell, you were alive and kicking for the entire exfoliation, screaming with each inch removed. I'd hear nothing from this prison that could compare to what I've seen and heard in person from my cage. Hell didn't make me tougher. It made me crueler. I could listen to just about anything and not even cringe. Seeing it, on the other hand, still unsettled me, more because I knew how it felt.

I let myself doze off. I could nap anywhere and in almost all states of emotional distress, not including a vehicle. Die once in a car accident, and it pretty much cured you of road trip naps. There weren't many people I trusted enough behind the wheel to sleep. But the moment a trusted loved one was in the driver's seat, I was out cold. Miguel was one of those people. Although I sat in another prison because of his favors, I trusted him with my life, just not my freedom. It could be worse. I didn't know how, but I was sure I'd learn that answer soon enough.

On my knees, hands behind my back, I got as much rest as I could. I needed to conserve my energy and sanity. It wasn't hard. I'd slept my way through hell, and this cage wasn't worse. I stayed on the edge of full sleep and wakefulness. It was the kind of rest where I wasn't entirely under but not quite awake. It's what my grandmother used to call a 'relax'. "*A wee doze,*" she'd say. I'd kill for a night of actual sleep, but I was too scared and too sore to allow myself to fully sleep. Every few minutes, my body felt heavier, and my shoulders slumped forward. My eye and temple throbbed, and my neck was sore from being punched. It felt like I had hit my head with more force than I had thought. *Rude of them not to catch me as I went down, if I say so myself.* Though, I wouldn't have caught someone I purposely knocked out, either. I guess that made us even in that area. It was hard to throw stones when I'd have kicked them while they were down. I went toe to toe with monsters. Picking up a rock and braining them wasn't beneath me. I didn't follow a fighter's creed. I followed the rules of the street. I fought dirty and to the bitter end. I wasn't big enough to do it any other way. I learned how to fist-fight from kids who had no special abilities. They showed me how to use every possible way to win, especially the more questionable and treacherous ones.

I opened my eyes when I felt myself slip further into a comfortable slumber. I shouldn't be this relaxed. The head injury made me feel lazier than I should be. The parts of my mind that should be on full alert were groggy and soupy. I wasn't just tired. I was inching toward the edge of unconsciousness. My head started to throb like I had been kicked by a horse. I have had concussions before, not from being kicked by a horse but the same kind of pain. This felt closer to something being broken. I'd be pissed off if they'd dented the titanium plate in my forehead. It would mean surgery again if I lived. If my parting gift from this fleabag hotel was another craniotomy, *pissed off* didn't cover the seething rage I'd feel. I hated hospitals as much as I hated sitting in stone clinks.

I sensed the witches at the door before it swung open. My necklace heated, and my skin crawled with spiders. They felt like hell and demons and decisions they'd pay for. The scent of dabbling in torture and hell filled the room. I was thankful, for once, to smell fresh blood. It covered the repulsive odor of the septic hellhole I was in. Through the door came the two soon-to-be-dead aspiring witches from the hotel — Witch One and Witch Two. They were smug, staring at me on my knees, just as I would have been. Though, I wouldn't have been stupid enough to tie my enemy up and leave her heart beating or come into a room with someone ten times more powerful with a dozen ways to kill them at my disposal. I wondered how they had made it this far when they were clearly lacking in the commonsense department. Clearly they weren't the brains of this operation, or it would have failed by now. They were the weakest links, which was probably why they were sent into a room with a full-blooded witch. They were expendable.

"Dumb and Dumber," I muttered.

"Ailis, how are you feeling?" Witch One asked. It was an odd question. The concern in her voice was weirder, given she was the one who had rattled my brain to begin with. But I'd have been concerned if my sacrifice wasn't in perfect health as well.

"I'm not a big fan of your accommodations. They're underwhelming. Not even a coffee or a bagel. Shit service, if you ask me." They hadn't asked, but I needled anyway. I gave them a bored look. I shrugged as best I could do with my wrists shackled at my back. "I've felt better. But I've also felt worse."

"I'm sure you have. I've heard a great many things about you," she replied. "You've been unconscious for just over twenty-four hours. I think you hit your head a little too hard. I apologize for that."

"My, my, aren't we all of a sudden civilized?" I rolled my eyes. "I don't accept your apology."

"It doesn't matter. It has been given."

I smiled, followed by a small laugh that faded to a tired sigh. "I don't know what you've been reading, little bookstore witch, but I need to accept the apology for it to clear the slate between us. Until then, you carry the stain of your wrongdoing. Too many stains aren't good for the soul...what's remaining of it, anyway."

"You'll be gone soon enough, and it won't matter," she responded.

"It won't matter? Do you know nothing about the magic you're trying to use or the world you're stomping around in? It's like the blind leading the blind." I shook my head at her idiocy. "Again, you have no idea what you're talking about. If I'm dead, you'll carry the taint on your soul forever. There will never be a chance for me to forgive you. I'll be dead, and the stain lasts beyond my death." I schooled her for no other reason than to waste their time. "Why do you think murderers go to hell? There's no one left to absolve them." Sure, they didn't need to know murderers went to hell regardless of who forgave them — a life for a life and all that jazz. But I'd still say what I had to say to rattle them with. Sure, lying is a sin, and I didn't need any more sins to count in the end, but I was pretty sure there was a clause that said you could lie during life-or-death situations. Fingers crossed, because won't I look silly when I'm being tarred and feathered for telling fibs to psychopaths?

"If you feel well enough to argue, you are well enough to begin." She may have tried to ignore my comment, but I watched the fear set in behind her eyes.

Even a bookstore witch understood the weight of imbalance. I wanted to laugh that this, me not forgiving her, was what she was concerned about. But I didn't bother pointing out the obvious. The stain from me was mere wrinkles over her soul compared to what she carried around from bargains and tortured souls. It smeared her aura like black ink dropped in water. I could see it like a shadow that stood too close to my own. There was so much taint on her soul. It looked like it was almost well done.

"To begin what?" I asked.

"We need your help raising Chac. You are who we've been waiting for. Only your blood will do," Witch Two stepped away from the wall, just inches from my knees. I looked at her feet and raised my brows, an acknowledgment of how close she was to me. She stepped back a foot, and I smiled. *Petty, I know.*

"Haven't you heard? I'm the Mother of Prostitutes and Abominations of the Earth," I said with more pride than I should have. They both stared at me like I'd grown an extra eyeball in the middle of my forehead. "I take it neither of you have read the Bible? I'm the Whore of Hell. The Whore of Babylon. You don't know the story, I'm guessing? I'm not exactly a good sacrifice. I'm not a virgin, and I'm unquestionably not the poster girl for religious purity. Sadly, hell has already used me up."

"Power and sacrifice come in many forms. You should know this." Witch One spoke to me like a child. "You will help us now, or you will suffer until you do."

"No. I'll take door number three. You can kill me," I answered. Pain burst across my cheek. The slap jolted my already knocked around brain. This was going to do wonders for my concussion. Dying of brain damage? I didn't even factor that into my 'what-could-and-would-go-wrong-when-I-went-with-the-witches' plan. "Beating me isn't going to make me help you, either. In all the stories you've ever heard about me, have you learned nothing? I spent an eternity in hell. Nothing you can think up or do will come close to what the demons and devils can and will do to me. This is nothing more than uncomfortable foreplay, but I can nap through it. Because when the demons come, that's when the real torture begins. Trust me, you'll know soon enough. If you manage to raise whatever demon spawn you've agreed to bring to the surface, he's going to burn you all." I laughed out the last of my comment. I couldn't help it. Call it nerves or call it amusement, but I laughed at the two dead women standing in front of me. They were on borrowed time, and soon the debt would be called in. "We're all going to die. I hope he kills me last, so I can watch you get your just rewards. I would bargain with him just to watch you all die. I'm that level of petty."

Witch One hit me again. "Enough games! We're done playing. You will help us, one way or another."

"No, I won't. Kill me now, meat suit, because if I don't die tonight, I'll hunt you until my last breath," I replied. "That's if, by some miracle, one of you lives through your deadly demon games."

"Are you threatening us?" she asked, a hint of a laugh filling the room.

"Did it sound like a compliment?" I replied.

"Enough of this. We have Sofia," Witch Two said, cutting between my back and forth with her counterpart. She was the voice of reason between the two. Her grip on her sanity, and likely reality, was firmer. She'd be harder to needle, but it could still be done. With enough time, I could make even a devil grow irritated by me. Some would say it was a skill that came naturally to me.

"Hit me again, and one of you will hurt along with me." I spit out a mouth of blood from biting my cheek when I was hit. *So that's who was screaming bloody murder since I woke up.* I had wondered who took up room two. It appeared we both ordered the same room service. I laughed on the outside but winced all the way down to my soul. I wasn't Sophie's biggest fan, nor was she mine, but I didn't want her dead for it and certainly not at the hands of absolute bat-shit crazy wannabe witches. I was fine with choosing my own fate but not that of someone else's. Did it change how I'd proceed? No. I didn't want her death on my hands, but I would risk a lot more than just me and Sofia for this to end. I'd have to hope for the best and prepare for the worst.

"And what do you expect to gain from taking Sofia?" I asked. The more time I got them to spend on me, the less time they had to torture some other poor soul—even if that soul was someone who hated me. "She doesn't strike me as a good sacrifice."

"We will kill your precious little wolf if you don't help," Witch Two said.

I laughed a little too suddenly, making them stare at me in confusion. "And? She wouldn't be the first creature I've watched die, and she certainly won't be the last. Go ahead. If possible, could you make it quick? She sure is a bloody screamer, and I could really use the rest."

"Heartless bitch," Witch One muttered. "You'd let your friend die in your place without so much as batting an eye, and you have the nerve to call us evil?"

"First, I just finished telling you, I'm the Whore of Babylon. Were you not listening to that part?" I said and smiled.

"You'd let your wolf die in your place," she accused, her voice thick with disgust.

"I'm not going to help you to save her life if that's what you're waiting for." I shrugged. I fought the urge to smile as I stared into the eyes of each witch, and both flinched. "You are holders of information you should not have. If you walk out of this hovel with a pulse, you'll die for that knowledge. They will hunt you for it. Mark my words."

I warned them both, but neither looked troubled by the threat they made. "Regardless, Sofia isn't *my* wolf or my friend. Even if she were, nothing you could do to her would make me help you summon a demon. Sofia is probably a great gal, but she's not worth the death of millions of innocent people. None of us are. Not her and not even me."

"Are you certain of that?" Witch One asked. She itched for more pain. My pain. She would make an excellent addition to hell. She was already on the fast track to a promotion. She was a breath away from becoming a walking demon. After a few years in the pits, I'm sure she'd be one of the tortures and would be delighted to take the job. Maybe. Hell had a way of taking the fun out of things like this. Any passion once turned into a job, sucked.

"Do not make this any more difficult than it already is for you," Witch Two added.

"Good cop, bad cop. I've seen this movie before. I die in the end, no matter what I do," I answered. "I'm not making this difficult, but I'm not going to make this easier, either. You're going to kill me whether I help you or not. As tempting as that offer is, I'd rather not damn all of humanity on my way out."

"We haven't hurt you nearly as bad as we can, but that is up to you. Do this of your own free will or do this by force. This can be a clean deal or a messy one...your choice." Witch One began the bargains. Every bad guy movie had a deal that was too good to be true. They never panned out, not even in the movies.

"No matter what you tell yourself, this isn't going to be clean, ladies. You have no idea what you're meddling with. You're all going to die, and it's going to paint these fucking walls in your blood." I laughed again. I couldn't help it. They were nothing more than toothpicks for what would come out of hell. He'd clean his teeth with their bones after he flayed them. "I'll see you in hell, because that's exactly where you're going."

"We didn't kill anyone," Witch One said, as a matter of fact.

I smirked. Did they really believe that? Could anyone be so diluted to think their actions, even indirectly, didn't have consequences? "What you did directly resulted in someone's death. You don't have to be the shooter to be guilty. Just handing the killer the gun is enough to make you responsible."

"We made a deal with him. He is responsible for the deaths." She sounded like she was trying to convince herself more than me. Her voice was a little too shaky to be confused with confidence.

"Oh, Jesus, this is rich. You're so clueless that I don't know if I should feel sorry for you or not. He may have agreed to take the blame, but that doesn't clean the slate. What was done by your hands must be answered for." I laughed until my eyes watered. "It doesn't matter if you made a deal for world peace, ending famine or curing every disease. The road to hell is paved with good intentions and littered with the bones of those who thought they could get around the responsibility of those deals. You could have done it all for the right reasons and would still have no soul in the end. You sold it the moment you signed the pact. Where the hell did you think your soul was going when this was all said and done? Never, in the history of *ever*, has someone gotten out of a demon deal with their souls, no matter what you were told. Just answering the damn call taints your soul, never mind everything that follows." The stupidity of them all was more than I could handle. I laughed a little harder this time. Not even my first-year students were this foolish, and many of them gave me perpetual anxiety, fear they'd summon by accident or sell their souls for a higher grade. I sighed long and hard and blinked away my tears. "Oh, this is too much. You're going to die and don't even understand why. Hell is going to have a field day with you all. It's always roughest for those like you, thinking you don't belong there. Trust me, you belong there."

"You lie!" Witch Two screamed. She stepped forward.

"You and I both know I'm not lying," I replied. "Be careful what you wish for, lest it come true."

Witch One put her hand out to stop whatever new violence was about to erupt from her counterpart. "I've had about enough of your tales. You will not scare us. We are committed. We have earned our freedom. We are deserving."

"On that, I agree. You deserve exactly what's coming for you. Read the fine print, ladies. The devil is in the details. There is *no* freedom to earn. He's bought and paid for it. You may be free right now, but it all has a price. I hope your soul was worth it. I hope you got everything you wanted out of this, because you're going to spend all of eternity paying for it." I grinned with the knowledge. Sure, I might die, but I'd see them on the other side, and it would make my trip to hell worth it. Hearing them suffer would be music to my ears. "No matter what you were told, no demon, great or small, gets out of bed for less than eternity and a day with your soul. Buckle up, witches. It's going to be a bumpy fucking ride. I hope you know just how stupid it was to choose a Lycan as your sacrifice. You're in for a hell of a time when they come with questions."

"Chac will not kill us. We have a binding deal," Witch Two said. But I heard the fear in the back of her throat. She could swallow as hard as she could, but I still heard it. I don't know who they were trying to convince, me or them, but they still pressed this one issue — as though my agreement would save them.

"A binding deal for your freedom, your soul, unlimited power and whatever else you've asked for, and all you need to do is summon him? Not happening. But, say you're right. Say you get out of this alive *with* your soul, however tainted it is. By some miracle, I'm wrong, and you walk away. You may have made a bargain with a demon, but you cannot bargain with the hounds of hell. They're coming on the heels of that demon. You all will die, whether you have a deal with the Grand Poohbah himself or a bloody fairy. Either way, I hope you like dogs. If Chac — this god you think you're summoning — comes to the surface, he will bring the hunt with him. If you open the gate for him, he will have the power to command the wild hunt, and they're starved for sinners like you and me. There is *no* pact in heaven or hell that'll keep them at bay."

Sure, I could have told them they weren't going to raise a god, but I never gave the bad guys a head start out of the front door. I liked to keep the path clear for myself. To be honest, I didn't know what they were going to drag up. I knew who they thought they'd get and who they wanted, but they fumbled around in the dark, and Lord knows what they'd pull out of the pits. At best, they'd yank up a lower-level demon, and I'd be able to control it. At worst, it would be Chac.

"You lie," they said in unison.

"You will be the first the wild hunt takes. No tainted soul will walk the earth." I snickered. "If I've said this once, I've said it a million times... Don't screw with something you don't know all about. Hell, no matter how smart we think we are, is something we will never understand."

"Your tongue is slick with lies," Witch One spat back.

"And yours is about to be cut from your mouth. I'm looking forward to watching," I answered. "You, all of you, deserve what's coming. And for once, I'm happy to have been invited to the show."

"All good plans have a plan B. We have negotiated for power or eternal life. Demon or Sire, either option is fine with us." Witch Two was impressed, arrogant to the bitter and blood-sucking end. Witch One didn't seem impressed that their master plan was now common knowledge, but I would keep goading them until I got what I needed...information. I'd draw it out as long as I could, see what other nibbles I could collect with their loose tongues and need for reassurance. Information was power, and, in my position, a leg up could make all the difference. So far, I knew there was at least one vampire here, the entire group of witches and likely the traitor—all wrapped up and waiting for the other half of my plan, which was still a work in progress.

"Eternal life? Sire? If you think your little vampire is going to turn you and you'll live forever, you're not just ignorant, you're running full stupid in your tank," I replied. "What makes you think the council would ever allow it?"

"The vampires will welcome us and all we can do for them." Witch One was as smug as her friend. Sure, to secure a witch was a boast for any vampire nest, but they weren't witches and not worth the skin they stood in or the trouble they'd bring.

I chuckled. "*Our* council, you idiot. The Coven. Did you not think of who governs and polices the magic you're using? They'll hunt you down and kill you. I've already sent word to them after our first meeting. Do you think you will be able to defend yourselves, as brand spanking new fledgling bloodsuckers, against dozens of the most powerful witches to ever walk the earth? They have more power in their pinky fingers than I will ever have," I answered, and it was mostly true. They were what terrified all witches, regardless of their bloodline. "They will *never* allow a witch to fall into the hands of vampires. Throughout the entire history of witches, you've never heard of a witch-turned-vampire surviving long enough to make the history books for a reason," I explained, and it was the god's honest truth. Consorting with hell was a death sentence, and vampires were an inch away from hell. "And if they get here before you're turned, I hope you have a better excuse than wanting power and eternal life, or you'll be burned at the stake. You really should invest in reading glasses the next time you join a club. The fine print alone will kill ya."

But it wasn't the entire truth. The Coven, the Assembly of Witches, was very real and very scary, and no sane person would want them knocking on the door. But I hadn't told them. I would have, but up until now, I wasn't aware of Plan B. It's not like I could just email the Coven and inform them of my suspicions. I'd have to go through intermediaries and schedule a meeting, fly to London and wait for them to see me—and that's if they agreed there was proof enough for them to waste their time on me. There was a process for everything, and witches were no different with the red tape. Even if I had gotten there and managed to swing a meeting, the Coven wouldn't have stopped the witches here in Mexico. The Coven believed in freedom of choice and wouldn't intervene until wrong-doing had been done. Suspicion would ruin a reputation, but I doubted that was a major concern for these witches. Anything more than gossip would need concrete proof. Unfortunately, the Coven wouldn't burn them without it. A history of fires set before guilt was proven had made the Coven hesitate with the matches. They were all about ensuring the witch was at fault, which, as a witch, I could appreciate. But won't they look silly when they're running for their lives later? If they killed the dark witches ahead of time, there'd be no dying because of them later. Though, I wasn't exactly an impartial vote on this matter. I was chained up, hoping I wouldn't die in the end.

Whether I was telling the truth or not, I'd use whatever I had to break their confidence, cause doubt and fear. The more you feared, the more hesitant you became. Regrettably, for me, the downside to them being afraid was the pain they dished out to me because of it. Witch One came for me again. Her face was twisted in hate and doubt. But this time, I was prepared. I rolled onto my back and kicked out with both my feet, connecting with her knees. The pop of her kneecap echoed in the stone room. Her legs buckled, and she went to the floor like a sack of stones. The sound of her bones hitting the rock sent a shiver through my body. Her pain and rage rained down on me in fists, but it was worth it. I had warned them. The next one to come for my pain would share in it.

They say there is always something bigger and better out there than you. Neither Witch One nor Witch Two were my bigger and badder. What they were raising, on the other hand, would be. I was out cold before I could argue my point. *I hate the dark.*

Chapter Five

Being unconscious had its perks. For one, you can't be scared when you're out cold. Two, nothing hurt when you slumbered in the darkness. Unfortunately, for some of us, our need to survive outweighed our desire for rest, and we woke up. I groaned as I came around for a second time. My brain felt like it was in a bucket being kicked down a hill. The room spun, and small sparkles filled my vision. The witch hadn't done much more damage with her fists, but the knock of my head against the rock most certainly had. I was one more punch away from having my brain leak out of my ears.

I had been dreaming of me and my father, sitting at the beach in Van, waiting on my mother to finish her yoga. It was a memory more than a dream. My mother did her yoga every day on the beach, an hour before sunset. We lived a block up the road and wandered down every evening. Me and my dad would eat ice cream and make castles in the sand. Some days, we'd swim. On other days, we'd use sticks to practice drawing symbols of protection and minor spells for growing plants in the winter and healing small injuries. Although my parents were hereditary witches, my father loved earth magic. He always had the smell of the ground before it rained, while my mother smelled of the air just before lightning struck. Their scent, grass and ozone were why I sat outside when a storm was coming. Every breath reminded me of days none of us thought would end...until they did. Waking up from that memory made me a little more bitter than I had been before I'd been knocked out.

"Is it true?" Sofia's voice brought me out of my deep, fist-induced bleariness. Although it was nothing more than a whisper, it echoed in my ears, and I winced at the piercing sound of it.

"Is what true?" I answered back through the walls, saddened to hear her voice. My throat was raw, and my words came out like a growl. I swallowed against the feeling of sandpaper.

"They will rot in hell for this?" she asked. "They sold their souls, and now they'll die for it?"

I thought about it for a moment. I didn't know if I was right or wrong. I only knew what I hoped for. "Yes. No. I don't know. I think so. Even if they didn't sell their soul to the demon they're summoning, their choices up until this point would seal their fate. Their actions, whether direct or indirect, ended innocent lives. When you take a life, you owe a life. If you take a soul, you owe a soul. Balance is always restored. Whether that comes today or a year from now, I don't know."

"And if they become vampires, then what? They get to live for hundreds of years with no punishment?" she asked.

"If they aren't hunted down by the Coven... It's not like life will be a picnic for them, Sofia. Becoming a vampire isn't freedom and isn't without punishment. They'll be hunted by everything else, including their own kind — witches. No good witch out there would stand by and watch them keep their freedom. We'd hunt them down and kill them for it," I replied. "They're signing up for a life I wouldn't wish on anyone. I'd sooner go back to hell than be a bloodsucker. It is not like in the movies. It's not glamorous. Their lives are utterly horrific. They have decades of torment at the hands of monsters, their creators, before they have enough power to leave. And that's pretty iffy. Most die at the hands of their own makers or because of them — witches turned vampires, with no one else to go. They'll be everyone's meat. That is a fate worse than hell. I'd rather go to hell than be hunted by my people or spend a minute at the mercy of a vampire."

I shuddered with memories. I had been in a house after a team had exterminated forty-eight vampires. The newest ones had been abused and passed around like new toys. They had been beasts, starved and animalistic. Their creator had a sweet spot for the young ones. It looked like a junior high classroom had been butchered. The Master was hunted down by his own people, and pieces of his body were delivered to the families of those turned. The vampires thought it would be considered a gift. It wasn't taken that way. It scared the crap out of the families.

"Nothing the vampires could ever do to them is payment enough for what they've done." Sofia brought me out of my twisted thoughts. "If they live for any length of time, no matter their conditions, it will be too good for them."

"I agree," I answered. Although I thought differently, vampires were mighty creative when punishing their own, and I wasn't going to argue opinions with her. From what I'd seen since getting to Mexico, I understood Sofia's need for revenge. Her people had been slaughtered and left gutted for the world to see. I doubted any punishment would sate that hunger for justice deep within her. I'd been there, and nothing short of being on a spit in hell would be punishment enough. "They'll get what's coming to them, Sofia, one way or another. If they were smart, they'd take death by my hand and not the coming demon, vampire or witch. In comparison, my hand is a mercy."

"They don't deserve mercy." Sofia's voice had so much hate behind it.

"No, they don't. But nothing I can do will ever be enough. I simply can't give them what they deserve, and it's not worth selling off a piece of my soul or letting the ground open up to dish it out. I want to, but I won't go to hell for them. I won't give them that. They've taken enough already."

"It's never enough, is it? The evil ones never get what they've earned." Her voice broke, and she started crying. "They're going to kill us. I'm going to die in here with someone who doesn't care enough to fight for her life."

"If you're talking about me, I care, Sofia, more than you know."

"People who care about living do not come to Pack, do not threaten our Lycaon, our leader, and they certainly are not calm when they're chained up by witches. Hell, you're basically tempting them to kill you with that mouth of yours," she replied. "I've heard all the stories about you, Ailis. You're jogging your way back into hell and whistling Dixie the entire way."

"Had they been professionals, I'd have kept my mouth shut. But they're not. They're not even amateurs, for Christ's sake. The angrier I make them, the most mistakes they'll make. I'm counting on them to forget to do something or trip up. Them being angry will save my life in the end. Pissing them off forced them to walk away to cool down, leaving me alone to think." I rolled my eyes at the last comment Sofia had made, even though she couldn't see it. People always made assumptions about me. "You've heard rumors, and that's all they are. If you heard the truth, you'd know it's nothing more than bravado. I'm scared. I'm always scared. I have so much fear in me. I'm surprised you can't smell it thick like blood coating the walls. But being scared isn't reason enough for me to give in to the panic of it. I'm not freaking out because I have to stay calm enough to think of a way out, or I'll stay stuck here, chained up by witches, and I will die because of it. I don't want to die, and the only way I'll live is to be rational and grounded. I'll save my absolute bat-shit crazy breakdown for when it won't kill me," I answered.

Most people thought my ability to remain calm in the face of uncertainty was a lack of fear. It wasn't. I was on the verge of vomiting, and my eyes prickled with unshed tears. I was well and truly scared, but I was also good under pressure. Half a lifetime of being hunted by demons and the cursed made for a well-practiced skill. "In the words of Poe, 'That which you mistake for madness is but an over acuteness of the senses.' For the record, the last time I was on the road to hell, I wasn't whistling. I was screaming and running and begging. But if all I ever have is one whisper left, I'll never give it to the bad guys. They'll never hear my plea for mercy. They simply don't scare me like hell does."

"To die laughing must be the most glorious of all glorious deaths," Sofia finished the Poe quote. "Odd choice of poets for the situation, no? His poems don't exactly strike the hopeful chord."

"Edgar Allan Poe is perfect for this moment. He portrays universal emotions, like fear, grief, loss, unrequited love, living a macabre life, burying your enemy alive in the cellar and being scared out of your mind by a bird," I answered and closed my eyes. I needed to focus now.

"While we're quoting poets, the witches are preparing for our deaths." Sofia pointed out the obvious. I bit my tongue rather than snap at her comment. Sofia filled the silence with unnecessary noise. Scared and uncomfortable people did that. I didn't blame her, but I did need a moment of clarity and hush to think.

"The poetry was for your benefit, no one else's. I needed you to calm down, for your mind to focus on something else. I can't hear anything over your crying. I'm sorry, Sofia, but I need you to be quiet," I answered. I wasn't being rude yet. Her sniffle was louder than I wanted it to be. "Shh, Sofia. Please. I need to listen to my surroundings and think. The witches will come back, and when they do, I don't want to be caught screwing around. They're stupid and desperate, and I don't want to be kneeling here when they return with newer ways to make me help them."

I didn't bother to tell Sophia that she'd likely be the new way to force my hand. Whatever I said helped. She tried to swallow it, but I could still hear her sobs muffled. It was better than the echo of scared crying. I took that opportunity, not knowing how long she'd be able to keep it together, and listened for any sound of life outside of our rooms. I heard nothing. I felt nothing. Not close by, anyway. I felt power, but it wasn't close enough for me to worry about it right now. I had other things on my to-do list that didn't include the what-ifs. The witches would be back. I didn't need to see their schedule to know they'd come and ask again. The next time I was sure Sofia would be used as up close and personal motivation. I didn't want to see her die, too. I wasn't a Sofia fan, but I didn't dislike her enough to watch her try to heal the loss of her head. Up until meeting the witches of this fine establishment, I didn't think I hated anyone enough to see them without their heads. But I could live with seeing *them* without their heads.

"They want your blood," she whispered. "I heard them talking when they brought you here." When I didn't respond, she took it as an invitation to keep chattering. "They said they need your blood to break a curse on a demon in hell, that your parents twisted it before their deaths. I heard them talking about a spell to release him, and it would take powerful souls and blood from your line. They said your parents cursed Chac to the gates of hell? I didn't know witches could do that."

"Witches can do a lot of things we don't advertise for fear of being snagged like this and forced to do magic we don't casually do," I answered. "It does explain why they came back for me rather than move on to a new victim. They did say that only my blood would do. I had assumed it for a more powerful sacrifice."

"Does what they said mean anything to you?"

"Yes, it does. I was there the night my parents died," I replied. "I told you the condensed version the first time we met."

It wasn't common knowledge how my parents died. The paper had reported a house fire, killing two. That was the night I met Samuel. Although it happened when I was a child, I remember it like yesterday. Every time I smelled a campfire, it reminded me of the night my childhood home went up in flames. Our home was filled with lower demons tasked to take a full-blooded witch. They had come for me, unprepared to face the wrath of my mother and father. I was shoved into a circle of protection and watched my father battle the demons with energy so raw and angry that it sizzled in the air and burned the house plants in the living room while my mother cursed the name of the demon who had sent them. I knew, even as a child, with the way my mother looked at me, that her curse and saving my life would be her final act as a witch and as a mother. She would damn the beast before her last breath to keep him from coming for me again.

I didn't have the skill I have today and couldn't help them, although I tried with all my might and soul. I conjured shadows of beasts, moved chairs in their way, wrapped cords around their necks and shoved demons through windows and down the stairs. I did all I could, but it wasn't enough. I still have a small scar on my left hand from where I had used my fingernails to open my flesh to draw symbols on the floor. I called out for aid to anyone listening. The marking I had found in the back of my mother's grimoire had the name 'Samuel' written below it. At the time, I didn't know who Samuel was or why my mother would have his name in the chapter about protection, but in my panic, I would have called an angel, even knowing that call would likely kill me. Angels weren't dogs you could command. Contrary to popular belief, when an angel came, everyone died in the end.

With my own tiny well of magic gone, I watched as demons attacked, one after the other. I remember how red and shiny with blood the floors were and being upset by it. My mother had just had the floors polished, and I was angry they were making a mess. I sat on the floor, knees to my chest, hands over my ears, and cried quietly. With the house in flames, the demons not relenting, both of my parents stood in front of my circle, giving the rest of their magic to my protection. The demons came in waves, and my parents stood their ground until the house burned around them. They never screamed. I remember that as clear as day. They held hands until the very end. The last words they said were of love for each other. I still remember what their hands looked like, clasped together.

By the time Samuel arrived with a group of witches, it was too late for my parents. With a wash of power, Samuel and his friends sent the demons back to hell, where they belonged. He knelt at my circle, and with a push of my hand, I dropped the spell and crawled into his arms. I had tried to be strong and not cry much. For some reason, I thought my parents would have been proud of me if I had been as brave as they had been. But the tears had still come. That night was the last time I had seen my parents and my childhood home. Their sacrifice bought me a dozen more years and change, and for that, what kid wouldn't be grateful. The night I got into a vehicle with a drunk driver, I pissed it away.

"The demon, Chac, has been whispering to the witches, telling them that your blood and a spell spoken by you is the only way out," Sofia added. "I don't know if it matters, but they said his true name is Chaxel…"

"No!" I cut her off. I knew what name was about to fall from her lips, and it sent my pulse hammering in my ears. "Do not say his name, Sofia. You do not want to be the person who knows his true name. For most devils and higher-level demons, knowing their original name could end your life."

"Oh, I didn't know just speaking it would make a difference," she whispered. "I thought you should know what you're up against."

"Hell. It's always hell," I answered. I blinked away the threat of tears at the thoughts of my parents' final moments. "The witches could drain me dry, and I wouldn't have enough juice to break a curse tied by my parents. I'm not strong enough. My parents were powerful witches, and I'm simply…not. I'm a shadow of them. When the witches find out that I can't do all they want, they'll go on the hunt for more souls to butcher."

"I'm sorry, Ailis," she whispered. "I'm sorry for what I said before about your family."

"Don't worry about it."

"Do you have a plan yet?" she asked, thankfully changing the subject.

"I always have a plan. It's time to go," I finally said after taking a few minutes to get my bearings again. I may have woken up chained to a floor, but I've woken up in cuffs before. I didn't come all this way and take this kind of shit and abuse for nothing. My therapist hadn't just taught me how to control my fear. He'd also given me tools to combat what caused the anxiety in my soul. After Miguel, who used to train me weekly in self-defense and technique, my therapist found someone to teach me how to get myself out of situations little witches usually found themselves in. She had been worth every penny I'd spent, especially now.

"Oh, my God. Please don't leave me here. I'm sorry I was a bitch to you. Please, Ailis, I don't want to die," she begged. Her desperation was pliable. It felt like a blistering hot tongue against my soul. "I'll do anything, just don't leave me. I'll give you anything you want if you take me with you. I swear…please. If you want my protection, you have it, I swear. I have your back for as long as I'm alive. I'd rather die out there, trying to protect you, than in here. I can smell vampires. You can't leave me to them, not again. Fuck, not again. I can't do it another time. I can't play their victim once more. Please. I'm not strong enough to do it twice."

"Shh, Sofia, I'm not leaving you here, and I sure as hell would never leave someone to the mercy of a vampire. When I said I didn't give a shit about you, it was only so they didn't think you were important to me. Being cared about isn't a good place to be when you're chained up. They'd have gone straight to your room had they thought I cared." I shook my head, although she couldn't see it. "Bloody hell, Sofia. I'm a lot of things, but I'm not the kind of person who would leave someone behind."

"Thank you," she replied, her voice still holding a measure of unshed tears.

"Just don't eat me, and we'll call it even." I tried to calm her. If she started crying too much, I wouldn't be able to hear if Dumb and Dumber were coming back.

"What can I do to help?" she asked.

"Calm down and pay attention. That's what I need from you right now. You can have a breakdown later when you're free and clear. But right now, keep your head in the game. If you hear someone coming, let me know. We only have one shot at this, so don't piss it away on tears."

Her sobs ended in almost an instant. A few sniffles and the louder cries stopped. "Okay, I can do that."

"In case this is a bust and they come back before we're free, how much more can you take?" I asked. "If I need you to buy me more time to break free, can you do it? Can you take it? If we hear them coming, can you cause a ruckus that brings them to your room?"

"I can take it," she replied. "I'll do what I have to. I swear I can take whatever we need to do to get the fuck out of here."

"Okay. Keep your mouth closed and ears open. I don't want to die for nothing."

I didn't feel bad for being hard on her. I had been in her shoes before, needing a heavy hand to pull me out of spiraling. With her paying attention to anyone coming, I focused on my cuffs. Each one was shaped like a horseshoe, with a small bar across the end. The cold iron was better to escape from than the newer cuffs used by the cops. Police-issued restraints and handcuffs were harder to get out of and usually cut the skin when you pulled against them. Most attempts were unsuccessful and left you with scars to remind you of your stupidity.

Regardless of what was strapped around my wrists, I didn't have the kind of hypermobility needed in my thumbs to escape without a world of pain. It would hurt like hell to pop them out of joint and back in. If I didn't do it right, I'd break my thumbs or need surgery to repair what desperation had forced me to do. If I left with wonky thumbs but still had my life, it would be worth the doctor's trip later. I moved the cuff up as far as it would go, pinching and scraping my skin. I was thankful for tiny wrists right about now.

My breath hitched in my throat as the metal dug into the wounds on my arms. A thin bandage wasn't enough to protect my skin from the digging metal. I bent my wrist and pressed my thumb against my forearm, slowly stretching out the muscles and ligaments. Once I was sure I wasn't going to break my finger, I twisted it until the joint gave. The pop was audible. My scream was swallowed into nothing more than a hiss. I felt dizzy for a few seconds as the pain flooded my body, my brain's way of telling me to stop. I breathed through it and slipped the one cuff down, back over my injuries and hand and repeated for the other side. The cuffs dropped to the floor.

Popping my thumbs back into place wasn't as painful. Thankfully my thumbs had lost a lot of sensation by then. Once back into place, I rested on my hands and knees until the nausea faded and the vertigo was gone. Deep breaths in and out of the septic stench and I was good as new-ish. I pulled the useless amulet from around my neck and chucked it into the corner. The jade was pretty, but that's all it was. The fact it was made from their hair grossed me out. I stood and rotated my shoulders. They were knotted from being pulled behind my back for over a day. I moved my hands down my body and did a mental check of injuries. I was in rough shape. Under my clothes felt crunchy, as if I had bled from wounds I didn't remember. The witches likely dragged me into the room rather than carried me. My head swam like my skull bones were separated into four parts. I ran my hand against my frontal bone over the titanium. It didn't feel dented. My brain felt like it was about to leak out of my ears, and my worry was over a piece of metal in my head. I wasn't vain at all.

One step at a time, I told myself. I took a few deep breaths, calming myself. I pressed my hand into my chest, trying to will the tension out. Rubbing in circular motions, erasing the tightness, the doom I felt slowly disappeared.

"Ailis?" Sophia whispered. "Are you okay?"

"I'm good," I replied. "Just checking myself over before our mad dash to the finish line."

"You need to know, they have Anna. If she's still alive and you have to pick between us, take her," Sophia said. "They brought her to the club and snagged her a few minutes later. It's how they got me. I went after them."

"Why didn't you guys call out to your people for help?" I asked. "When they took you, why didn't you call for Miguel?"

"Would you call someone to die in your place?" she asked. "They tried to torture Anna into sending out a call for help, but she refused. She's just a kid, Ailis. If you have to choose who to save, pick her. I'll take her place willingly. There's nothing these bitches can do to me that I won't take for a child a dozen times over. For a kid, I'd take it all."

"Shit." I groaned out the word. "Can you shift into your Lycan form?"

"No. Well, yes, but not right now. They have me bound with silver and little colored rocks," she answered. "I can't get it off, Ailis. My arms are bound with silver."

"If I take the silver off of you, could you shift?" I asked.

"Yes. But how will you get it off me?" she asked. Sofia's voice was panicked, worried that if she couldn't get herself out, I'd leave her.

"Let me worry about that," I replied.

I reached for the doorknob and hesitated. I stared at the symbols painted on the door. If it didn't open, I'd know I was another monster. Part of me didn't want to try. I didn't want to know if I was one of the villains of this story. The door didn't fry my brain when I touched it. It clicked open without so much as a shock. The spells on the door were for evil. I wasn't evil. *Paint me surprised*. I won't lie, I didn't think it would open. Up until then, I had doubted my scruples. The next person who called me evil, I'd throw this in their face — if I lived long enough to be petty once again.

I sent my energy a few feet from my room, like a spider web of aura, my awareness. I couldn't extend it more than two or three feet, like some of the level two and three witches that belonged to the Coven had learned to do, but it was enough for when I really needed the extra help. I felt nothing immediate. Wherever we were, we were alone. I slinked out of my prison into a stone hallway and opened Sofia's door next to me. I ducked my head in and looked around. With the coast clear, I slipped in quickly.

"I plan to take them off with my own two hands," I said as I shut the door behind me.

"Thank God. I thought you were going to leave me." Sofia looked relieved. The tiny slice of light that came in under the door showed fresh tears in her eyes. "When I heard your door open, I thought you'd bolt."

"Christ, you sure have a low opinion of me."

"I'm sorry, but most people would just run to save themselves."

"Believe what you want about me, but I'm not most people. I wouldn't leave someone behind, not if I had the chance to help them," I answered. My heart palpitated at the thought of Cisco. He didn't hand me over to the bad guys. I wasn't going to hand one of his people over, either.

"If half of your people wanted me dead, I probably would have bolted," she replied.

"Only half? Mere days ago, it was your entire Pack. I'd say things are starting to look up for me." I grinned, and she huffed a laugh. "Let's take a look at the damage, shall we?"

Sofia was bound with one long silver chain. It was cooked into her flesh, down to the meat. It looked like blistered and bloodied steak, raw and oozing clear fluid as her body tried to heal itself. My throat clenched. I could smell her roasted meat. The scent reminded me of why I don't eat animal flesh. I turned from her once and gagged. I couldn't help it.

"I'm not gonna lie. It's really bad," I finally said, swallowing down my heaves. "It's literally cooked into your flesh and meat. I think I can see bone in some places."

"You need to pull the silver off," she replied. "That is going to be the bad part. Silver is how we're bound. We can't shift with it on, and it slowly leaches our energy."

"I thought that was a myth," I replied, taking another look and trying to figure out how I'd remove it without ruining her remaining skin.

"I wish."

"I'm so sorry, Sofia. This is going to hurt. The only spell I know for pain would knock you out, cold. And I don't think I'd be able to carry you out of here."

"Don't worry about the pain. I've felt worse," she replied, and it hurt my soul to hear her say it.

I touched her shoulder and gave her a squeeze. "I hate that we have pain in common."

"We have more in common than either of us wishes to say out loud. Hell isn't just a place found in the pits, Ailis," she replied, and I left it at that.

She didn't make a sound as I pulled the chain out of her skin. It was like a dog who had a choker on and had outgrown it years ago. The sound made me gag again, like skinning a raw chicken. She sat perfectly still, her eyes on the door. I wondered how many times she had silver cooked into her for her to be so calm about it. She was either used to it or just that desperate to get the hell out of Dodge. I didn't ask. It wasn't my business if she was used to it, and it was a stupid question if she could put up with it just to get out. I dropped the chain to the ground and pulled the silver loose from her wrists. Once she was free, I helped her stand. I quickly rubbed my sticky hands on my pants. Until I showered, I'd feel her burned flesh on my fingertips.

"That was so absolutely disgusting." The words came out of my mouth before I could close it. I felt my face heat up. "Sorry, Sofia."

"Try hearing it from the inside, like peeling tape off a dog. I almost puked on you."

"Thanks for not doing that." I smiled and was glad I hadn't insulted her with my comment. "Can you shift now? Do I need to make you angry or scare you or can it just pop out whenever it wants to? Tell me what to do, and let's get the hell out of here."

She stared at me for a moment. I think she was trying to see if I was serious or not. "No. None of that. But I will need your help."

"How?" I asked. My voice was rushed. I wanted to get out of there now, and I felt like we were taking too long. I kept glancing over my shoulder, half expecting the villainous calvary to be standing behind me. "You have to fill me in, Sofia. It's not like there are any books I could have read to prepare me for this. I checked online, but there's no book called, 'So Lycans are real, here's everything you need to know in five minutes.' Start talking because up until recently, I didn't even know about you."

"Sorry. Usually anyone around us is Pack and already knows. Everyone else we kill. I'm kind of glad I didn't let anyone kill you now," she joked. If she could find humor in the moment, she had a good shot of survival. "Remember when we met, and you pushed the essence of my wolf back down? I need you to pull it back up. I don't have the energy to do it myself. I'm healing too many injuries. My wolf won't come. If I use up all my energy to shift, I might die. My heart could stop. My wolf won't risk my life on a maybe. She'll only come now if it's life or death."

"Someone should tell her that it's kind of life or death here," I replied, and she shrugged. "What happens if I pull it up and you still don't have the energy? Will you be standing here all hungry? I mean, are you going to eat me for that energy?"

"I guess we'll see." She huffed a laugh and saw the fear on my face. "Sorry. I've never been this injured without the Pack to help me heal. I don't know what will happen."

"I'm sorry you've been this injured before." I gave her a weak smile.

She nodded. "I guess you can say we've both been to hell. We just took different routes there and back, but the scars look like we took the same bus."

"If you eat me, make it quick. Go for my heart first," I answered and changed the subject from the emotionally hard stuff to our pending doom. It was easier to deal with and talk about.

"That's not a quick kill. You can live without your heart long enough for you to know you don't have one anymore. It doesn't look peaceful, and it certainly isn't the quickest way."

"It's creepy that you know that." I gave her a look that said I was a little suspicious of how she'd come upon that knowledge.

"I'm assuming it's the same with humans as it is with deer," she answered. "I'll start the process. Once you feel my wolf, I'll let go, and you do the rest. Pull it up to the surface and release it. My wolf will know what to do after that. Sometimes, with new shifters who can't control when they change, stronger Pack will pull and push their wolf to get them used to how it feels, sort of like what you can do, only less uncomfortable."

"I can't believe we're about to do this," I mumbled, scared at what would come next.

"Don't worry. We've taught this technique to others, and it has worked out fine for them."

"Other what?" I asked.

"Like the wererats," she answered. "I taught it to their Alpha, Levi, personally. He's a friend."

"Wererats? What the hell are...? You know what? I don't even want to know. Learning about you all hasn't really been a walk in the park. I don't need another group of people wanting me dead," I replied.

"Oh damn, Ailis. For a witch, you certainly lead a sheltered life. How do you not know about weres? It's not like their secret will end in your death. I mean, they'll kill you, but not because of some oath. They'll simply do it to keep themselves safe," she asked. "How have you not even bumped into one? The were population is huge in Canada."

"My areas of expertise are demons, not furry things that'll eat my face off. I try to stay the hell out of business that isn't mine. And I sure as hell don't go hunting for things that may or may not be real. I'm not that stupid."

She motioned around the room. "And yet, here we are—a Lycan and a witch in a dungeon because a myth sold us out to demons and his servants. Do you know how ridiculous it sounds that you don't know about shifters?"

"We can argue about my monster blindness later," I replied. She sounded like Samuel. He had been trying to train me for years, to become a better witch, to learn of every beast out there. I was of the mind that the less I knew, the less will knock on my door. '*Foolish witch, they'll still chain you to the floor of a dungeon, whether you're on a first-name basis or not,*' he'd told me "Let's get this show on the road so we have a later to argue about my stupidity."

"I wouldn't say you're stupid, just…not very bright when it comes to the *monstruo*," she replied.

"Monstruo… That means monsters, right? Or are you about to give me another nightmare to worry about?"

"It's what my grandmother used to call the creatures of the night...monsters."

"Oh, thank God. If you were about to spring another creature on me, I was going to leave you in here," I replied. My Spanish was rough, but some words stuck. Monsters were one of them. I had heard Miguel curse them out enough times that some words I'd never forget. "How do you want to do this? What kind of show am I in for?"

"I'll start. I'll give you a signal, then you take over," she replied. "It'll be like any other time we've shifted."

"I've never seen one of you in your full glory, let alone shifting. The closest I've come is seeing claws."

"Shit, I thought you had for some reason," she groaned. "Maybe close your eyes for this? It can be scary the first time. You'll hear my joints popping. It'll sound like bones breaking, but don't worry, they're not. It may sound wet and smell a bit like blood and wet fur."

"Isn't there a way to do this that doesn't include me yanking your wolf out? I don't have a good feeling about this." I didn't think I'd die, but I also didn't think her aura would appreciate me rooting around looking for stuff to grab onto.

She smiled. "Yeah, I could eat you."

"Very well, wolf tugging it is," I replied.

"On the plus side, you've already been clawed up. If I scratch you, you're no farther behind," Sofia said and winked.

"Great. Thanks. Miguel said my chances were slim for infection, and I cleaned the wounds with holy water, just in case. I'm sure if you cut me up, that just ups the chances that you'll have to kill me in the end," I countered. "So, please keep your paws to yourself."

"If it makes you feel any better, I don't want to kill you anymore," she said. "Holy water? That's a nice and painful touch. If it works, it may help us with people who are attacked if we can get to them soon enough."

"I was told you have to do it within twenty-four hours, give or take," I added, in case it was important. "Keep soaking them until it doesn't hurt anymore. Only then will you know the body as be purified."

"We're talking like one of us isn't going to make it out of here," she mumbled, more to herself, but I heard her.

"We *are* going to make it. Focus on the end game, and we'll be home free soon enough. Ready?" I asked, without a shred of doubt that I'd keep Sofia alive long enough for her to save herself. Myself, on the other hand? I had serious doubts.

In almost every situation I had found myself in, when it came to dancing with the cursed, I questioned my ability to stay alive. But I never once questioned what I would do to keep innocents above the dirt or how many bad guys I'd take down in my attempts to win. I stepped back and closed my eyes. I could feel Sofia's energy building like a cup filling with water. I stretched my aura toward it. At first, the energy clawed at me, but I kept reaching. I envisioned a wolf in my mind's eye, and I grabbed onto her by the scruff of the neck. I didn't have time to coax it out like you would a scared animal. The wolf, in turn, didn't like the rush job and clawed up my arm in untrusting protest. They weren't physical cuts, but I still flinched at the pain of them. They dragged down my mind and hurt just as bad as the real thing. But I didn't let go. I couldn't. I ate my screams and yanked.

I wrapped my arms around the wolf and fought it to the surface. The first sound I heard was a slight groan from Sofia, followed by joints popping and what sounded like someone walking on gravel. I heard Sofia's skin slip like something wet being flopped onto the floor. I swallowed the urge to vomit at the sounds she made. I pulled the wolf to the surface and let go. I quickly took another step back. When I finally opened my eyes, Sofia knelt in complete Lycan form. I couldn't see every detail in the darkness, but I could see enough to want the hell out of that room. My survival instincts were much like a squirrel on drugs, twitching to run into traffic. Anywhere was better than here. Standing mere feet from a Lycan was everything I thought it would be and she warned me of—absolutely terrifying and one of my worst ideas to date. One look at her jaws and I knew being eaten by her would not be a good way to go.

Chapter Six

When I had thought of what a Lycan would look like in full form, my imagination hadn't even come close. In the back of my mind, I thought it would be similar to a horror movie, all claws and fangs and fur. It was so much more than that. Sofia stood a good foot taller than she had in human form, and she had already been five foot ten. Under the muscle and thin layer of fur, she retained her humanistic traits. Her eyes were the same ones I had just looked into, only much larger and dominating as she took in her surroundings. Her long snout twitched as she drew in a breath, but it was her mouth that took all my attention. Saliva coated her tongue as it brushed against sharp canines three times the size of a wolf's teeth. Spittle hit the ground when she closed her mouth, and I swallowed my urge to scream. The small moan trapped in my throat brought her ears flicking toward me. She reached toward me, her claws long and threatening. My eyes grew wider, and I shook my head. She instantly dropped her hand when I took another step back.

"Jesus H. Christ," I whispered.

"It's okay." Sofia finally spoke. Her words sounded odd, like she had rocks in her mouth and was new to the communication game.

"Just give me a second," I whispered. The room prickled with her power. The smell of nightmares filled my chest. "Sweet Mother Mary, you're fucking massive."

"Calm down, Ail...Alish...Lish." She couldn't pronounce my name with teeth big enough to snap me in two. It made me wonder if that was why Miguel had called me Lish. "I won't hurt you."

"Are you hungry?" I asked. I couldn't keep the fear from my voice. "You look like you're hungry."

"Not for you," she answered.

"So, you know, I'd probably taste like trash, all hellfire and matchsticks," I replied. "I'd likely upset your stomach."

"I'm sure you'd taste just fine. I mean...not that I want to eat you, just...never mind." Her laugh sounded like a dog trying to sneeze. I smiled at her poor attempt to make me feel better about the flavor of my damned soul. "You smell like a cat more than anything else. The scent is more pronounced now that I've shifted. Do you have a familiar? I can feel the warning climbing up my spine, telling me you're not worth eating."

"I've been told I do, but this is the first I've heard that the smell of my cat is a warning," I replied. "I appreciate you trying to make me feel better, Sofia, but let's skip the small talk and get going. If you're not going to eat me, let's get the hell out of here."

"Sorry. I'm nervous. I talk a lot when I'm uneasy," she replied.

"I've noticed, but it's better than your crying," I answered, and she growled at my comment. I huffed a laugh and motioned to the door. "Ready to probably die?"

"I'd rather die fighting than tied to the floor," she replied.

She nodded once, and I took that as she was ready to roll. I inched open the door slowly. I unlocked my shields, my aura, enough to include Sofia. It felt weird to have her inside my aura. I had only just started learning how to do it, and having an extra person in there with me made my skin crawl. It felt like her naked skin was touching me, as though she were close enough to be lying on top of me—an invasion of space, mind and soul. It wouldn't protect us from any direct attacks, but it would hide the smell and energy of us. With a vampire and Lycan helping the witches, I'd take no chance we'd be caught before the grand escape.

"Stay close or my shields will come down, and the bad guys will know we are out," I said. "Whoever is up there will sense us. And if one of your people is here, they'll smell us."

I could feel Sofia at my back but heard nothing from her. She was quieter than I thought she'd be. Dogs aren't this stealthy. For some reason, I thought she'd be just as loud as a regular dog, but she was silent as a wolf in the night and inched along in complete silence. The only noise was from my own shuffling feet. The hallway was stone, and it echoed every breath and movement from my shoes. Ahead, there was one way in and out. I liked the odds that no one would sneak up behind us, but I hated that we only had one exit. I liked options, but only ones I could take advantage of, not the monsters'.

The hallway extended thirty feet in front of us and five feet behind. Every few feet, there was a door on the left or right. Hotel Hostage was well equipped to hold a dozen. I stopped at every doorway and checked inside the rooms. Each was identical, and all were currently empty. They hadn't always been. The smell of fresh blood was enough to tell me we were much too late. I felt bad for being thankful there were no others being tortured for no other reason than knowing I wouldn't save them. I knew I couldn't launch much of a rescue mission had we found more victims. Although I could do nothing for them, I still wanted to know how many I'd leave behind for later...if there was a later.

"If you smell someone, warn me," I whispered.

"I smell death. There's blood and meat. But I smell nothing living down here."

"Are we in a basement or deeper underground?" I asked.

"A basement. I hear walking above us and smell fresh air," she answered. "It doesn't smell wet enough to be that far underground."

I nodded. "How many people are up there?"

"Really? How the hell would I know that? How about you tell me?" she asked, and I almost laughed. "I have no idea, Lish. I'm not a psychic. There are a lot of footsteps at once. Do you want me to guess?"

I was thankful it was dark, so she couldn't see how red my face was. "I suppose not. Sorry. I don't know why I figured you'd know. I thought maybe you would be able to smell them or something."

"If I was calm and uninjured, I could probably smell a few different scents and make a pretty good guess. But down here, there's too much happening for me to pick each smell apart from the other. We're too close for me to really smell anything more than a witch and a cat. Can't you just magically get us out of here? Like cast a spell or something?" It was her turn for a silly question.

"Really? I'm a witch, not a genie or a leprechaun who grants wishes. You watch too many movies," I responded. I shook my head and knew she'd seen it. Her eyes were perfect for the darkness—or so that's what the lore said.

"What? Are leprechauns real? Can you summon one or something?" she asked. Her tongue slid an awkward way over her teeth, and the 'L' sounded off. "I've never seen one before. I thought they were a myth."

I nodded. The surprise in her voice was much more excited than I had been when I'd found out about Lycan. Though, if one were standing in front of us, she'd be as scared as I was to learn of her people. "Yes, they're real, but I haven't heard of any in Mexico since the early fifties. Even if they were kicking around out back, they aren't exactly something I'd want down here."

"Can't be any worse than what's upstairs," she replied. "I'd take a granted wish over torture any day."

I huffed a laugh. "When leprechauns grant wishes, it's at your expense. Wanna lose ten pounds? They'll cut off one of your arms. Want to be a blonde? They'll give you the hair from your best friend, scalp and all. They're devious little creatures and cannot be summoned. They're not demons, and I'm thankful they're not. I'd hate to be chasing those bastards around. Even if they could be, they wouldn't help us anyway. They'd probably kill us for bothering them, kill us for sport or just kill us because they could," I answered. "You and I aren't in any condition to take on one of those creatures. It's best just to leave them alone. Leave genies alone, too.

They're worse than leprechauns. They're vengeful as all hell. They're like the plague in how many people will die in painful ways before they're captured. I'd rather a demon grant my wish than a genie."

"Not really like the fables, are they?" she asked, and I cringed at the thought of being near one. Leprechauns wreaked havoc in Ireland. We didn't need them to muck up Mexico, too. "Aren't you a demon or something close to that? Couldn't you use demon-y stuff?"

"For the last time, no, I'm not a demon. Hereditary witches were cursed by a demon. It doesn't make us one any more than Lycan are."

"You smell like one." She pointed out the obvious.

"You spend a lifetime in hell and see if you come out smelling like roses. They cooked off my soul. It's bound to leave a lingering aroma," I responded and kept inching ahead. "For the record, you don't smell that great either, by the way."

"I'm sorry for what I said to you at The Pale Horse. I didn't mean it." She tried to clear the air. Everyone with a conscience who thinks they're going to die always tries to make amends during their final moments.

"Yes, you did," I replied. "Maybe not all of it, but some of it. I get it. I'm not part of your world, but I'm stomping around on those who are part of it. It's okay, Sofia. All that requires forgiveness is forgiven."

"When you woke up in that cell, I didn't smell your fear, not how I should have. And when the witches came into your room, there was no surprise. You came here willingly, didn't you?" she asked, and I nodded. "Why?"

"To kill them. The witches won't stop until they rip the gates of hell off its hinges to release a jailed demon, and it's going to take a lot of death for that to happen. Unless someone stops them, they'll keep taking your people. If I wouldn't come, more would have died. And when the demon is strong enough, he will kill us all," I replied. "So, I came willingly to save who I could and stop this from continuing."

"A risky plan."

"Not one of my best, I'll give you that, but I was out of options and was the most expendable person here. I don't have a family. I don't have anyone depending on me. But I have people I love, people who need me to be brave. I want them to live, and unless I came here, they wouldn't have survived," I explained, and it made perfect sense to my soul. "What kind of demon-loving hag would I be if I didn't witch up and kick some ass?"

"I may have meant what I said when I said it, but I take it back now. You came into this hellhole to help my people, not stomp around on us. I let my anger blind me from the truth. I'm sorry," she replied. "Thank you for helping end this and for not leaving me behind."

"Don't sweat it. When we're home free, you can buy me a drink, and we'll call it even." I paused and turned to face her. I knew what she was looking for, what she needed, to settle the guilt in her soul. If she was going to die, she wanted a clear conscience, and I could give her that, if nothing else. "I forgive you, Sofia, for what was said between us. You're in a bad place and are looking for absolution. You have it. I absolve you of anything said or done between us."

"Thank you." She nodded in the most awkward of ways. "You really love him—Miguel—don't you?"

"Yeah. I tried not to, but it isn't something I can just magically stop doing. I would have, right after we stopped seeing each other, if I could have. But there are some things magic can't fix, and love just so happens to be one of them," I answered. "I don't think I'll ever stop. To be honest, I don't ever want to. Until my last breath, he'll be the only man I've ever loved. If that means a war with Caser and your people, I'll add it to my to-do list right after murder and mayhem. At this rate, I'll never leave Mexico."

"I have your back," she said, touching my shoulder. It took everything in my power not to squirm away from her claws. "You have my protection, if Miguel is who you want. I mean, if I live, I'll stand for you against those who challenge you. I may not look like much, but I would fight for you."

"If I live, thank you," I answered, then laughed. "I don't think I want to see the rest of your people if you think you don't look like much. Trust me... You're fucking terrifying, Sofia."

"Thank you." Her laugh was uncomfortable.

That was all the time we'd spend on bonding. I hadn't bothered asking for forgiveness for hurting her with my words. I didn't need it. I was going to the same place with or without it—Hotel Fire and Brimstone. Their sauna was to die for, and their services were better than this rat trap. I turned from Sofia and inched forward. We didn't have time to talk and braid each other's hair. The more we chatted about things that didn't need to be said, the higher the risk was of being caught. Bonding over hurt feelings was not how I wanted to go out in this world.

The hall took a sharp turn, ending at the foot of a stone staircase. I stopped at the first step, and my necklace pulsed. It had been steadily vibrating since I'd woken up on the floor, but now it throbbed hard enough for it to feel like a heartbeat. It wasn't hot, but it was a warning in a sense. I turned around and glanced back down the hall we had just walked. I shook my head. I was somewhere between confused and uneasy. It felt like missing a closet when looking for the boogeyman.

"Hold on a minute," I said. I couldn't push my aura any farther from us, but something rubbed up against it. Magic. Energy. Something I couldn't quite put my finger on.

"What?" she whispered.

"There's something or someone down here, Sofia. My gut is telling me that if we go up these stairs, we're making a mistake," I replied. She followed me back around the corner. There weren't any more doors to open, but I felt something tickle the back of my neck. I closed my eyes and tilted my head. A soft, muffled voice echoed, as though someone were whispering from another room in a house. It wasn't loud enough to track, but it was there in a haze of soft energy. A slight breeze carried a voice in a hush so low we almost missed it. "Do you hear that?"

She paused, her ears turning, her nose twitching. "It's so faint, but I think it's coming from upstairs."

"No. It's too close for that," I answered. I closed my eyes and listened again. You could never truly trust your eyes. What we saw was often deceiving when it came to magic. I could hear the slightest muffle, like a weak scream from down the block. Sofia bumped into my back when I stopped. I ran my hands up and down the walls to the floor. "It's behind this wall. It looks stone, but it's wood. I can feel it."

"A door? Why can't we see it?" she asked.

"Magic," I replied. I pushed a little energy into the wall, and it shuddered.

"I see a doorknob," she said, and I opened my eyes.

In front of us stood a hidden door. "There's either something in there that should stay hidden or something we weren't meant to find. Either way, I'm opening the door. Get ready to run. If it's a slice of hell, I'm running, and you had better be right behind me. Sofia, no matter how much I'll want to save you, I'll know I can't, so I won't try. You'll die down here, alone."

She nodded. "Understood. If you run, I run, no stopping."

"If we bolt, get the hell out of here. Don't stop for me. I'm who they want. If you stay with me, you'll die with me. I'll go one way, and you go the other. Go for help, and I'll stave off the inevitable until you send assistance for me," I said, and she nodded.

I opened the door, and for a split second, I couldn't make sense of what I was seeing. I slammed my mouth shut to keep myself from screaming. I charged into the room at full force. I threw my shields around the room to block our noise. It was the widest I had ever attempted, and I felt the instant drain on my energy. Inside the stone prison, a very much alive Cisco was strapped nude to a table with a vampire feeding on the inside of his thigh. His neck was bruised and scarred from the wounds that had been inflicted previously. His entire body, top to bottom, looked like someone had taken a bat to him. Had he been human, the beating would have killed him, let alone his being used as a blood bag.

I did not have the speed of a monster, but I had the rage of a witch. Sofia was at the table before I could blink. She grabbed the vampire and snapped his neck. I grabbed the only wooden object in the room, a small chair, and smashed it against the wall. I drove a broken arm of the chair into the chest of the vampire. Sophia was gnawing at his neck when he burned to ash. The burned bloodsucker slipped through Sofia's hands into a pile of dust on the floor. It was a cleaner death than he had deserved. It was a kindness I didn't want him to have. The hateful part of my heart had wanted him to suffer as Cisco had, even for a moment. Instead, he was given the mercy of death. Later, if I lived, I'd regret that part the most.

I turned and ran to the table Cisco was bound to. "Cisco," I called while Sofia snapped the leather straps holding him down.

He opened his eyes in a panic. "It's not real… It's not real. They're not real. You're not real."

"Sofia, he's going to freak out. He can't lose it. Keep him quiet." I called out to her.

Sofia pulled Cisco into her chest. "I'm here. We're here, Francisco. It's Sofia and Ailis. We're here. We're real. Smell me. Smell your Pack."

Cisco rolled off the table and staggered to my front. He was covered in fang marks and wounds that should have killed him days ago. He grabbed onto my shirt and pulled me to his chest. Had he been at his full strength, the force of his shake would have rattled my brain to mush. "Kill me. I won't help you, you fucking bitch. I don't care who you pretend to be. I'd rather die than help you do a damn thing. Kill me!"

"I see you haven't lost your charm, sissy," I answered him as only I could, with memories only he and I shared. "It's me, Little Red. I only kill monsters, and you, Grannie, aren't a monster. You're just a cocky wolf who carries his gun like a gangster."

Cisco's eyes went wide. "Ailis? Miguel's Lish?" He turned to Sofia, who stood in her wolf form and breathed in her scent. "Sofia?"

Sofia nodded. "We thought you were dead. Ailis watched them kill you."

Cisco pulled me into his chest and hugged me until it hurt. "I thought it was lights out for me, until I woke up, almost healed," he answered. "They kept coming in and telling me to help them. They believe we have to be a willing sacrifice for their god. They can't kill us unless we agree. Hence, why I'm still alive, because I refused. They came in here looking like everyone I care about, trying to get me to agree."

"I'm glad to see you still have your head." I smiled.

"If they would have cut my spinal cord, I'd be a goner. But they needed me. The vampire wanted to feed from me for the power I gave him, until it was my turn to play the victim in the circle," he explained. "The vampire is how they've overpowered our people. They were lured by one of our own and subdued by a bloodsucker."

I touched his face and felt the threat of tears burning my eyes. "They made me watch the video of you on your first day with them. I thought you were gone, and it killed me inside that I didn't save you."

"I wouldn't have wanted you to try. You didn't come because of me, did you?" He staggered back to the table on weak legs. Sofia helped him back onto the blood-covered slab. "Please tell me you didn't do this for me. They keep talking about what it would take to get you to finally come."

"Would I do that?" I asked.

He looked up and nodded. "Yeah. You're a foolish little witch and stubborn like Miguel. Of course, you would."

"I didn't come for you, Cisco. You're just a bonus. I came for them," I answered and pointed to the ceiling. "They're up there. But now, we have a problem. I don't have the energy to change you, Cisco, and fight them. And you're in no condition to shift yourself."

"They want you bad, Ailis. You need to get the hell out of here," he replied. "I don't know what they want, but I think all of this was to get you here. Everything I've overheard has been about you, Ailis."

I nodded. "They want me to break some curse twisted by my dead parents. Not gonna happen."

"What's the plan then?" Cisco asked. "I take it there isn't a rescue party coming?"

"You're looking at it," I replied.

Cisco's smile made me flinch. He had been too weak to heal the broken teeth. "If you think Miguel isn't tearing this city apart looking for you, you don't understand how deep his love is for you. You are the moon that his beast howls to."

"I don't know if that's a compliment or —" I started.

"It's very much a compliment," he interrupted. "His wolf answers only to you, his bonded mate, his living soul. It is why Caser cannot command him as he can the others. Rest assured, Ailis, Miguel will find you. He'll sniff you out."

"How come none of your people could feel you?" I asked. "Miguel couldn't sense you — or whatever you all call it."

"All members of a Pack are linked. It's kind of like whispering to each other. Some of us are better at closing that door, while others we can hear nonstop," he replied. "My wolf knew if I sent out a call or my people knew I was still alive, they'd come for me. Neither me nor my wolf would risk Pack for any reason, not even to save my fur."

"Silly fool, maybe we could have helped you sooner," I said, touching his hand. That little act of kindness softened his face.

"And maybe you all would be dead for trying," he replied. "This bloodsucker could have called on his people, and there may have been an outright war. I couldn't risk it. One life is too many to lose. A war between Lycan and vampire would take the lives of innocents. I'd rather die than be the cause of that."

"You're a better monster than I am," I replied and winked.

That earned me another one of his scary grins. "Uh-huh, and that's why you're in this room with Sofia and not long gone."

"Don't go messing with my street cred. It took a trip to hell to earn me my reputation, and I'm not about to lose it in a hellhole," I said and started to pace. I did my best thinking while beating a track into the ground.

I glanced back at Cisco and Sofia, working out a plan in my head before saying anything out loud. Sofia's burns were starting to heal, but her energy level was too low to fight a roomful of witches. I didn't want to say it, but I couldn't depend on her to do much more than get in my way. And Cisco? Well, he really did look like he had just had his head almost cut off and was using every drop of energy to keep it in place. He was beaten, burned, cut up and used as meals on wheels for the vampire we'd just killed. There was no way he'd make it out of here on his own two feet, which happened to have fang marks all over them. I had to look away and think. I couldn't problem solve with him in my line of sight. I couldn't lose my temper...not yet. I couldn't break down in relief that he was alive, either. But I couldn't think my way around the problem. I couldn't get Sofia, him and Anna out while also keeping myself alive. I couldn't leave anyone behind, though. I groaned, frustrated at the lack of options. This must have been why so many hunters out there worked alone. People only complicated things.

"Sofia, how fast can you run if you carry Cisco?" I asked.

"No. Leave me here until it's done." Cisco lifted his hand. "I'll slow you down, and all of us will die."

I ignored him. "Answer me, Sofia."

"I can carry him. I can do it," Sofia said. "I may be low in the Pack, but I'm strong enough for this. I won't fail you."

"Do I not get a say in this?" Cisco asked.

"You want a say in how you're rescued? I see your ego has survived this ordeal." I huffed a laugh. "I'll keep that in mind for the next time I have to drag you out of a hellhole. This absolute shitshow is my trainwreck waiting to happen. You're just catching a ride."

"You sound like Miguel," Cisco replied. "Bossy."

"Okay. That's the plan, then." I touched her arm. My hand flinched. My eyes said she was a wolf, but my brain wasn't expecting her to be hot and furry. "This is it, Sofia. Whatever happens up there, run. Get the hell out of here and get Cisco to your people. Go get help, and if Anna is still breathing, I'll keep her alive until you come back for us."

"Is that why you helped me shift? You wanted me to leave you here before we even found Cisco?" she asked, crossing her massive arms ending in claws. I had to look away. I remembered exactly how those suckers felt, cutting up my arm. "You planned this all along, didn't you? You wouldn't leave me behind, but now you expect me to do it to you?"

"I helped you shift so you'd have a chance, so that you could run faster than anything else here," I replied. "I'm sorry, Sofia, but you're nothing more than a soul for the taking up there. You'd be a body for me to trip over. I knew I wouldn't be able to protect both of us and Anna, if she's still alive. But in your wolf form, you can run and get help while I hold them back. And now, you can save Cisco in the process. Please, Sofia, do this for me. If I die tonight, I want to know that I saved two people. Let me have that. If I go down, I want to be smiling. I want to know I didn't lose completely."

She nodded. Her eyes glittered. "You won't lose."

I unclasped the charm from my neck. It was the first time I had taken it off since the day Miguel had made it for me. "Lean down so I can put this on you."

"What is it?" she asked but still ducked down for me to slip it on. She trusted me enough to let me put it on her before I answered her question.

"It's a charm necklace. It'll warn you of harm from spells and the cursed. Think of it as a pager. It'll vibrate against your skin if you're in danger. But if it starts to heat up, head in a different direction," I answered. "It's a warning and nothing more. The rest, I'm sorry, is up to you. Also, it was a gift from Miguel, so I expect it back."

"It didn't protect you all that much," she countered.

"Sofia, I had every intention of coming here. I planned on them taking me. I knew they'd come back the moment I heard Anna was missing. The charm *did* help me where and when it needed to. I'm alive, aren't I? It's always given me a heads-up every step of the way," I responded. "Don't be a hero up there. Just run. Run as fast as you can. There's a Lycan up there, the traitor. If it catches up to you, kill it. Don't ask them questions, and don't try to figure out the why behind what they've done. Just kill them."

"Happily," she replied.

"Her," Cisco added. "It's a woman. That's all I know. I've heard the witches talk about her but never heard her name."

"Kill the bitch," I added. "I'll do what I can to keep them back. Focus on getting out of here and kill anything that tries to stop you. It doesn't matter what you see. It doesn't matter if they threaten to kill me. Don't be another victim just to try to save me. They're planning to kill me anyway. We don't all have to die tonight."

"That's the same thing he says." Sofia motioned to Cisco.

Cisco nodded. "Don't become a hostage to save another hostage. You'll all die instead of just one."

Sofia picked Cisco up, and I grinned. It looked all wrong. Cisco was a hulk of a man, muscular and imposing. But in Sofia's arms, he looked small and breakable. They noticed my look and snickered with me. With Cisco in her arms, Sofia followed behind me. I turned to them both. "They die, all of them, for what they've done. If it's the last thing I do, they die. It won't be what they deserve, but it'll have to be good enough."

Sofia huffed. It sounded like when a dog wanted your attention or had a bug up its nose. "Like you just said, don't be a hero."

"A hero doesn't stay behind to kill everyone, Sofia. Rest assured, I'm not a hero. But they need to be stopped. If I don't take my shot tonight, I may never get another one. They'll keep killing until they get what they want. They'll unleash hell, and we'll all kick the bucket in one swoop. If it goes south, I'm merely taking the fastest route to my grave," I answered. "Rather selfish of me, when you think of it. If this plan tanks, I will go out in a blaze of glory and leave a mess for you all to clean up."

We reached the top of the stairs, and I took a deep breath. It was now or never, and now that I stood at the door to my fate, my stomach twisted into a knot. I didn't know what would happen once I opened the door, but I knew what I'd leave behind the moment I stepped through it. A slab of wood stood between the life I wanted to have with Miguel — family, home, love and the unknown. I wished more than anything that I had said so much more to Miguel before I'd left. He deserved to know how deeply I cared, how much I valued who he was, even his furry side. But we don't always get what we want or deserve. Sometimes we get stuck with the shitty end of a stick and have to make do. I tucked the memory of Miguel and all the maybes and could-have-beens into my soul and would let that love carry me forward. I breathed out a lungful of pent-up air and shook out my hands. It was time to face the music, which was starting to sound like the theme song to *Jaws*.

Sofia leaned down to my ear. "Eight voices, one is muffled. I smell fresh blood. Anna, I think. And one that smells familiar, the traitor, but I can't really smell them clearly enough to give you a name. The smell of hell is blocking it out. They're to the right. Fresh air to the left."

The smell of hell was an apt description. The witches had a circle in place if Sofia or Cisco couldn't smell past it. But I could. It was matchsticks and burning metal, with a hint of cooked hair. The blood would have to be Anna's, if we hadn't found her tied or dead in the basement. I sent up a prayer for Caser's daughter in case the man upstairs was watching the shitshow that was my life. With the way I run things, I'd be surprised if I didn't have a peanut gallery in the clouds, waiting for my next stupid move.

Cisco grabbed my arm and squeezed. "Whatever happens when you open the door, whatever anyone has ever told you, you don't deserve the fate you've been dealt. You're better than you think you are, Ailis. You came into hell for us, and I'll never forget it. Pack will never forget it. And when you go back down to the pits, I will find you when it is my time, and I will protect you. I give my word, from this life and to the next. Thank you for one last chance."

"Tell Miguel... I..." My voice caught in my throat. I pursed my lips, holding in the sound of my heart breaking. "If I don't make it, tell him I'm sorry and that I..." My eyes watered, and I cleared my throat. "That I have loved him from the start, and I'll love him until the end."

"He knows. We all know," Cisco answered.

"You can tell him yourself later. I'm not your errand dog," Sofia said but smiled to show her tease. Seeing a Lycan grin looked terrifying, but I appreciated it just the same. "You'll see him later. I will pray to Fenrir for your protection. We will get help, and I swear I'll come back for you, even if I must come alone. I won't leave you here."

"Good luck. Whatever you do, don't stop, no matter what. I don't care what you hear. Just run," I said and counted. At three, I opened the door. I threw my aura out, a web of power and did my best to clear a path. I screamed to Sofia. "Run!"

Sofia didn't skip a beat. She ran and didn't look back once. She held Cisco in her arms and was gone in a blur. She was a flood of fear and speed. I caught her out of the corner of my eye. She burst through the window, and my shield snapped. I pulled it back in and around myself. Sofia and Cisco were long gone by the time the bad guys realized I had opened the door. I smiled. No matter what happened, I'd got them out. It was better than I'd thought I could do. I'd thought for sure everyone would die tonight. *Two down...* One more soul and I'll have won more than I thought I could.

Chapter Seven

"Of all the gin joints in all the towns in all the world…" I smiled at a surprised room of witches. "No? No one is going to finish that line? Oh, come on. It's perfect for this moment."

Eight sets of blinking eyes stared back at me. A pin drop could have echoed. I wondered how long it would take before one of them snapped out of it and spoke. Without taking my eyes off them, I took in my surroundings. And as usual, unless I wanted to toss myself out of a stained-glass window, there was only one doorway exit, a wooden one that looked like I would have better luck kicking my way through the rock walls. Just once, I'd like to be in a situation where the exit was right next to me rather than the other side of the bad guys.

The one-room building we stood in was floor-to-ceiling stone, save a few boards and windows. It looked as old as the ruins, only this building was in better condition, as if someone had tried to take care of it or the sturdy door had kept the tourists from destroying it. An old wooden cross hung at the front. The hanging Jesus was long gone, which felt fitting, given why we were here. Not even Jesus wanted to hang around for the show. I envied him a little. I'd have disappeared if I could have, as well. This once safe-haven didn't scream sanctuary in the least. I wondered if it would still be considered sacrilegious if the church was broken-down and hadn't seen its glory days in what looked like a few decades.

The old stained-glass windows along the walls had been replaced with weathered wood. The glass behind the altar was cracked and barely holding on. It reminded me of my soul—chipped, cracked, battered and in need of a complete renovation. The building felt like someone stepping over your grave. I shivered with the kind of unease that only came with hauntings and hell. Either of those two were possibilities at this point. I wouldn't be surprised if the place had a ghost or two. If this had once been holy ground, there had to be an old cemetery close by. Old death equals old power and old souls. Why a spirit would hang around after death was beyond me. This world was bad enough when you're alive. To hang out for more was just crazy. Unfinished business, I've been told. I don't care what kind of baggage I still had to go through. The moment I check out, my shit is dealt with. *So long, suckers.* Heaven or hell, I was out of here.

The hairs on the back of my neck stood on end. My skin crawled with the history of the place. It felt like ice gliding down my spine. The past of this church was dark. I could feel that darkness dance over my aura like an army of ants. But that was true of almost every old church I had stepped into. Most religions had a twisted beginning, built on bones and broken souls, and had always felt like waking up from a nightmare. They made my palms sweat, my heart skip beats and dried my mouth. The fresh blood on the floor and the staticky energy in the air didn't help matters.

Raising a demon in a church was just too comical to comment on. At the front of the room, seven witches stood around a fresh circle. They hadn't even tried to stop Sofia. Though, given her speed and surprise exit, they'd stood no chance of catching her. They stood as they had in my dream, following the first crime scene. In my dream, around the circle stood seven witches, nude, save shoulder-to-toe red cloches. I couldn't see their faces at the time, but I saw them all today, and I'd never forget a single one. The wolf in my dream stood to the right, not a part of the magic but as guilty as the rest.

The group of seven opened up for me to see Caser's daughter, Anna, tied in the circle on her back. Her blonde hair had streaks of red from a head wound. Her eyes were closed, and I was thankful for that small miracle. I was surprised to see that she would be playing victim again after an oath was given for her safety—and that changed everything. Anna became a reason I had to stay and not just torch the place. Anna opened her eyes and found mine. I didn't know if she thought I was there to finish the job or if she was just scared. She screamed through the gag, and my heart broke for her. I shook my head and lifted my finger to my lips. Within seconds, she quieted. Nothing about me looked approachable or kind, but at that moment, she understood perfectly. I wasn't there to hurt her.

To the very right of the room stood one of the first women to go missing, the Lycan from my dream, who had started to laugh when Anna had screamed. One heated glare from me and her laughter died. I'd felt her energy as soon as I opened the door. I recognized her face from the file Caser had given me the night one of his people died for attacking me. Evette, Caser's partner, stood tall and proud, and I wanted nothing more than to wipe that smug look off her face. Evette had gone missing early on. At first, Caser had suspected she had been challenged and killed, but because of her tie to Caser, no one was brave enough to step forward. Challenges were supposed to be done within Pack, in front of witnesses, so it had made perfect sense to Caser that no one admitted to killing her. How wrong he had been.

Evette had the most to gain and most to lose by working with the witches. I felt my hate for her settle into my bones. I didn't hate many people. It was a waste of energy. But Evette I'd hate until my last breath. She not only sold out her people, innocents, but she offered a child up on a silver platter. That, alone, was worth being dragged over hot coals into the lower pits of hell for the devils to teach her a lesson.

"Why?" I blurted out. I looked from Evette to Anna. "You sold out your daughter? For what? What could they possibly give you that is more valuable than your own child?"

"Oh, she's not mine," Evette answered as if that were a good enough reason. "I wasn't good enough to breed with. But if you must know why, being in second place for the rest of my life isn't worth much."

I turned the force of my stare back to her. I was disgusted. No one else noticed, but I saw her take a step back. "Oh, sweetie, just because you were sleeping with first place doesn't mean you were in second. You're not nearly that important. Caser didn't even look for you. You were listed as dead, lost to a challenge."

"As if I'd lose," she answered. She sounded sure of herself, but the look on her face said her ego was bruised.

"Why did no one come looking for you, little wolf?" I asked. If pissing each and every one of them off was how I'd buy time for me and Anna, I would. "Why was there no missing person report issued? I read your entire file, and there was not a single notation that you mattered much to anyone. Your report was a few sentences and a photo. You're not good enough to breed with and not good enough to look for. I can see why you'd team up with these wannabes. You weren't going to get anywhere on your own, that's for damn sure."

"None of that is important anymore. Soon, I'll be in first place, and the rest of this won't matter, will it?" She smirked. As though, somehow, when this was all said and done, her slate would be wiped clean. "With Damon at my side, no one will be brave enough to challenge me."

"Oh, I think not. You're living in a dream world if you think the shit you've done won't matter to the others, whether one lone wolf stands with you or not. *If*, and that's a very big if, you make it out of here alive, the Pack will never forgive you. No one will. They'll know what you did. They'll smell it on you. They'll never accept you after all you've done to your people. There will never be a place for you, anywhere, in your society. You'll be first of nothing. The only thing that won't matter is you." I knew nothing about Pack, but I knew enough about hate to know it burned your ass every chance it got. Hate spent like the dickens in hell.

It would buy her a first-class ticket into the pits. Whatever the outcome, she'd die for this, either by my hands or Pack or hell. I wasn't picky enough to care who took her life, as long as she found herself in an unmarked grave. I made a mental note to remember the name Damon. He must have been the hate I had felt the night I met Pack. If I lived, he wouldn't.

She smiled. It wasn't a full '*I win*' smile, but it was cocky. I could relate. Smugness was in my blood. I smiled back. "You're dead. You all are."

"Not from where I'm standing," she replied.

"The night is young," I answered and turned my attention to the witches. I made eye contact with each one. Twit and twat, with their combined room temperature I.Q., stepped forward. I paused to eyeball the rest. Each flinched just enough for me to notice when I made eye contact. I was petty enough to smile when I saw their fear.

"You must understand, by now, how important you are to us." Witch One was the first brave witch to open her mouth. Of them all, she had guts. I prayed I lived long enough to see them splattered on the walls of this gin joint. "Do you know how difficult it has been to get your attention?"

"You could have simply made an appointment to meet with me like any sane person would. This…?" I motioned to Anna on the floor, "Jesus, this wasn't necessary. Better yet, you could have summoned a demon in my backyard rather than all of this. That would have gotten my full attention. I'm a demon expert, brain trust, not a detective. I don't pay attention to bodies on the ground unless a demon is attached to their deaths."

"Oh, we summoned many demons in Vancouver, close to home, but none managed to grab your eye quite like hitting close to your heart."

"Oh, yes, because wolves are so very close to my heart." I shrugged and feigned interest but flipped through the rolodex of information in the back of my mind. Over the last year, a dozen lower-level demons had popped up here and there but had been sent packing pretty damn fast by local practitioners attached to the police department. Mannix had dealt with most of them and hadn't once mentioned it to me. It wasn't anything that would typically catch my eye unless someone said something in passing. I was thankful for that. Gaining my attention meant countless lives had been lost.

"But Miguel is." Evette piped up from the corner. "You, witch, were my ticket out of Caser's shadow."

"Does anyone here have a spray bottle or a muzzle? Or could you tie your dog up in the backyard? I have a delicate sense of smell, and she stinks like a dead bitch," I asked and got crickets. Evette's reaction was a mix between growl and *hrmph*.

Witch Two broke her silence. "She is a means to an end, such as yourself."

"You should have selected better on both accounts," I replied.

"Your blood is all we need, willing or not," she answered.

"Ah, yes, to break a curse," I said. Her face paled. "The walls down there were thick, but noise has a way of carrying in a void of silence. You say you need my blood to remove a curse in hell. Silly little witch, you need more than blood. You need the spell to untwist. Without that, you're back to square one."

"You are most correct," she replied and pulled out a slip of paper no bigger than a recipe card. "He has given us the spell, and we do not need you to say the words."

My eyes widened, not in fear but in surprise. I don't know why their stupidity caught me off guard at every turn. "First, whatever you have isn't the spell. The original spell was four pages long, and good luck understanding Theban script. It isn't something that can be translated into English without dropping words and meaning. Theban takes decades to learn, passed down through generations. When it comes to hell, I wouldn't be so willing to make mistakes with a spell."

I flat-out lied to them about the spell. Sure, my mother wrote every spell in Theban, but if you knew what you were doing, it could be translated, though rarely into English. Latin was the usual language. The curse my mother had used, I'd never forget. Her final words, which were five in total, were stamped on my soul. *Secures. Chaxeleon. Infernum. Aeternum. Chac. Secure Chaxeleon in hell forever. Tie Chac to the pits for eternity.*

"And second, you put an awful lot of your eggs in one basket for mortal beings. You take the word of a demon as though the cursed thing would never lie to you. News flash! They lie better than any other. Whatever the hell you have in your hand is not what you think it is." I had no idea what they held, but I knew I needed to buy as much time as possible. For once, arguing with idiots didn't seem like a bad way to spend my night. I was glad to spend my time doing anything other than dying.

"I may not be able to smell a lie, but even I know you would lie to save your own skin," she replied. "Including lying about this spell."

"When you were in Vancouver, you should have taken a few classes. Here's a little education for free," I replied. "My blood is *not* going to break whatever curse was woven. Only the blood of the person who spun it will work. The curse you're referring to was twisted by two level three, full-blooded witches. Do you know how unbelievably powerful that curse would be? My blood, even if it could work, would not be strong enough to undo the bindings of two hereditary witches, ten times my power. The point is rather moot, though. This all rests on the willingness of me, my blood and a spell you don't have. What the hell do you think the devils are going to do when they feel you mucking around with the gate?"

If I woke up tomorrow, I'd be adding deception to my lecture list. A good lie could buy you time. A great lie can cause doubt in your opponent. And I needed both, time and doubt. Sure, I also could be dragging out the inevitable, but I was willing to risk it for another few minutes with a pulse. Witch Two didn't so much as bat an eye. She wasn't buying the horseshit I was selling. Her counterpart, however, looked worried. Her eyes darted between me and the others.

"Your lies will follow you into hell, where you shall burn for eternity," Witch Two finally answered. "I have read the books on curses, along with articles authored by you, yourself. The time for arguing is over. Your games and lies have come to an end. Chaxeleon will rise."

My heart skipped a beat at the mention of his full name. The memory of the night my parents died flared to life. I shook the thoughts from my mind, willing myself not to delve too deeply into them. "Do you know who you are trying to raise? He's not just any demon," I asked. They nodded as if they had a clue. They didn't. "Chaxeleon was so powerful, it took devils to lock him away in the first place. To bind him, it took the joined efforts of two hereditary witches and some of the most powerful devils below. Do you really think me, one solitary witch, and you, a bunch of hacks, can raise him? You're off your broomsticks."

I counted the seconds passing in the back of my mind. I had no idea where I was or how long it would take Sofia to run for help. She was in bad condition, burned and blistered, carrying an even worse-off Cisco. I couldn't stall forever, but I'd try for as long as possible. Even a minute could mean the difference between a dead solitary witch and a live one.

"You forget, witch," Evette spoke up, drawing all of our attention, "about feeding the Gods with the souls of Lycan. There are no more powerful souls out there than ours."

"And you'll rot in hell for that," I replied. "But none of this even matters. I only stuck around to see what was going to happen next, oath breakers. I've never seen an entire room of witches dragged into hell." I fought the urge to smile. It didn't matter if I died tonight. I wouldn't lose in the end, and that settled my soul like nothing else could. A brief flash of confusion on their faces, and I lost my fight not to smile. "You gave your word that Anna would go free. You all are oath breakers. You will die for this, just like your little Plan B in the basement did. Your ticket to immortal life was a heap of ash on the floor the moment you broke your word."

My laughter bubbled up and filled the room with the sound of my taunting them. It was all nerves, but they didn't need to know I was scared to my core. I was always afraid. My scent would be no different today than it was a year ago. I watched as the knowledge of my words sunk in. I killed their way out of this mess. The bloodsucker would not be coming to help them. The room filled with static. They collectively lashed out, and I dropped to my knees. The combined power of seven witches, wannabes or not, was a lot to take in. They were backed by stolen power from hell. It tasted familiar, and I wanted to vomit—but I took it.

I had used a lot of energy getting Sofia, Cisco and myself from the basement. I'd feel every sting the witches doled out while I conserved my remaining energy. It wouldn't kill me—not fast, at least. But I didn't strike back. I wasn't here for their deaths only. That would need to wait. My focus was on Anna first, kill the witches second, then the traitorous dog whenever I could spare a moment. Witch One stood in front of me. Although I wanted retribution, I held back. I'd need every drop of energy I had left. She knelt and lifted my head.

She pressed a knife against my stomach. "No, you're the only witch who dies today."

"Wrong again." I spit the words in her face.

She flinched as if I had burned her with my saliva. She pushed the knife into my stomach, and my flesh parted as if to step aside and invite the blade in. It slid in like a hot knife to butter. It felt like being punched in the stomach while something burned me from the inside. The cut to the skin hurt more than the blade going through my meat. The world faded around the edges, bringing her ugly, hate filled face into perfect focus. She was smiling. Her eyes lit up like a kid in a candy store. I had once thought she'd blend in well in hell. This only confirmed it. The room tilted to the side as my brain caught up to what was happening to my body. My blood pressure skyrocketed, and little sparkles of twirling light danced across my line of sight. I dropped forward, gasping for air. The room was a dull echo, eaten up by my pounding heart. Fighting my natural urge to fight back, to run, to get the hell away from that which was causing my pain was one of the hardest things to do. The flood of adrenaline sped my pulse and breathing. My legs twitched as they prepared for a mad dash I wouldn't take. Every fiber of my being told me to run, but my soul was firmly rooted in place.

"I hope you're the last to die," I muttered.

The witch dragged me by the hair to the head of the room and pulled me to my knees in front of the circle. I held on to my bleeding stomach and tried to put as much pressure on it as I could. Struggling would have only made me bleed harder, so I let myself be heaved like a bag of trash across the room. In the circle, Anna's frozen stare found my eyes. The look of terror on her face steadied my resolve. Children should never be in the position of thinking they were going to die at the hands of monsters — human or not. No one should ever face this fate. But I had a soft spot for kids, whereas most adults brought it on themselves by putting their noses where they didn't belong.

I smiled at Anna, giving her a soft look. I didn't have a maternal bone in my body, but whatever she saw on my face eased the lines around her eyes. I tried to will her to be calm. Win or lose, this would be over soon. I slumped forward in a display of weakness. It wasn't all show. I was growing dizzy from blood loss, and my stomach burned like hot coals sitting just behind my wound. I groaned as the beginnings of heart palpitations began. Soon, I wouldn't have enough blood to keep the cursed thing beating. If the witches didn't outright kill me, I'd bleed out, die of shock, sepsis or organ failure. So many choices, and yet all were still better than being killed by a demon, which was also high on the list of probabilities. *Yay me.* It wasn't often I had a menu of death to choose from.

From the corner of the room, a lanky woman stepped forward, extending her hand. The witches blocked most of my view of her. "Give me what I've paid for." Her voice raked down my mind and sent up warning flares. Her voice had a familiarity to it like I had heard it before but couldn't place it. But all monstrous people sounded familiar to me, as if hell itself echoed from behind their words.

I hadn't sensed the woman when I'd first stepped into the room, and I still felt nothing much from her…not a prickle of power or show of force. Whoever she was, the others stepped away from her. Witch One handed over the knife she had just used to stab me with. The woman cleaned my blood from the blade into a small glass vial. With not another word exchanged, the woman and my blood walked out of the church. As curious as I was as to who she was and why she took my blood, I brought no more attention to myself. My hands dropped to the floor while the group began to discuss who would die first, me or Anna. The wolf wanted Anna out of the picture immediately, while the others thought keeping me alive increased the risk to their lives. I couldn't argue with that last part. They should have killed me the first time they'd met me.

I inched my bloody hand forward and touched the edge of the circle. I felt no hum of power or burning threat that said if I came any closer, I'd be fried to a crisp. They hadn't set the circle yet. *Stupid is as stupid does*. It was wide open, so I took it from them. I crawled into the ring on the floor, running my bloody hand over the part I had destroyed with my knees on my way in. I was a hereditary witch. My magic was in my blood, my rituals all required a drop of my blood to invoke, or they wouldn't work for me. I closed my eyes and envisioned the ring around us, building an invisible wall between us and those in the room. With my blood, I willed the wall to take shape.

I felt the first tickle of magic taking root as the loose hairs on my head began to rise. I felt my aura fill with energy, the rush of it making my head pound and my stomach hurt as the muscles tightened. The air around me smelled of ozone and matchsticks. The energy was sticky at first, appealing to the part of my brain that wanted to survive, trying to convince me to keep it all for myself. Magic was a heady beast, enticing as any vice could be. It rubbed along my soul like a lover's caress, tempting me to take more than I needed, more than I could handle. But any more than my aura could hold and I'd burn it from the inside out. I pushed the energy from my aura into the circle.

Tutela, I thought to myself. I didn't need to say the word for protection out loud. It was one of the few spells taught by my parents that I still use to this day. It was such a part of me that a simple thought could spin the spell and set it in place. My cat, so far, was the only one to cross a set circle of mine. That should have told me everything I needed to know about how important that little beast was to me and my survival. Opening my eyes, I could see the shimmer of my gray and red smoky-edged aura, tainted from hell, at the edge of the circle. My circle wouldn't keep out the more powerful from hell, but it would keep the witches at bay. For those who could break it down, my circle would hold long enough for the minutes I needed.

The first rule of a stab wound club was to leave the damn knife alone. Since lunatic one was holding the said knife, I had few options to help myself before I passed out. Blinking away tears and fatigue, I ripped a strip of my shirt off and balled it up. Taking a deep breath and clenching my teeth hard enough to crack my jaw, I pushed the fabric into my stomach wound. Putting in a small plug hurt more than the knife had. A wave of heat and nausea following my attempts to stanch the bleeding almost took me out. My stomach muscles protested, but for once, I was thankful for my body's reaction to the pain. A person's body wanted to live and did all it could to keep a person alive. It often clamps down around any object that has entered the body, cutting off the flow of blood. My shirt wouldn't do much more than slow the bleeding, but unless a surgeon strolled through the front door, a dirty shirt would have to do for now.

Once I was sure I wasn't going to pass out, I leaned into Anna's ear. "Whatever you do, Anna, do not open your eyes. Do not scream. Do not make a sound. No matter what you hear, keep your eyes shut. Can you do that for me?"

Anna squeezed her eyes and nodded slowly. I hated what I was about to do, more because I was risking her life in the process. With choices at a premium, I sent up a prayer to any God listening, to keep Anna alive long enough for Sofia to return with Pack. I willed as much of my aura as I could into the circle of protection in case I failed. Anna could hold out in the circle until her people came for her. Nothing short of the bottom pits of hell was going to put a dent in this circle.

"If this goes sideways, do not leave this circle until your Pack comes for you," I told her, then thought better of my messaging, given one of her own people sold her out. "Do not break the circle for anyone but Miguel or your father. I don't care who steps up to the circle or what promises they make, do not break it for anyone. Nod if you understand."

She nodded again. With her eyes still shut, small tears rolled from the edges, and my heart broke for her. That she was still tied up made me want to scream. The only knife in the room was currently being scraped of my blood. I'd figure out a way to get her free if we lived through the next few minutes. We had a fifty-fifty chance, and those odds, when it came to gambling on the gates, weren't bad at all. Well, Anna had those odds. I wasn't so lucky. I'd have better luck winning the jackpot in Vegas than walking out of this mess.

On my knees, using the blood from my stomach wound, I drew symbols on the stones. That I'd found someone who knew them wasn't sheer luck. During conversations with Samuel, he'd pointed me in the right direction. He couldn't outright tell me the secrets he held, but he always found a way to lead me to what I needed. To have this knowledge wasn't just stupid. It was a death wish. But for once, I was thankful for fools. It took me the better part of a day, calling those I wasn't supposed to know and asking questions I shouldn't have the answers to. But once I found the man with the information I desired, a few threats later and I had what I needed. I should have felt bad for making the threats I had. I'll call him when I get home and apologize, if he hasn't already blocked my number and moved out of the country, cursing my name on his way out.

With the symbols painted, I pressed my hand into the marking in the middle, a mirror of what was carved into the gates of hell. I poured my aura into symbols and called on hell with everything I had. I swayed on my knees as the energy flowed from me and into a spell I had never cast before. I kept myself upright with my bloodied hands, and in the back of my mind, I stood in front of the gates, prying them open. My bloody hands painted the gates, and my call was heard. The moment they squealed on their hinges, I was shoved out, my mind fully back in the circle. The squeal echoed throughout the room, and the remaining windows in the church burst, showering glass down like sharp raindrops. I kept my hands pressed into my circle, over my symbols. The power in the room grew to a deafening level, and the force blew me back through my circle, leaving Anna unprotected. Had it not been for the rope nailed to the floor, she'd have been blown across the room with me. The others, outside of my circle, took the brunt of it, hitting the walls with crunches of bone and slaps of meat on stone.

I did not summon the demon who had called himself Chac. Nothing could have forced that out of me, not even the life of Anna. I had summoned the one thing we're never allowed to call...Hellhounds. If my call was righteous, they would come. If not, they'd come for only me. It was the deadliest of summons, and I was sure it would stain my soul until the end of time. It wasn't a kind of magic one could practice, so it was cast with only hope to power it. Practice didn't make perfect. It would have made me dead a lot quicker than I was about to be. All I had was trust that it would work. There was no other choice. But both me and Anna would die if I didn't try. My last-ditch act of desperation would be glorious and perhaps as stupid as the man who had saved the markings for me to threaten out of him.

On my back, I struggled to breathe. The wind had been knocked out of me when I'd landed ten feet from the circle. While I tried to relearn how my lungs worked, I heard it, the warning of their coming. The first thunder echoed through the room. Once my lungs filled, I could hear them—hell, wild and vengeful, coming like a hundred horse hooves on concrete. Every step exploded in my ears. Thunder vibrated down my spine. Each crackle reminded me of bone grinding on broken bones. I felt it deep in my chest as it rattled the little breath I had in my lungs. My ears popped. A high-pitched ringing sent my hands to my ears in vain. I couldn't hear anything but them. My heart pounded with the beat of their feet. It echoed in my skull like they were running across my brain. Static prickled the air and lifted my hair in a wind that wasn't there. Each new breath became harder and harder to take. The very air heated and burned as I sucked it down.

Inside my broken circle, Anna lay with her eyes shut, the wind stirring her bloody hair. The witches screamed and clawed at their throats. Their hair whipped around their faces in an impossible wind. The wood-covered windows peeled from their longtime resting place, slamming into the ground and smashing against the stone walls. The only door splintered and finally burst from the frame, sending shards of wood through the room. I shielded my face from most of it but felt slivers of wood embed themselves into my forearms.

They burst through the door, and hundreds of shapes and sizes filled the room. I moved to face them but quickly turned away. My eyes couldn't decide whether I could see them or the shadow of them. I caught glimpses of fur and teeth, claws and eyes so red they lit the room. Heat sizzled the floor, burning the wood wherever they touched. They could have been the size of pixies, and I'd have been terrified to my core. Their scent filled the room like dozens of rotten bodies burning in the pits. I gagged on heat and death. They smelled of times I'd sooner not remember. Each breath reminded me of when my own flesh cooked and hung from my bones. The smell was torture and hell and the very gates I had once walked through.

"No, no, no, no..." I shook my head, the stench of hell pulling me back to those long two minutes in a cage.

I don't know how long I sat there, terrified to my core, before snapping out of it. I wasn't in a cage. The smell of cooked flesh wasn't mine. The terrible sounds weren't coming from me. I wanted to scream and cry and curl up in a ball but forced myself to focus. I could cry later. I'm pretty sure I would, whether I willed it to happen or not. Tonight didn't look like a night I'd walk away from without shedding a few tears and ending my life.

"Anna." My focus shifted from hell to keeping an innocent from being dragged down.

My eyes scanned the floor for something sharp and large enough to cut through the ropes holding Anna. The knife was twenty feet away from me. I scurried on the floor, slipping in my own blood and debris, grabbing the knife the witch had stabbed me with and moved back into the circle. Anna was unconscious in the middle, covered in glass and pieces of broken church. I cut the ropes holding her down, trying to be careful not to slash her wrists in the process. With more effort than it should have taken, I picked Anna up. I wasn't physically weak on a good day, but today wasn't one of those. My body was beaten, bruised and bleeding and had seen better days in hell. My torn stomach muscles protested at the exertion. My legs shook, and my arms burned. But I got to my feet and started to walk through the room. I kept my eyes on the busted doorway.

One foot in front of the other, I carried Anne through the hounds, the screaming witches who were being ripped apart, a Lycan traitor who no longer had a head, a coming demon being sent back to his prison, and out of the front door. I whispered the only prayer I remembered by heart, and it was said while eating dinner. But I didn't think the big guy upstairs cared all that much. If He was listening, the words weren't really the point of it. Asking for my food and drink to be blessed had to count as a prayer, didn't it? I crossed my fingers, just in case.

I didn't look behind me. If the hounds were there, about to tear me down, I didn't really want to know. I moved slowly, too sluggish for my tastes, but made it down the three steps out of the church. The grass was damp, and a light drizzle had started. Hopefully, the calling of the hounds didn't also bring with it biblical flooding. I doubted I had the strength to build a raft at this point. I'd hate to make it this far only to drown. What an absolute waste of a good rescue this would turn out to be.

I walked until I had nothing left. I fell to my knees, dizzy from a head injury, a stab wound, the inside a church blowing up and blood loss. I was bleeding from a few dozen small cuts and a hole in my stomach. When my legs could give me no more, I crawled on my hands and knees, dragging Anna as far from the church as I could get. Half sitting, I gripped Anna's sweater, dug my feet into the earth, and pulled. Inch by inch, we moved. And once my stomach protested to the point of making me sick, I used the last of my energy to draw a ring of blood around both Anna and me on the ground. I leached from my aura, putting all my energy into a circle of protection, my heart and soul and the drips of whatever I had left. I knelt with Anna behind me. I glanced down at her and felt the first tear fall. The circle would hold until I died, and the blood was void of my energy.

Around us grew wild lavender. The air was filled with it. I wondered if Miguel would still be tracking the smell or had given up on finding me, missing the very thing that would point in our direction. Even if I didn't make it, I'd done all I could. That had to be worth something. If Anna had survived, I would have gotten everything I asked for. It was rare to be gifted every ask before death.

Chapter Eight

Anna's body shivered and twitched. Her chest rose and fell the way it would if she had run, full-out, for a mile...quickly at first, as though she couldn't get enough air, and finally slowing down to something I could barely see. I recognized those movements, the last-ditch efforts of her body trying to hold on to small shreds of life. She was paling and turning a sickly gray. Her skin was clammy and cold. Her body was fighting shock, trying desperately to keep going. She looked how I felt, close to death. I watched her, trying to think through my own disorientation. I glanced around, as far as my eye could see, and saw no lights, no houses I could try to drag her to. I didn't know where I'd get the energy to do it, but I would have tried. We were in the middle of nowhere, and I had no tools to keep her alive. I wasn't the kind of doctor you'd want on a plane unless there was a demon causing the deaths. I assessed Anna the best I could and felt the first tingle in my nose, a warning of pending tears.

I closed my eyes and reached out to her with my aura. My shields opened up just enough for me to sense her, but I found next to nothing on the other end. Usually, I could feel another person's soul when I reached out to it. I could feel their energy like static. I could see their aura shimmering around them as if they were standing in front of a light. Anna's aura was faded, so dull I couldn't see much more than a watery haze. I pulled my shields back up and prayed.

Her last breath came out long and hot and broke something in me that would never repair. She stopped breathing, and with one last shudder, her heart gave a final beat. She was dying in front of my eyes. I screamed wordlessly into the night. *Why can't I ever be on time?* I always got to the victim too late. I came when the bodies were cold and already toe tagged. I wanted to be on time for once. *Just once, let me save someone from the grips of death.*

"Oh, come on," I cried. It wasn't fair to live a life where I had to fight tooth and nail against evil. My blood was a lighthouse for monsters, and until I died, they'd never leave me alone. But because of one wrong choice when I was a child, it cost me my eternal salvation. Even in death, they'd never stop coming.

"Please," I whispered to any god listening. My bone-dry mouth made my words sound like a growl. "Don't take her."

My body was slow, and it felt like my limbs were lined with lead as I moved into position. I felt like I was going to vomit on her, not save her life. My pulse hammered in my neck. I tilted her head back and began chest compressions. Every pump felt like pushing a car uphill. With my shoulders over my hands, I leaned into it and began my attempt to save her life. I counted to thirty to the tune of the Bee Gees *Stayin' Alive*. It was how I had learned it back home and the only way I could remember it now. At thirty, I gave her two breaths. Back and forth until I felt her soul's fight to remain. Her pulse, though weak as a dying butterfly, returned. Her face was coated in blood, both fresh and old, but I could see a little color returning. Rage began to boil in my stomach for what had been done to her.

"Hold on, Anna," I whispered. "Please, just a little longer."

But I knew if I didn't think of something else, she'd die right alongside me. Time was running out for me. I could feel it trickle out of my stomach wound. If this was it for me, I'd eat up everything I had to give her a chance. I closed my eyes, and with a mental knife, I carved chunks of my aura off. It hurt as much as I thought it would, like cutting off my own skin. Siphoning energy from my aura was painful and left parts of me feeling like I had been road-rashed and rolled in salt. My aura, which usually flowed around me in wisps, was now close to gone. But I had no choice. I needed the energy but felt weaker for it. I was raw in parts and watery in others. It was like the day I was spat from hell, with a broken soul and a worn-off aura. When I went to hell this time, it would burn up my soul in a matter of seconds.

I pushed energy into Anna to keep her heart beating and saved the rest to call out to her people. I leaned forward and drew the only glyph I knew for Lycan on the ground in front of me, one I'd found in an old text. It was the same mark engraved on the back of the necklace Miguel had given me. For years, he had protected me, and I hadn't known it. With the symbol painted, I pushed the rest of my power, carved from my aura, into the mark, and I called the one person I knew would always be listening for me.

"Miguel!" I screamed into the night. "Help me! Please!"

But it wasn't Miguel who came. I wasn't so lucky, and I wasn't so surprised. It was time for me to pay for who I had called from the pits of hell. Before me was a hellhound. He stood in the shadows, but I knew he was there. I smelled him and gagged because of it. My soul recoiled from him. In a few short minutes, my sanity would retreat as well. He felt like the only thing the monsters ran from. If I could have, I would have run, too. But a person can't run from hell, especially someone like me. I was marked for the taking, whether I had called them early or not. I could never run fast enough or far enough. There wasn't a place where I could hide from a hellhound. It had been the only warning I had been given when I had threatened someone for the spell to call the very beast who now stood before me.

"Please, not yet. I can't die, not yet." I cried. I looked at Anna. She would be alone. She was injured, and her soul fought to live, but like her, it was weak. She would die without me to restart her heart if needed. "I'm not done yet. Please, let me help her first. Once I know she'll live, you can have me. I swear it on any oath."

The hound inched forward, and I cowered from the pulse of heat radiating from the shadows. As it stepped from the darkness, my body tried to shrivel into the smallest non-threatening being possible, which wasn't hard compared to what stood before me. The hound was the size of a horse. It looked like everything I imagined one would look like. A blood-soaked wolf, only this one wouldn't have fit in at the zoo. His claws touched the edge of the circle, and I felt the flare of my power along my soul. I knew my circle wouldn't keep out a hellhound. Nothing could keep out a hound from hell. They were neither good nor bad, and I wasn't powerful enough to try anything more than what I had done. I was depleted, exhausted, bleeding out and fading fast.

It finally spoke. "You knew the cost of our call. You hold the knowledge of our warnings. To call us means to forfeit your life for that summons." His voice was closer to human than animal. He reminded me of Sofia when she spoke. "Why do you fear me so? Your pain would end if you came with me."

I half smiled. "Not for long, though. Hell isn't exactly pain-free."

"You know better than most that the pain of hell isn't as bad as the pain up here," he replied. "Up here, it is endless. You suffer in ways hell cannot compete with."

I nodded. It was true. Physical pain doesn't hurt as much as emotional pain. "Please, not yet. I'll come with you, willingly, when Anna is safe."

He stepped over the line. His claws touched my hands. "You would stay for a monster?"

"Don't call her that!" I snapped and shoved his paw away. "She's just a child, and you won't fucking touch her."

"A child who will become one of the beasts. I can smell it on her. She will grow and become Lycan. She'll be just another monster to be hunted and killed," he answered. "She may not have claws today, but one day, she'll be just another beast like the rest."

"Don't say that." My voice was heated, but came out with an edge of whine, like a kid not given another cookie.

I didn't like him calling Anna a monster, but I didn't know how to react in a way that wouldn't get both me and Anna killed. I did my best to swallow my temper. I couldn't afford it. Between the power it took to keep my heart beating and stay conscious to help Anna, I couldn't give away my energy for something so trivial as anger. I looked up to the sky, to the stars. I found the Little Dipper, the cluster both Miguel and I would find when we were missing the other. No matter where we were, we were connected by that one constellation. There weren't many nights that had passed over the years where I hadn't looked up at least once to find it. It was a shared secret that once said, no matter what, it would be okay. Hell could swallow me whole, but somehow, I'd be okay.

"Miguel, please. Help me," I whispered. "I need you."

"You ask a monster to save you from another monster? You are perplexing, Ailis Petronilla Kyteler," the hound said, a slight lilt to his voice as if confused. If I didn't know any better, I'd say his words were closer to a tease than a question. I had always hated when demons and the cursed used my full name. It felt like they knew more about me than I did about them. That was never a good position to be in.

"Don't call Miguel that," I whispered. "He's not a monster."

"But these are merely the words you've said to him, yourself. Is that not what you last called him? Is that not what he calls himself at the end of each day? You gave him the shame he carries. Your words are a scar on his soul." The hound pointed out the hate that had spewed from my mouth just days before.

My eyes were growing heavy. I could feel the blood loss start to weigh down on the rest of my body. It took a lot of concentration to form my next words. "He's *my* monster, not yours. You don't get to call him that."

"And this one" — the hound motioned to Anna — "is she yours, as well?"

I positioned myself closer to Anna. "Yes. She's mine. You can't have her, either." My voice was panicked. The jolt of fear woke me up. If I didn't stay conscious, Anna was as good as dead, and this was all for naught.

"How could you stop me? You're bleeding all over her. There's more of your blood on her than her own. Your energy is spent. Your aura is torn to shreds. You have nothing to offer me. Not even your soul is worth anything to me. It's been ripped apart once already. You smell like the others in the cages — death and suffering."

I picked up the only weapon I had, the knife that had been used to stab me and held it out. My hands shook in effort. Hot tears rolled from my eyes. They burned lines down my cold cheeks. I was going to die, and Anna would die with me. I felt like I had failed her, failed Miguel, failed myself. I had summoned the un-callable and sentenced us both to hell. "I will kill you before you take her. Do you hear me? You can't have her!"

The hound batted my hand, and the knife fell to the ground. "If one *could* kill me, you would not be the one to do it. You haven't even the strength to hold the knife, let alone kill me with it. You wouldn't be able to protect yourself from the lowliest creature right now. How do you suppose you'd defend yourself from me?"

"I'll die trying." I picked the knife back up and stared him in the eyes.

He may have been ten times my size and strength, but physical strength wasn't the only thing that mattered. I was more determined to keep Anna alive than he was of taking her. I squeezed my hand tighter around the blade and winced in pain. My hand throbbed from an already injured thumb and his swipe. He had barely touched me, and I was sure he had broken a couple fingers.

"All I can do is try," I said, my voice calm and determined. "But mark my words, wolf. You're going to hurt with me. If I bleed, so do you. If I die, you best believe I will take you with me."

"I'll make you a deal. Let me have the girl, and I'll ensure you live. She's nothing to you, Ailis. She will grow and become one of the creatures you hate. If you die to protect her, imagine all the others who will die because you weren't there to help them—hundreds, maybe thousands. Is this one little life worth that? She is a Lycan, one of mine and not yours. I will take her if I choose. Why not reap the reward now of stepping aside, rather than me stepping over your dead body and taking what is mine to have."

I shook my head, sloshing my bruised brain around. "She is worth it. Future lives aren't my responsibility. I can't save everyone. But this life, right now, is my responsibility and can be saved. You don't get to have her. She is innocent. You can't take an innocent."

"I'm making an exception with not killing you outright for calling the hunt to your door. I can certainly make an exception for the little one, too. You'll do anything to survive. Why not cut out the middleman and get rid of another monster now rather than later?" he asked.

I swiped at the hound. A drop of his blood fell into my circle. I felt the walls of my circle strengthen. "Get the fuck away from her. I will end you. Do you hear me? I will eat everything in my soul for more energy to kill you. Even if I fail, I'll have done everything in my power to save her, and you will hurt for it."

"You will die," he said, like it was written as fact somewhere.

"We all die someday, but today is not her day. She will go home. She will grow. She will marry, and she will have children of her own. And you will have nothing but me, a worthless and tattered soul. I will see you in hell, and I'll smile every time I see you walk past my cage." I yelled into the face of hell itself. "You don't get to win. Even if I lose, you lose with me. But mark my words. You will *not* take an innocent while my heart still beats."

"It is slowing as we speak. Another few minutes and the girl is mine to do as I please."

The hound moved, and I sliced his paw again. His nails rested on the edge of my symbol. The blood from the hound flared my glyph. The power pulsed and pushed my circle to full strength. I felt a tug in my belly button. It was unlike anything I had ever felt before. Raw power. Neither good nor bad, just power. I screamed into the night as it rolled through my body. I could see Miguel in the back of my mind. It was like a scratch on the eye. You could see that scratch in your line of sight, but each time you tried to look, the mark moved.

"*Ailis?*" In my mind's eye Miguel looked up while driving. He swerved to the side of the road, cursing. "*Ailis! Hold on, Lish. I'm coming.*"

I teetered to my side, half on my rear and half on my knees. It was a relief, not for me, but for Anna. I just had to hold on a little longer, and Anna would be safe. I cried. I didn't have enough in me to fight off a fly, let alone a wolf spit from the pits of hell. But I would kill myself trying. *"I'm sorry, Miguel. I found Sofia and Cisco. He's alive. Sofia has him. I sent them for help. I found Anna, but I'm not going to make it this time. I need you to know how deeply I love you. No matter what I said, I wouldn't have left you behind. I couldn't. But I'm sorry that I'm leaving you now. Remember who you are, and know I love every part of you. All of you, even the parts you don't love about yourself."*

I felt Miguel's anguish, his horror, as if it were my own. I could almost feel his heart breaking. His desperation pierced my soul, and I cried. *"Hold on, Lish. Please, don't give up."*

"I'm not giving up, but Anna... She needs what I have left, Miguel. I called the hounds from hell to help me. I can't hold the circle, hold back the hound and keep both of our hearts beating. I need to choose, and I pick her, an innocent. I'm sorry. I'm so sorry, my little monster. I love you more than life. Follow the lavender." I smiled. I had been given the gift of a final goodbye to him. *"I'm not scared anymore. I have your love to bring with me, and it's enough. Thank you, Miguel."* I ran my hand over the symbol, smearing it into the earth and closed the link between us. I reached for Anna's hand. "Hold on, just a little bit more, Anna. Help is coming. Your people are coming."

"Why did you close him off? You said you love him. Why would you not want him with you?" the hound asked, confused. "Why wouldn't you take his energy to save yourself? He would have given you his very life to keep your heart beating. When a Lycan answers the call for one of their people, they can keep them alive with their own power. Why not take it?"

I smiled through the tears. "Because I love him. I don't want his last memory of me to be feeling me die," I answered. "And I would never take his life to save my own. I wouldn't take anyone's life for mine. I'm selfish enough to want him to remember me as whole, but never selfish enough to allow someone else to die in my place."

My pulse fluttered in my neck. I was running out of time. I stared up at the sky, and for the first time in a long time, I truly prayed. I asked for guidance, help and enough energy to save Anna, nothing more. I wasn't greedy enough to ask to save my own skin. Tears rolled from the corners of my eyes, and for a moment, I could hear my cat purring. I huffed a small, satisfied laugh. I always heard my cat when my heart was breaking the hardest. A hiss rolled through the air, followed by what I could only describe to be a high-pitched warning snarl. I grinned. It wasn't the usual gentle purr I heard but the sound of an alley cat ready to fight.

"Cat?" I whispered as the sound grew closer, not knowing how he could be there but certain he was.

Cat tore through the night and lunged into my circle, filling it with a shriek that was all warning and a willingness to fight to the death. My circle welcomed my cat, and I knew it was because we were bound as familiar and witch. He placed himself between the hound and me, spitting and swiping at the beast from hell. Cat's hair stood on end, and his fluffed tail twitched from side to side. His growls were unlike anything I had heard from him before. Wisps of heat and energy pulsed through my circle, firming up where it had been fading. He swatted the air between us and the hound, growls pouring from his little body. We wouldn't stave off a hellhound, but we would make a damn good attempt.

"Cat? How are you here?" The moment my hand touched my cat, my body calmed. The pain was still there, but the horror of it all was gone, replaced with hope. I didn't waste my hope of my own life but that of Anna's.

"Your familiar has come," the hound said. "I underestimated you, Ailis. Not a single soul has succeeded in calling their familiars to my front. But this one came without your call and has come of free will. What a rare treat for me to be surprised."

"I offer you one warning. Don't touch my fucking cat," I answered. "You'll return to hell mauled, dragging a laughing witch and a very much alive cat hanging off your throat. It's your choice on how you want to go home, embarrassed and torn to shreds or in one piece with some dignity."

Cat clawed at the hound again, drawing blood. It was a warning, and I was sure it would be the only one. Cat turned and crawled up Anna's legs and perched on her thighs, eyes fixed on the hound. After a few high-pitched growls, he turned his attention to me, licking the wound on my forehead. His tongue felt like hot sandpaper, but I didn't push him away. Even though it stung, it was oddly comforting. There had been many times I had come home, beaten up from a job, only to wake up to Cat cleaning my wounds as I slept.

"Help me, please," I whispered to my cat. "Just long enough to save Anna, that's all I'm asking. Just until help arrives."

Waves of energy rolled off my cat, and I pulled on everything I had left within my own soul. I knew if there was one more burst, and I'd be dead. I looked at Anna, bruised and battered. Helpless. Crusted blood coated her ears and nose. She had a head injury, and I knew from experience she'd die without medical treatment. A bomb ticked away in the back of my mind as I thought about the choices I had. There were too many outcomes, too many endings I didn't like. I couldn't keep both of us alive, and I was thankful she wasn't awake to know I had to decide who I wanted to live more—me or her. She shouldn't know her fate rested on the shoulders of a witch who hated monsters and had a soul that stank of hell. I fell to my side. I coiled my energy in my chest. I'd never choose myself over a child, furry or not. I could save her if I was willing to give everything I had to protect her.

The words I had said to the witches in the basement came to mind—"*Be careful what you wish for.*" Tonight, I would get everything I wished for if she lived, but I would pay for it. Sofia and Cisco would live. The vampire was dead. The witches were torn to bits. The Lycan traitor's head was clean off her body. There's no deader than that for them. But now it was time to cover the cost of my asks. I never deluded myself into thinking I'd get out of this alive. I knew I'd have a debt to pay and would pay it without question. Owing a favor to a hellhound would be almost as bad as owing a favor to Miguel.

"I feel the energy rising in you, little demon. The familiar will fare just fine. Not even the gates will touch a familiar, but I'm curious as to who you will sacrifice, yourself or the girl? Whose heart will you use that power to keep beating?" the hound asked. He sat and stared. When I didn't answer, it was answer enough for him. I would sacrifice myself. He rested down on his chest, propped in front of me. He was close enough for me to feel him. I reached my hand into his fur, just over his heart and looked him in the eyes. His eyes were orange and brown and reminded me of Miguel's. The hound didn't flinch or move. I balled the energy into my hand.

"I will use it to stop your heart," I replied. "Please, don't. I don't want to hurt you, but I will to save her. I will kill you and me for her. Please, don't make me do this," I whispered. "I'm not asking for my life, only time. Just until Anna's people get to her. Please. I give myself. I won't fight you. I'll come willingly if you please just give us a little more time."

He leaned his head forward and breathed in my scent. "You smell of tears and truth. You will kill me for no other reason than to protect the child. I wondered how righteous of a call it was that you sent out, how willing you were to die for that call, how ready you would be to die for the child, an innocent. Are you willing to accept your fate, the one you called to your front door? To pay the price for our call?"

"I'm willing," I answered. "Let her live, and I'm all yours."

He lowered his head onto my body. It was lighter than it should have been. When I didn't object, he moved closer. "I will wait here until Pack gets here for Anna."

"You're not going to kill her?" I asked.

"No. I do not take innocents," he responded.

"It isn't that I'm not grateful, but why? Why barter with me to begin with?"

"To see how pure your soul was," he replied. "I will remain here with you for your sacrifice. You were willing to give your life, your soul, your being, for three of mine, for the innocents lost and the ones who would have been lost. We do not punish for this, but I had to know if you were righteous or selfish. Had you been selfish, this would have ended badly for you. I will guard you until you're found."

I closed my eyes. "I'm going to die here with a hellhound—not how I thought I'd die. At least I have my cat with me."

"You've had many close calls, little demon. This should not be a surprise to you. Your wounded arms should have told you that you would touch the end, and it would taste like Lycan."

"I'm not a demon," I answered. "I'm a witch."

"Same difference. Where do you think your energy comes from for the magic you use? What do you think the taint on your aura is from? Those who can wield magic can tap into hell, harnessing the energy," he said, and I frowned. That was news to me. In all the books I had ever read, no one had ever documented where the magic came from or from where we pull the energy. There was speculation, of course, but nothing concrete. "It is a trade with the pits, power moving both ways. You get some of their energy, and they take some of yours from your aura. The larger the need, the greater the payment."

"I thought only dark arts users pulled from hell?" I asked.

"You all do," he replied. "And that is why the bigger magics and spells, the higher the price. It costs you your soul. It injures your soul so deeply that it dies. Small taints can heal. Large gashes cannot."

"Some users call on their gods and goddesses," I countered.

"You believe a god gives you magic but not hell? You are a perplexing witch."

I grumbled. "How do we not know this?"

"Your Coven does," he replied. "Almost all higher magics know, but rarely do they speak of anything that links them to the beasts who terrify you all."

"And like them, I'd rather not be called a demon," I replied.

"You can call yourself whatever you would like. It doesn't change what you are. You're cursed, like those behind the gates. It is what makes you a witch. Just as a curse has made the blood drinkers, the wee folk, most lingering spirits, right down to the banshees and shifters."

"I'm not evil," I whispered. As I sat with a hound I called out of hell, I was starting to doubt that.

"I didn't say it made you evil. Only your choices can decide that for you," he answered. "How you decide to use your abilities is what decides the road you'll walk. One leads back to hell."

"I'm going back anyway." I coughed up blood.

"This is true. You cannot buy your freedom from hell. But you can earn a way out quicker."

"How?" I asked.

"That is for you to learn, not for me to tell," he answered.

"I remember your voice," I whispered and smiled. "I remember you called me 'a little demon' when you chased me from the gates. You found me again."

"And I remember your voice and the feel of your soul. When I heard you call out for aid, I came, curious as to why you'd wish to taste hell so soon," he replied.

I tilted my head to the side. I could hear my name faintly. I couldn't remember if I heard it when I had died the last time, like someone calling out an order up. "Do you hear that?"

"Rest, witch. It's not long now," the hound replied.

"Death hurt more the first time." I gripped the fur of the hound and my cat. I was so tired. As soon as the purring started, the pain faded, like sleep washing over me. I felt heavier but peaceful in the knowledge that I'd won. Those I set out to save would live. Those who deserved death were gone. I got what I bargained for. "Miguel, I love you."

"He knows," the hound answered back. "Close your eyes, little demon. Rest. I will keep watch. And if you do not wake, I will see you in hell."

I rolled my face to the twinkling sky. For the first time in my life, the night was beautiful. I wasn't afraid of the dark. I smiled up at the stars and felt the hot tears roll from the corners of my eyes. "Mom, Dad, I'm sorry. I can't hold on anymore. Wait for me. I'm coming home," I whispered with my final breath.

Chapter Nine

Death doesn't hurt, not like how staying alive does. Survival alive bleeds the soul dry, slow and deep and leaves you feeling like death isn't that bad of an option. The road to get to the end, those final moments, though, is painful and messy and scary. But once you take your last breath, the pain and fear leave your body in one last shuddered breath. It's painless and worth letting go for. In some religions, it's the greatest thing a person could do. Everything we've ever done leads up to this final moment, your last hold on life, and if it goes as planned, it's glorious. It isn't like in the movies, where people cling and fight to the bitter end. Death has a certain peacefulness to it that allows us all to let go and ease into the finality of life, going wherever it is our souls belong. For me, it was the pits. For others, I prayed they didn't follow me down. But I knew a few dozen I'd see there and be glad to make their acquaintance once again. *Petty, even at the end.*

The moment I released my last breath, my muscles finally relaxed, and the pain was nothing more than a bad memory. It didn't hurt as much as it had the first time, mangled in a vehicle, bleeding out and dying. I only remembered flashes of that wreck, being pinned between twisted metal and limbs from other passengers. I was the only one to make a sound, although it was nothing more than a bloody gurgle. The rest of my friends had died on impact. Voices from outside of the car grew quiet, and I was gone. That part, being gone, didn't hurt. It was a relief. Broken bones don't hurt when you're dead. Waking up in a cage? Now that's a different story—a two-minute story that would take decades to tell.

On the ground, outside of a church hell would be proud of, I slowly inched my way out of this world and wasn't scared of what was soon to come. This time around, I wouldn't be alone, and I had a heart full of reasons this trip down would be worth it. As I faded, I heard Sofia's voice, dull and distant. It echoed all around me.

"I challenge your claim! I am Sofia Maria Gonzalez Lopez of the Los Luna Pack. You will back away at once or suffer the wrath of my wolf." Sofia's voice rented the air. "I challenge you. If I win, I get them both."

"And, if you lose?" the hound asked.

"I won't lose, hound." Sofia laughed.

"They are mine," he replied.

"No, they are innocents, and I claim them under law." Her voice vibrated the very earth my broken body curled on. "I claim my friend, Ailis. I told her I'd come back, and I'm not leaving without them both. You can go of free will, or I will send you back to hell without your head. Choose before I make the choice for you."

"You're already bleeding, wolf," the hound said.

"This is the only blood of mine that shall fall," Sofia said. "But I will bathe in yours before you're able to take them from me."

"A night of surprises." The hound laughed at her words, as though he didn't believe them. Even as I tiptoed my way back to hell, I had a smile, doubting Sofia would be his end. I could feel it in my fading soul.

"I challenge you," she said again. "Fenrir, protect me and mine." Her words carried a power that rattled my bones. "If I shall fall before my war is won, carry the souls of those lost to the heavens. They are deserving of your grace. I am ready for my next post. I am ready to die."

"Sofia Maria Gonzalez Lopez, I feel the power of your soul. You are worthy, and they are yours. I will see you at the gates, noble one," the hound said, and the smell of hell was gone.

The moment the hound pulled back from my circle, darkness pulled me back under. I felt safe in the dark for the first time. I was relaxed, calm like nothing could get to me as long as I stayed tucked into the nothingness. There were no nightmares or reasons to cry. There was no pain and no misery. As I wrapped myself in the quietness, a flash of blinding white light filled the dark, and my chest heaved as though my bones were breaking. Pain radiated throughout my entire body. It felt like pins and needles stabbed every inch of flesh, followed by a burning fire. My lungs felt like they were going to explode—too much air, too rapid, too hot. The pain was incredible and didn't let up for a second.

"Breathe!" Miguel screamed. His voice was an echo. "Damn it, Lish, hold on! Please, come back! Keep her heart beating!"

"Clear!" A man's voice pulled me from the fog I was curled up in. His scent was off, and I didn't like it. He didn't smell like Miguel or his people. He smelled different, something I would have normally backed away from.

"If her heart stops, she goes to hell," Miguel called out. "Seconds down there are lifetimes up here."

"Clear!" echoed into the night.

"For me, please, stay with me." Miguel's voice felt like a slap. "I love you. You promised me you wouldn't leave me. You gave me your word! I can't do this without you."

"Clear!" The man's voice yelled from far away. My chest burned. Every fiber in my body felt like it was engulfed in flames. "Jesus, get that cat off her."

"Levi, leave the fucking cat alone." Sofia's voice cut through the night.

"It keeps biting me. How the hell do I work on her with her cat biting me?" the man replied. "Take the damn thing off her. Her stomach wound is pumping out all over the ground. It won't matter if her heart keeps beating if she bleeds out."

The darkness ate at the edges again. The pain was doubling back. Every inch of my skin felt raw and rubbed in salt. My aura was nearly gone, eaten up to keep my circle, and it hurt the most around my heart. It felt like I had carved it out of my chest to save Anna. Little by little, what remained of my aura was slipping off like Sofia's skin had. A person couldn't live for long without an aura. Soon, my soul would burn up, bombarded by everything evil on this side of the gate.

It was a painful way to die. Death didn't hurt when the people you loved let you go. It's when they held on that your final moments felt like being electrocuted while your lungs were blowing up. Why couldn't they just let me go in peace? It didn't have to hurt like this. The only time life was gentle was in death, and I couldn't even have that.

"Please, Lish," Miguel's voice whispered over my soul and for the briefest of moments, I was calm again. "Hold on. I love you. Don't leave me. I'm begging you."

In the darkness of my fading soul, I heard the padding of many feet. Curled on my side, a wet nose nudged my arm. I wasn't afraid. It felt familiar. I smiled when I could smell Miguel. A wolf curled around me, holding the scent of home and promises and all the parts of life I had fought to keep. I pushed my face into his fur and breathed in the smell of love and hope. He smelled of everything I had ever needed in life — protection, family, a future, and not facing the world alone.

"I need a favor." Miguel pushed his mouth to my ear. These were the exact words he had used to bring me to Mexico. "I need you to live. I need you to come back. I can feel you fading. My wolf can feel you leaving. Please, don't go, Lish. I'm begging you. Come home. Come back to me. I can't promise it won't hurt, but I swear I'll be at your side."

I gripped his wolf tighter, holding on to the only lifeline I had. I had two choices — lie here and die, or fight to the bitter end. "Help me." The wolf stirred, hearing my ask, and started to crawl with me holding on, out of the deepest pits of my soul.

I will see you in hell. But not today, hound of hell.

I reached up toward Miguel's voice and fought against the pull at my feet. I wasn't ready to go...not yet. I just needed the reminder, a reason to keep fighting, someone worth living for, someone who wouldn't leave me to suffer alone. I wasn't ready to leave him. Not now. Not ever. I fought to get back to him at every turn. Every chance I had to call it quits in life, I had never once thrown in the towel. There had never been a day I gave up or gave in. If hell wanted me, it would need to come and get me because I wasn't walking that road willingly.

My chest felt like I was being kicked. *Crack.* It sounded like a bone breaking. My lungs expanded to the point I thought they'd burst. My body jerked, and every nerve came alive. In the distance, I could hear sirens and feel myself coming back into my body. I was filled with pain before the world faded again and the pain dulled but didn't stop. When I couldn't smell hell but could hear Cat purring, I gave into the heaviness and endured because that was life, pain and horror, love and everything worth rubbing your soul raw for. With one hand gripping Miguel's wolf in the distance, I held on for dear life.

"You can't bring a cat into an ambulance," a man's voice yelled too close to my ear. "It's not sanitary."

"Oh, and you are perfectly hygienic? You're a fucking rat, Levi. Wash the damn bus after," Sofia replied. "She's a witch. This isn't *just* a cat. It's her familiar. Unless you want her to die, I suggest you do your fucking job and leave what you don't understand alone. Every time you take the cat away, she flatlines. Use your brain."

"You don't have to be so mean. You could have just explained why the cat was important," Levi responded, his voice hushed. "I'm sorry. I didn't understand the connection."

They spoke softly as they worked on me. I picked up on an apology from Sofia, but the tension in the ambulance still popped my ears. When the doors slammed shut, I felt the exact weight of a cat I knew like my own soul. He curled on my chest and purred. The pain stopped in an instant. My aura, although hanging on by threads, didn't feel like it was about to blow away in the next light breeze. My eyelids lifted every so often, and blazing white light shone into my eyes. A hiss from my cat finally left me in the shadows of my soul. The next time I came to, I was in a hospital and could hear just enough to know a witch was talking to Miguel. I only caught bits and pieces, as my mind was scattered between the living and wanting to curl into a ball and sleep. She had been flown in from Costa Rica to see if I had been cursed by a demon.

"She hasn't been cursed," Sofia said. "I think she did witch things. When I found her, she was in a powerful circle, bleeding out, after fighting off a group of witches to keep hell closed."

"Witch things?" Miguel's soft laugh felt like a warm touch. "I believe she ran out of energy and used her aura as a last resort."

"This explains the aura connection with her familiar," she replied. "And the reason why I can't get around the cat. It is keeping her alive. Her familiar is sharing auras, healing Ailis."

"What do you need from us?" Sofia asked. "I'm not moving that cat if it's the only thing keeping her out of a hole in the ground."

"Until I check her out myself, I won't be leaving. Samuel has asked for me to check the soul of his only granddaughter. That is not a task I can simply do from here, and I'd not leave my oldest friend without answers. He is worried, and now that I'm here, I understand why," she explained with a voice meant for grandmothers. "I must feel her soul with my own, and I can't get through her shields or that of her familiar. I need you, Miguel, to let them know I'm not a threat. I'm here at her family's request. She trusts you. Every time you go near her, Miguel, her aura responds to you. It reaches for you. I believe she will listen to you and only you."

"Reaches for me?" he asked. "That explains why I can feel her before I can see her."

A light laugh filled the room like a warm breeze. "Before you even walked into the room, her aura shifted, reaching toward the door. And in return, yours reaches for hers."

"Like a soulmate," Sofia whispered.

"That is exactly it. They are bound as only two true mates can be. Please, Miguel. Samuel is expecting an update on his grand, and I'd like to settle his worry sooner rather than later," she answered.

That last part made my heart feel a little fuller. Samuel had always introduced me as family, but I had thought that was just a polite way of saying, 'She's an orphan.' Until now, I hadn't known he thought of me as family—as real family. I lowered my shields to Miguel's voice, relaxing into the warmth of the witch's aura rolling over me. She felt like standing near an oven, in the winter, with cookies baking. A bit of taint stained her here and there, but I got the sense she was a good person with just one touch. I knew Samuel wouldn't have sent someone to do harm, but one can never be too sure until they felt their souls, and hers was everything I wished mine was. Such grace and love… She was a warm blanket to my tattered beast of a soul.

I felt Miguel step closer before I could smell or hear him. "Lish, Samuel has sent help. Let her in. If Samuel trusts her to touch your aura, I trust her as well. I'm right here. I'll keep you safe, I promise."

I eased down my shields. It felt like having road rash and cleaning the wounds with grains of rock salt. My aura was almost drained and thinned to the quick around my heart. I had eaten up everything I could to do wild magic and build a circle of protection. Her touch was calming, but I was happier the moment she was done and I could lock myself back up. The witch told the doctors the cat was laying on that part of my aura for a reason and to stop trying to shoo it away, lest they wished to keep restarting my heart. The cat was sharing his aura with me until I was strong enough to heal on my own. She placed a few stones on my bedside and left me to heal in the only way an aura truly could, with time, love and care. With her magic, my cat and the Pack each taking turns to curl around me, sharing the aura of their wolves, I finally slept deeply, unafraid of the dark.

* * * *

The Pack had found me in the field, thirty feet from the church. I had been curled around Anna, the knife still in my hand, Cat sitting on my hip and a beast from the pits of hell at my feet. They had to wait for the hound to leave the circle, for it to fall, his claws digging up the earth and bringing my magic down as he left. I don't remember everything after I called the hounds. I had complete blanks when I tried to think back to that night. I was told the witches had been found ripped into tiny pieces. One of the hounds I had summoned had stayed in my circle to protect me. He had shared his energy with me, willing my heart to pump until help arrived. With my heart still beating, I got to skip another lifetime in hell. The hound stayed true to his word and didn't budge until Pack came. Miguel and Sofia worked on my chest until Sophia's friend, Levi, a wererat, had arrived with the bus, and they got me to the hospital. Miguel told the hospital that I had been attacked by a demon. In a way, I had been. Those witches were as close to day-walking demons as any demon from hell. Lies and truth can be a funny thing, worked together and twisted until they formed a different kind of truth.

When I finally came around without passing out again, I was in a hospital bed, covered in tubes and wires, with a chunk of aura missing. Sofia, an ER nurse, filled in the missing pieces from that night. She had brought her entire Pack to my aid when she couldn't find Caser or Miguel. The strongest members had left in search of me and Anna. Sofia, one of the lowest in the Pack, had demanded the rest go with her. She was willing to fight them all for aid. Sofia challenged the biggest Lycan there, the one left behind to protect the weaker. He's now in a hospital bed of his own. He didn't win the challenge. Never doubt the resolve of a survivor. The rest feared Sofia's wrath enough to follow her into hell. She knew she led them into what could have been a slaughter, but she led them anyway, to come back for me and Anna. Sofia and a dozen of the weaker wolves took to the fields in Lycan and human form, following the scent of Cat. Sophia had said the smell of Cat she had picked up on me earlier that night had filled the night air. She followed the smell, but the cat ran faster than her and was lost to the darkness, leaving behind my smell as breadcrumbs.

Along the way, they had attracted other monsters, coming to see why the Pack was running through territory not of their own in Lycan form. Those who stood against them died in that field. The lowest of Pack went toe-to-toe with vampires and never once flinched. Some, who were still untrained, never having once seen a fight with a monster, didn't so much as flinch. Their wolves knew what was at stake and tore through the fields with pure resolve. They may have been Beta to the others, weaker, but they had faith that couldn't be shaken. Innocents were down, and not one of them would stop for any reason. They were guardians through and through. Her pride in her people, as she told her story, was almost tangible. I felt it in my soul as her eyes glittered.

Sofia had come, scared, still bleeding from her time in the dungeons, back to the place where she had been tortured. She'd come back for me, to what could have been her death, because I hadn't left her or her people behind. She'd run blindly into the unknown because she was Lycan, and that was what they do. Sofia was the first to find us, directing the others to form their own version of a circle of protection around us. The others had fanned out, ready to take on anything that came their way — anything except the damn hellhound at my feet. Sofia didn't flinch, though. When she'd come into the clearing, she'd challenged the hellhound. If she won, she got us. If she lost, the hound got us all. She was too weak to shift, but she was willing to fight him with a stone in one hand and a knife in the other.

They didn't fight. Miguel had got to the field just after Sofia, running from the other direction, tracking my scent through the backroads. He had gotten there in time to see Sofia preparing to attack a hellhound, with tears rolling down her cheeks, her terror souring the night air and screaming a prayer for her soul should she fail. The hound had left, but not before dipping his head.

Sofia had done what her kind had been doing since striking the deal to guard mankind. She was willing to die for them. It didn't matter how scared she was. She'd still stood firm, holding nothing more than hope and a rock. But her truest weapon had been her soul and wolf, readying to burst from her skin the moment it was needed. The shift would have killed them both, but death scared neither. Bearing witness to the bravest act Miguel had ever seen, Sofia got a promotion for her bravery. She now works under Miguel as his first lieutenant. I didn't know what it meant, but Sofia was thrilled, so I played along. She and I would never be best friends, but we understood each other a little better now. It's easy to hate someone when we see parts in them that we see in ourselves, the parts we don't want to remember or face.

I was told that the Pack burned what they could. The church was knocked down after the witch from Costa Rica walked through the cells to make sure no souls or energy had been trapped. A priest blessed the ground for good measure. Miguel had gone back and salted the earth. One could never be too safe. No one would be using the crumbled church for future spells or serial killing. The salt cleaned the slate. Burying it removed the temptation.

Cisco had been placed in the room beside me. After twenty-four hours, he'd pushed a single bed into my room and slept an arm's reach away. The nurses tried, in vain, to move him. He wasn't budging, and he also was in perfect health once again. But no one in Pack was willing to leave me unattended for even a minute. Cisco's constant chatter was oddly peaceful. And whenever I woke up screaming, he was there, curling around me, telling me I survived, that I wasn't back in hell. You can't buy love like that. It was the type of love that usually took growing up together to build, but Cisco loved me like a sister, like family, like a Pack member. And my cat loved the heck out of him. That beast loved no one. *Well, maybe me.*

When Miguel had gone to pick up Sofia and found her already gone, he had thought she'd gone to claim Cisco's body on her own. At the morgue, a few of his people were already waiting there with a van for transport. Sofia hadn't shown up. Inside, Miguel had signed the papers and had been presented with a body that smelled nothing like Lycan. They're still not sure who owned the body, but it wasn't one of his people. The rest of Pack heard the news that it wasn't Cisco's body an hour after the witches had taken me. When Miguel called and I didn't answer, he'd come running. He'd found my letter and sent out a call to his people. Wherever I was, Anna would be there, too. *Two birds, one stone.* Although the trail kept turning up cold, he hadn't given up on me. Did I really think a *Dear John* letter would stop him from coming for me? No. I had hoped he'd come for me, but I'd also prayed he wouldn't put himself at risk. If he had died to find me, I'd never forgive myself. I didn't want to live bad enough to drag that kind of emotional baggage around with me. I had enough as it was.

Of the parts that I remember from that night, I remembered Miguel clear as day. Just before I lost consciousness, I heard his voice calling my name. It rolled through the field with the wind. I remembered when he was working on my chest. I could feel him, hear him begging me to live. I stayed with his voice until my heart started beating on its own again. I think it was his voice that kept me from packing it in and walking the road to hell. I don't think I'll ever forget hearing him pray, under his breath, for me to live, for my life to be spared, that he'd trade places with me in hell. He offered up his own soul for my salvation. He'd willingly climb into my cage and serve out my sentence. He knew better than anyone what that meant. If that wasn't stupid love, I don't know what was.

The Lycan who had helped the witches, Evette, had been found. Well, her headless body was. The hounds had torn her up bad enough that her tattoo and Pack branding had been the only way to identify her from the pieces of witches. Her head was later delivered to the Pack, dropped on their door like a jug of milk. No one knows who dumped the trash on Pack's steps, but it was tossed in with the rest of the garbage. I didn't know her, but I hated her enough that I was glad she was dead. She'd wanted power, she'd wanted to rule and she'd do anything to get it, including the slaughter of her people and the attempted murder of a child. She couldn't just be happy with what she had. Those who reached too high are at risk of losing it all. And she did, along with her head, when she'd landed. Evette had targeted me for power and power alone. Along with my blood and spell to lift a curse, my sacrifice would have been enough to raise the demon. I had been the last piece to the puzzle, the final ingredient. But like my grandmother had always said, "*Make sure you read your spells thrice. Get one part wrong, and you're dead.*" None of them read their spell three times, given they'd lost their lives over it. Though, who would have thought a hell-bound witch would be able to call the un-callable and damn them all to hell? I sure as hell didn't think it would work.

When I finally woke without the haze or pain that made the world tilt and my stomach heave, I knew I was going to live. From the first time I opened my eyes, my bed was surrounded by Lycan. Someone was always on guard, their backs to me, as a show of great trust, like a cat showing their belly. The Pack stood against anything or anyone that came into the room. Miguel had been scared my aura was damaged and would invite demons to try for me. But unlike the last time I'd skinned my soul alive, I had Pack and my cat, and not a single demon came this time. Not even a nurse could get by without being heavily scrutinized. The Pack had two nurses, and both monitored everything done or given to me. Sofia made enough threats that the staff started to ask for her when they came into the room. No one knew about Lycan, but they knew enough about monsters to not argue with Pack.

There was a small sofa ten feet from my bed, where the nurses took turns sleeping. Sofia was one of them. The moment I saw her, I felt the weight of my charm placed back around my neck. She had given it back when they were working on me. She thought it would help. I don't think it did, but I appreciated whatever attempts they all made to make sure I was still alive.

Samuel sent me a bouquet of dead flowers to symbolize he was angry with me for charging headfirst into hell. In the very center, a live daisy, my favorite of all the flowers. He was mad but happy I made it. He'd give me a stern talking to once I recovered. I didn't look forward to the talk, but I looked forward to the hug that always followed. I've lost count of the number of one-sided conversations he and I have had over the years, but each one always ended in a hug and a kiss on my forehead. This time, I'd probably agree with him. If I kept down this road, it eventually would come to a very dead end for me.

"Could I have a moment?" Caser called from the door.

The Pack didn't move.

"It's okay," I answered from my bed, and they moved to the side. Sofia looked at Caser, then at me. She had given me her protection, and apparently, that extended to her Pack leader. I smiled. "I'm okay, Sofia."

Caser's laughter calmed the nervousness in the air. "You'd think I didn't scare them as much as you do, little witch."

I shrugged, then winced. "Do I apologize for that?"

"You saved the life of my only child, Anna, and at a deadly expense to yourself. You called your own wild hunt. Do not apologize. That is a great power, Ailis," he replied. "You can have a little leeway today."

"What do you mean, I called my own wild hunt?" I asked.

Caser pulled a chair up beside my bed. "To call the hounds of hell to your aid, to cleanse evil and those who broke their oaths to you. Anna told me the parts she remembered. That is what the hunt was designed for. You're simply the only one who has ever done it outside of Pack. Any other time someone has tried, the hounds had come and simply killed whoever tried to call them. It is why they are considered uncallable. I would not attempt it a second time, though. Your call was righteous, but those are far too rare to count on."

I raised my eyebrows. "You don't have to tell me twice. I don't really remember it, anyway."

Caser smiled. "Come now. Let's not start lying to each other, after we've shared so much between us."

"No, I don't remember all of it, Caser. And I don't want to. The parts that I do remember are enough for me to not speak of it and want to forget." I shook my head, trying to rid myself of the memories he'd dredged up. "I killed them, Caser. I did that. I willed that. I begged for it. I promised them death. I feel no pride in what I've done. I don't feel powerful. I feel like I took eight lives."

"Even a righteous kill grates on our souls, Ailis. If it didn't, it wouldn't be righteous, and you would be dead."

"Dr. Kyteler," I corrected him. "I didn't work my butt off to not be called doctor every chance I get." I smiled. One of my first friendly smiles used on Caser. He laughed again, and I reconsidered my stance on the matter. My friends didn't use my title. "I suppose Ailis is fine. The doc says I can leave in a few days. I'll be out of your hair, hopefully, after the full moon."

"Thank you for what you've done for me and my Pack. I will never forget it." Caser stood. He squeezed my hand. "From this life unto the next, you have my protection."

"Gee, how generous. I'd prefer cash to pay for my holiday. It was over ten grand, and I got to see the pool once—which you all ruined, I might add—and I ate there twice, not to mention changing my flight at the last minute. You all can damn well pay for the holiday from hell," I joked.

He leaned in. "Unto the next, Ailis. It's protection in hell that you can't even bargain for down there. It is a soul debt, something we don't give to anyone. It's a long time to be tied to someone like you. I have a feeling you'll keep me busy, and I will die regretting this."

I spent a moment staring down at my blanket. My pulse thumped in my throat. What I had to say next could end me in the very bed used to keep me alive. I glanced around at Caser's people. I didn't want to put them in the position of having to choose between me and their leader, but that's where I found myself. I was stuck between Caser and the man I loved, Miguel. I swallowed the urge to be sick and bit the bullet. In truth, I doubted he'd risk outing his people and leaving me for dead in a public place.

"What about Miguel?" My voice was weaker than I wanted it to be. I sounded pathetic and hopeful. I didn't really want to ask the question for fear I'd learn the answer, and it wouldn't be what I could live with. I didn't want to know if this would be my last few days with him. "I can't cut him out like that. He is my person. He's my friend. This is going to kill him. Bloody hell, this is going to kill me, too. I'm sorry, Caser. I know I said I'd leave him, but I can't do it. I *won't* do it—not for you, not for anyone. For as long as I have left, I can't spend that time without him. I know I said I would, but I can't. I'm sorry. I just can't do it. If I survive the full moon, I still won't leave him."

"I didn't think you would. But I wanted to know if you were worth it. I wanted to see if you were worth protecting with the lives of my people. If you didn't care, you'd have left without another thought, and I'd have killed you if you came back. But...but, if you loved him, you'd stay and fight for him. You'd risk it all for him because he's willing to risk us all for you. I wanted to know if you loved him enough to fight for him or if you were tormenting my boy. I guess I needed to know if you were worth me and my people putting our necks on the line for you. I don't want to fight to the death for someone unworthy of my blood."

I shook my head, irritated. "If you didn't think I'd go, why play the game?"

"At first, I thought I'd win. I didn't think you cared so much for him. I know now that I won't win," he answered. "Plus, if I force it, Sofia will kick my ass. She challenged my third and won, then challenged a hellhound, and it backed down. I won't be getting on her bad side anytime soon."

"She's a good one to have in your corner," I said, and I meant every word of it.

"You did good, Ailis. You have the protection of this Pack. And you have mine unto your next life."

"Mine, as well," Sofia spoke up, her back still turned to us. "From this life unto the next. No one should see hell alone."

I turned my head to the window, breathing a sigh of relief. Dust in the air, shimmering in the sunlight, caught my attention, reminding me of turning the vampire to ash in the basement of the hellhole we were held in. My heart pounded with urgency. A memory of Cisco rolled through my mind. "The vampires, Caser. They were involved. We killed one of them who was...drinking Cisco." My throat reflexed with the urge to be sick. The thought of what it had been doing to Cisco, bleeding him slowly, made one of the monitors beep from a rise in my blood pressure. "But they all must know what was happening to your people."

"It's okay, Calm down. We paid them a little visit. All is sorted," Cisco called out from his bed.

"When did you leave the hospital?" I asked him. "I thought you were all pain and poor me? I heard you whining to the nurses about your bruises."

"I'm never too hurt to collect my pound of flesh." Cisco rolled onto his side and grinned, propped up on one arm. He looked perfectly fine to me. "I'm just here for the sponge baths, little witch. I'm good to go and will check out when you do."

Caser leaned into my ear. "They paid dearly, Ailis. I doubt they will make a play for power any time soon."

"Everything has a price."

"And we all paid. I'm sorry you may have paid with your life." He touched my arm, freshly bandaged.

"All good things come to an end, sooner or later," I answered. It was a load of crap, but it was all that I had.

I finally broke down and cried. The tears were slow at first, like a memory coming to the surface. Caser left me to my tears. Death, hell, demons? None of it seemed so scary, knowing I'd have a hellhound or two down below when I died. The Pack went back to their posts around my bed. They didn't gawk or turn around while I cried. They let me keep my big-girl persona intact. I wouldn't get my secluded island breakdown. The hospital bed was my island. I could feel Miguel before the door even opened. I felt the pull in my soul. He got back to my room, just in time, with snacks. He knew I loathed hospital food as much as I hated being in one. I'd rather starve than eat what they tried to feed me. I don't care what their dietitian said. Green slop in a bowl was not what would speed my healing.

"Where is my cat?" I asked him. My cat had left the hospital this morning, out through the door, on his own.

"At my house. He was on my front steps when I went home for a change of clothes," he replied. "The hospital staff were happy to let him out of the front doors. The cursed thing kept attacking anyone who came near you. Me and Cisco were the only ones who didn't get mauled by the thing, so the beast is with me until you're cleared to leave."

"How the hell did it even get to Mexico?" I asked. "He didn't jog here."

Miguel laughed. "Samuel called the night we got you to the hospital and asked if the cat made it. After you and he last spoke, the cat showed up at his house. Samuel shoved the little monster into a carrier and onto a plane. He had a friend pick it up and let it loose once he was near your hotel. The cat tracked you from there." Miguel kissed my forehead. "Samuel said he knew you'd need the help from your familiar to save your life and soul when the thing clawed at his door. Samuel and the cat have been looking out for you since day one."

I nodded and smiled until the tears came back. "He was right to send him. Without my cat, I would have died. When he found me in the field, I had nothing left to give. I had already eaten up most of my aura to save Anna. Without help, I really don't think there would have been anything left for you to save."

All the fear I had been holding back poured out of me like a broken dam. Every doubt I had ever silenced, the terror I swallowed, the pain I ate down... It all washed out of me, rolling down my cheeks in hot salty tears. Miguel curled into my bed around me, his heat wrapping me in a feeling of immediate safety, as it always had.

"It's okay. Let it out. I can smell your fear. Give it to me to carry until you're strong enough to face it," he whispered, kissing my temple.

"I was sure I was going to die," I choked out. "I called out to my parents to wait for me, that I was coming home. Then I heard your voice. I saw your wolf, Miguel. He came for me, and when I asked for help, he pulled me out of the final darkness."

"I could feel you holding on. We both could. Neither of us was willing to let you go," he answered.

I tucked myself into him and let the fear roll out of me. He didn't let me cry alone. He held me and listened to my story and every fear I had struggled against, the pain my body and soul endured and the sadness I felt when I had thought Anna had died. Then came my guilt for who I had called to help us. He told me it wasn't my fault. The hounds only took those who had earned it. Those who died had been deserving of it. He reminded me of my goodness and that I wasn't a monster. He said all the right things at all the right moments. Hearing his voice and the love within it glued together a few more broken pieces. We may not be able to go back to what we had before, but whatever we'd become was better than what we were doing. Sometimes love was enough. We would have what we have and be thankful for it, wherever that led us. Probably straight to hell. It's where we both go when we're dead, anyway — me to a cage and him at the gate. Why not take the fast lane there and enjoy the ride with someone you love?

Chapter Ten

I spent my days with Miguel after being released from the hospital. The first few days, I lounged in his bed, curtains closed, sleeping in the safe smells of Miguel and his wolf. My aura, although almost fully healed, was still as raw as fresh skin and needed the constant touch of someone else's to keep me from being an emotional wreck, which happened more often at night. Whenever my dreams became too dark, his wolf would find his way in and guide me back out to Miguel. The nights I woke up screaming, his Pack would come and roam the property while Miguel held me. He spent hours bathing me, loving every bruised inch of my body in ways I needed. It felt like we had all the time in the world to get to know each other again, with Pack watching our backs every minute of the day, allowing us to be safely alone. His people were protective of me after I'd dug my own grave for them. That tended to leave a lasting impression. It left one hell of an impression on me, and I was reminded of it each time I closed my eyes.

When the monsters haunted me while the rest of the world slept, I would turn on a lamp and look at the life Miguel had built in Mexico. On his bedside table was a framed picture of us from a Halloween party, him a werewolf and me a demon. The irony was not lost on me, looking back on it. Bits of the life we had once shared together were scattered throughout his house, including photos of me from after I had left. When asked, he'd shrugged and blushed. There had never been a day where he had let go of me. Every chance he'd got, he'd come back to Vancouver to check up on me.

Once it no longer hurt to move, I saw Mexico as I had intended — not running for my life or asking hell to lend a hand. Miguel showed me the places still left on my list of things I had wanted to see during my trip and a few places the tourists weren't allowed to go. Being a local had its perks, and they were absolutely breathtaking. When Miguel offered to show me a cenote without a fresh body, I pulled out the travel list on my phone, pointing out that the cenotes and ruins were already checked off. It may have been morbid, but I still counted them. *Been there, done that.* Just because I hadn't enjoyed the place and there was a body on the ground didn't mean I wasn't there. If I only counted the good memories in my life, I'd have no memories at all. He, of course, thought that was morbid and wanted to give me a memory better than blood and bones. Who was I to argue?

When we pulled into Caser's driveway, I grinned. Cisco was giving Sofia a noogie while Anna was on his back, pulling his hair. Caser stood with a hose in his hand, spraying them down like you would a dog chewing on a shoe. Everything about the moment was normal, and it made me thankful I'd caved to Miguel's suggestion. Several others were unloading their vehicles and gave us a wave as we got out.

"Where is this cenote you were talking about?" I asked.

"It's at the back of the property," he replied. "This land has been in Caser's family for as long as anyone has papers to prove it. His great-grandmother was a healer for the Pack and used the cenote in her practices."

Anna, who was fully healed, took up her place at my side, leading me through the yard and into the backfield. It was all rolling hills and trees for as far as my eye could see. She pointed out the different plants that grew wild and the use her greatest gran had for them. She pointed to a grouping of trees to the left. She had a stash of lavender she kept hidden away from her dad for fear he'd rip it out. One glance at Caser said he knew all about the plants but left them alone for his daughter. Although Anna was Lycan, she was following in the footsteps of the women who'd come before her. She would be a healer, a place of honor among her people. She gave me a few tips I didn't even know, should I ever be faced with another gut wound from a knife. Hopefully, I wouldn't need the advice, but I tucked it away as a possibility.

As we approached a tree line, I could hear the music. Calm energy pulled me forward. It felt like home. It felt like all the people you had ever loved stood just beyond the trees. A burst of power hit me but didn't push me back. Instead, it drew me forward. Laughter and yips filled the field, bringing a surprised laugh from my throat. For no reason, I was excited, happy and wanted to run. It felt like walking into a family's home, where everyone you loved was waiting to see you.

"What is that?" I whispered to Miguel.

"Pack," he replied. "It's the energy of a shift."

"Sofia did not make me laugh when she shifted. I almost puked on her," I replied, hearing her laugh behind me.

"This is unforced, unpanicked. When they shift together, they feed off the energy of each other. It makes for a smoother shift," he replied. "They are the younger Lycan who came to the field for you. They're on their first patrol — a trust earned to be unattended by an Alpha. The energy you feel? It is utter devotion and pride. It's their eagerness to be given this opportunity."

"I swear I can feel their excitement in my stomach. It feels…amazing," I said and burst into a run. The energy was coursing through my body, and I couldn't stop myself.

I broke through the trees into a small, lush clearing, just in time to see a dozen wolves streaking into the trees on the other side, leaping into the shadows as though they were made for the dark. Not once did my charm necklace vibrate in a warning. Miguel grabbed me from behind and spun me, bringing a scream from my throat. He pointed at the trees to our left. A gray wolf stepped out of the shadows just enough for me to catch a glimpse before it was gone. Their energy moved through the wind and kept me grinning ear to ear. It was unlike anything I had ever felt before. Though, if I were alone and felt that power rolling up my arms, I'd have run in the other direction.

"They will keep the perimeter around us." Cisco stepped up to my side. "If something wicked this way comes, they will call for aid and hold them back until help arrives. Though, I doubt very much there'd be anything left by the time one of us got there. Sofia runs a tight ship. She takes no prisoners. I hear she's a harsh taskmaster."

Sofia stepped to his side and elbowed him. "And you wonder why you get picked last to be on a team."

"Ready to see what all the fuss is about?" Anna held out her hand to me. She led me over a small hill to nothing more than a hole in the ground. Small yellow flowers grew around the edge, a few scattered rocks and a metal ladder attached on the far side. "Welcome to the Los Luna cenote."

I thanked my lucky stars that it didn't resemble anything like the last one. Though, the last one had stairs and lights and a little more flare than this one. This was nothing more than a simple hole. I peered over the edge. A small wind of warmth and salty air rose from the opening. I saw nothing but the darkness. I pulled back and shook my head. I wasn't going down there. *Hell no*. This is what horror movies were made of. The last movie I watched was about a group of women going caving, and the monsters ate them. *No thanks*.

"Trust me," she said, and I laughed out loud at her comment. "You'll love it once you're down there. The jump is part of the fun."

"Jump? You expect me to jump into a dark hole?" I asked and laughed even harder. "Why do we need to jump when there's a perfectly good ladder on the other side?"

"Yes, but that's the way the boys take," Sofia said from behind and took a running leap into the hole. I screamed her name, but she was gone in the blink of an eye.

Cisco stepped up to the edge with two mesh bags over his shoulders. "We have to climb down because the women refuse to carry their gear."

"I didn't know I had to bring gear," I replied, cringing for being unprepared.

"Miguel had snorkel gear sent over for you," Cisco answered. "Jump. You won't regret it. Trust us, witchy woman. If we wanted you dead, we'd have left you in that field and only grabbed Anna."

"Yeah, I see why you're picked last for games," I replied, rolling my eyes hard enough to see my brain.

"It's not dark at the bottom," he said and grinned when he saw the look on my face. I most certainly did not believe him. Cisco swung a bag over his shoulder and started to pull out round balls the size of baseballs. He twisted them, and little lights inside blinked on. He chucked a half dozen over the edge. "There, scaredy-cat. I brought you a flashlight as well, but jumping with one will likely smash it, or you'll hit yourself in your soft little human noggin. You humans aren't made like you used to be. You're all sensitive nowadays."

"He'll go on for hours if we let him," Anna said. "You wonder why my dad always has the hose out when Cisco is around? This is why."

"I know. I was stuck in the hospital with him…without a hose," I replied.

"Ready?" she asked, holding out her hand.

With a grin and a silent prayer, I grabbed Anna's hand, and we jumped. It was the oddest feeling, freefalling and not knowing where the bottom was. I screamed the entire way down. Once I hit the water and popped back up, I laughed at the rush of it all, although my still-sore stomach protested. But Anna had been right. Half the fun was in the jump. Anna pulled me through the water to the rock walls, warning me to always stay clear of the drop zone. Having someone land on your head was not a fun way to start a tour. The small lights Cisco had tossed down bobbed around on the surface while light beams from above illuminated the water in a beautiful show. Small lanterns were flaring to life as Sofia climbed the walls around us.

Miguel and Cisco climbed down a metal ladder, bolted to the rock and jumped the last ten feet, carrying the gear on their backs. Miguel helped me put on my flippers, goggles and snorkel while Cisco showed me how to work his underwater flashlight. It felt like holding a brick until it was underwater. With Sofia in the lead, we snorkeled through the tunnels and cave systems, long forgotten by everyone but the Los Luna Pack. I grew tired after a few minutes and clung to the rock walls. My stomach muscles were still too sore. Without me having to ask, a tether was wrapped around my waist, and I was pulled through the water. No one mentioned having to do the work for me and let me enjoy the tour without the memories of why my stomach hurt too much to carry my own weight.

Every so often, Cisco would snap a photo of us all, saying he'd tag me in it on social media, while Anna gave me the history of the cenote. The Pack had been using these waters for decades. Her greatest of grandmothers had sworn it held healing properties and could calm a wolf in seconds. It was considered a safe space for all Lycan who visited her father's territory. And everyone who came left their squabbles at the top. They were all wolves down here—no Pack, no lines in the sand, no plays for power.

"Most Packs have a sacred place of worship or healing," Miguel said, swimming at my side. He had spent most of his time pulling me through the water but wasn't fazed in the least. Lycan stamina at its finest. "The Noire Lune Pack, back in Van? They had a small chunk of Stanley Park, right in the middle, away from prying eyes."

"They don't anymore?" I asked and made a mental note never to venture into that part of the park again.

"Their Lycaon, Nathaniel, doesn't run things as of old," he replied and shrugged. "He took over as I was leaving to come back to Mexico. What I've heard, though, isn't all that promising. They've lost touch with who they are and why they are. But they wouldn't be the first Pack to go down that road—and won't be the last."

"And Caser keeps to the old ways?" I asked.

"The good parts, yes. He's outlawed a lot of the practices that were revolting or weakened and divided us. He's not bad once you get to know him. You'll come to see that what he does, all he does, is to help his people and those we are entrusted to protect. With great power comes great responsibility...and being called an asshole more times than not." Miguel's voice was soft and caring. Caser meant a lot to Miguel, but I had to agree with that last part. I had cursed him more times than I could count, and I had only just met the man.

"What's that?" I asked, pointing to a large cave carved into the rock.

"A place of worship for some," Miguel answered. "For others, a place to rest and heal. Before the time of hospitals and trained medical personnel in our Pack, the wounded used to be lowered into the cenote and placed in one of the caves. Healers would remain with them until they either died or healed."

I scrunched my face and fought to urge to cringe. "Are there old bones in here?"

Miguel laughed. "Probably, but not from Pack. The dead are burned. The smoke carries their souls to the gates for them to relieve an elder and take up their post."

"Do you really believe a puff of smoke is what sends them on to their next life?" I asked.

"Why not? A couple weeks ago, you didn't believe in Lycan, and now you're swimming in a Lycan place of worship with a group of us," he answered. "Faith and belief have nothing to do with what I can see and prove to others. It doesn't matter how farfetched it may be to others. It only matters what I know in my soul and what brings me peace. My belief hurts no one."

"Fair point," I replied.

"Are you two lovebirds coming?" Sofia called from the front of the group, treading water like she was born with fins and gills.

"Where are we going?" I asked.

Anna grinned. "We've saved the best for last."

As we swam, the walls closed in on either side. Although the two of us could swim shoulder to shoulder, it felt tight as the ceiling lowered above us. The stalactites, growing down from the cave ceiling, forced us under in some areas. And the stalagmites, growing up from the floor, made us weave around like we were in a maze. Each one I focused on with my flashlight looked like they were coated in tiny gems. It was beautiful, and this is what I would choose to remember — not the first cenote, but this moment.

"Take a deep breath and hold my hand. I'll pull you through the rest of the way," Miguel said, grabbing my hand and pulling my attention from a small silvery fish

I was following. "It's a bit of a distance, but nothing you can't hold your breath long enough for. Just don't panic, or you'll brain yourself on the rocks and stalactites."

I nodded and took a few practice breaths before holding and going under. Miguel pulled, and I kicked from behind. He was faster than I was, so I let him pull me while I shone my light on the world underwater. Small fish darted by, and the rock glittered under my light. I felt myself being pulled upward through a tunnel and couldn't help but to look behind me to make sure nothing was coming. That weird voice in the back of my mind, the one we all had, told me a monster was waiting for the moment I turned my back.

We broke the surface, and I gasped for air. We were at the end of the cenote in an almost perfectly round cave. A massive slab of rock, smoothed from years of use, stood before us. Lanterns hung everywhere, and little lights bobbed on the surface. It was a warm kind of light that made the cave feel bigger somehow. Each breath felt like breathing in home, laced with raw power. Two dozen Pack members stood on the rock, energy rolling off them like heat on cement. But I wasn't scared. I was calm and felt perfectly at ease. My soul stretched out toward them all, and I felt like hell could open up, and for the first time, I didn't fear what would happen. I knew the Pack would have my back, and I would have theirs.

"Ailis Petronilla Kyteler." Caser's voice brought my attention from the cave to the rock he stood on. "I welcome you to the Los Luna Pack. Step forward."

I frowned, the first start of panic setting in, and reached for Miguel. "What's going on? Did I do something wrong? Am I in trouble?"

"We're using the only loophole we have," Miguel answered. "A blood debt is owed to you for the protection of our people. You are receiving the blood oath of protection from our Pack."

"That's not necessary," I countered.

"Unless you want us to eat you for knowing our secret, I suggest you get your ass in gear," Cisco said as he climbed onto the rock. "Though, I *am* a little hungry."

"Your stomach was growling the entire time I carried you home from that church, sissy," Sofia said, giving me a wink. "You're always hungry."

Caser grinned and held out his hand. "It's okay, Ailis. This is the only way we can skirt the law. By presenting you with a blood oath, we will always come to your call. A debt is owed by me and my people. Let us give this to you."

I held Caser's hand and stood at his front. "I don't know what I'm supposed to do."

Miguel moved to my side. "When Caser finishes, you have the choice to accept and agree to keep our secret, being tied to us for the rest of your life and unto the next, or decline. If you decline, you will be graced with twenty-four hours to leave our territory and never return. Your ties and protection would be severed here. We could not interfere if any other Pack were to find out you know about Lycan."

I nodded and watched as the others shuffled positions. I could tell, by how each one felt against my aura, they were moving into power positions within their Pack. Caser stood in the middle, Miguel to his right. The rest stood behind them. Sofia, beaming, took her place directly behind Miguel, to his right, with her chin held high and proud. Cisco stood near the end with Anna at his side. He gave me a nod that said he was happy with his position within Pack. They all were.

Caser cleared his throat. "Ailis, you have bled for my people. You stood firm in the face of my ancestors, calling them to aid you in the protection of my only child and my people. I give to you my blood, my protection, my love. Do you accept the tie that will bind you to my people, forever protecting our secret, with your own blood, protection and love, unto your death?"

I swallowed hard, but the choice was simple. I looked at Miguel and smiled. "I accept."

Caser slid a knife across his hand and touched my arm. It was hard not to pull back and swallow my gag. He passed the knife to Miguel, who cut open his palm and placed it on my arm, offering his blood, protection and love. Each member of the Pack took their turn. Cisco was last, making the largest cut on his hand, placing it on my arm and pulling me in for a hug.

"You are our Grimmwolf now," he said. At my confused look, he grinned. "It means you are fierce and powerful like a wolf. It is a title given to those we respect that are not Lycan."

"Does it come with perks other than being covered in blood?" I asked.

"Nope, just blood and guts for wannabe Pack," he replied. Once he stepped back, the room erupted in cheers and laughter.

"Can I wash this off, or would that be rude?" I whispered to Anna.

"I don't know why you whisper. Every ear in this room can hear your heart beating." She laughed.

"Yes, you can wash it off," Miguel answered from the other side of the rock as he poured two glasses of champagne for the celebration.

Sofia followed me into the water with a small towel. "You're the first human to receive a blood oath from Pack."

"Hopefully, I'll live long enough to cash in on it. I'll find a perk if it kills me," I said, looking at the bright red marks left on my arm from a Lycan attack and thinking about the upcoming full moon.

"Don't think that way," she replied. "Have faith. I do. You got to the wound in time and washed it with holy water. It might work, Ailis."

I nodded and pushed the thoughts back down. I'd cross that bridge when I got to it. I closed my eyes and willed the sadness from my body, washed it away with the blood of Pack. If I constantly dwelled on the bad, I'd never have anything good to bring with me at the end of it all. Up on the rock, I lifted my glass with the others and sipped bubbly while being introduced to the others. Anna presented me with a gold wristband, their Pack symbol and the marking for Lycan was carved into the surface. It would be seen by other Lycan as a symbol of protection. Lycan would receive a branding with silver, but Caser was sure I'd have said hell no to being branded. He was spot on, but I'd have used more swearing to get my point across. When I looked at the Pack symbol, I glanced at Miguel with a knowing look. He had a small scar on the back of his neck that was identical. He had once told me a demon had branded him. Miguel shrugged, and I laughed. It's not like he could have told me the truth.

Not all of Pack was here, only half. Aside from the full moon, they were never all in one place together.

The other half were in full shift, scouting the property and ensuring the safety of those in the cenotes. With a few bottles of bubbly down, we swam through the cave and climbed back up to the top, and those who had been with us traded places with those on patrol. Those who had come to rescue me shifted back, cleaned themselves up at Caser's and joined us for dinner, which looked like it could feed an army. Tables of food kept coming, and small bonfires were set. Little lights within the trees came on while the music started playing. We danced like we all hadn't just endured hell. Toasts were made to the fallen, claps given to those who were once seen as the lowest Pack members, and tears were shed for the memories that would take more than a few dinners to get rid of.

This was how I spent my days leading up to the day I dreaded — moments made up of mythical beasts and love so deep it hurt. The new memories Miguel helped me make had scrubbed off the pointy bits of why I had come to Mexico. The cities he brought me to were incredible. The cobblestone towns felt like they held a piece of everyone's best memory. Each part of where Miguel had come from was exactly how I had pictured it in my mind. It was bits and pieces of who he was. If I shifted and died when the moon came, at least I got to see heaven with someone I loved deeply before the views from my cage in hell were less than desirable. And at the end of each day, as the sun set over paradise, I spent the nights in Miguel's arms at his home in Tulum.

Miguel's house reminded me of the place he had back home in East Van, right down to the paint on the walls. The smell of his home brought me comfort and eased me back into the memories of us together that I had tried so hard to forget. Even with the pending doom of a full moon, I felt safe, secure and like my ending could come and I'd be okay with it. I got to touch love again, and at the end of our days, that's all you could really hope for—being loved in our final moments. That love settled the parts inside me that thought I'd die alone, having never felt the calm embrace of someone I'd die for.

Miguel had insisted I stay with him for a few days until he knew my soul was okay. All the suffering and clinging to life would have been for nothing if I had died from a demon attack before the moon came and went. Although my soul was battered and bruised, it was still in one piece, minus a few bits I had left behind willingly. I didn't regret the bits I'd leave in Mexico. It had been worth it. Regardless of what he had said about my staying or why I had agreed, we both knew it was to be closer to each other. I had grazed the fingertips of death, and the call had been close enough for us both to need the touch of something purer than hell…if only for a few days.

* * * *

The day of the full moon, the decider of my fate, came hard and fast and felt worse than I thought it would. I wasn't kidding myself. I knew this day would feel like my soul was breaking open. But today I felt like I had more to lose than just my life, and it came in the blink of an eye. One minute I was diving in the cenotes, and the next, the day I might die, raised with the sun.

I spent the morning watching Miguel move with liquid grace. His only clothes were black shorts, which hung loose on his hips and showed off his muscular body in every detail. As his body heated up, that thin layer of fabric left little to the imagination. Each movement clenched his abs and drew my attention to his waist, hips and groin. My mind ran wild with what I knew was under the clinging piece of material. Training with Miguel was painful for my body and absolutely torturous for my libido. He was all business, and I was all cravings. Even after years of doing this, I was always the first to break and turn the session into something with less clothing and much more contact.

Although two years had passed between us, these last few days had closed that gap and made it feel like we had been together the entire time. I had spent every possible moment with him. But our break from the horror, from ignoring the payment to be made from demented witches trying to loosen a chunk of hell, had come to an end. I would be facing the music and paying for the reason I was called to Mexico, and Miguel was back to his usual routine of yoga, working out and sparring before work this evening. He, like me, compartmentalized. He also didn't bother pointing out the obvious. We were both scared of what the moon would bring, but neither of us said the words out loud. Picking at the scab wouldn't help. So, we went about our business as though I wasn't going to leave later to dig an unmarked grave that fit a witch of my exact size.

After what he had called a warm-up, he strapped gloves on us each and taught me how to defend myself. His jabs and movements had me spinning and ducking and hopping across the floor mats. For me, this was a full-body workout. For him, he hadn't even broken a sweat. I'm sure stamina was one of the perks of being a Lycan. So far, there were no perks, only targets on my back from being a witch.

"Pay attention and stop staring at my ass." Miguel's voice called me from my daydream. "Your bedroom eyes won't help you ward off an attack, Lish."

I grinned and moved my eyes away from the parts of his body I wanted to grab and lifted my hands back up to defend myself. "Why do you work out if you can shift into a Lycan and tear someone apart?"

"Which would you prefer to hit the news and social media, a fistfight or a wolf chewing on tourists?" he asked. "Would you like the world to see what you can do with a little hand from hell?"

"Good point," I replied. I swung at him, and he blocked me, pulling me into his chest. He kissed my nose once and pushed me back. I grumbled as I caught my footing again. "Not fair. You're faster than I am."

"And everyone who will ever step to your front will be faster than you. Get used to it or stop playing with monsters," he replied.

"I like playing with monsters." I winked, and he rolled his eyes.

"When you get home…" he started, and the instant sadness on my face softened his. "*When* you get home, and you will, the real monsters won't be nearly as fun as I am. You need to be ready."

"If, Miguel… If I leave Mexico alive," I responded. I jabbed again, and this time, he ducked to the side, batting my hand away.

"If you punch someone like that, you're going to break your knuckles or worse," he said. He ignored my comment, as he did every other time I had made it. He chose to have faith. I chose to be realistic. He walked me through jabs once again. "You need to use more than your shoulder to throw a punch. Dig into the ground with your right toe. Let the force of it carry up through your leg. Turn your hips and shoulders. Use all of your body."

"I remember how to fight, Miguel," I replied.

"Then why are you throwing punches like I'm filled with babies and puppies?" he asked. "If you're going to fight, then fight."

"I don't want to hurt you," I answered.

His laugh was sudden. "That's cute. Have you forgotten, so soon, what I am? You could hit me with a truck, Lish, and I'd get back up. Stop holding back."

My grin was a warning. "Very well, but don't complain if I leave you black and blue, and you have to meet up with your Pack after a wee witch kicked your ass."

Miguel held out his hand and motioned me forward. He wiggled his eyebrows, tempting me to try. I pulled off my gloves and tossed them to the floor. He mirrored me with a look of excitement. Like every other time he had trained me, I knew he liked when our sessions became full-contact and ended on the floor, my legs wrapped around his waist. I breathed in and out slowly, grounding myself. I circled around him as if stalking my prey. His body tensed when I stood behind him. I pushed my body against him, touching his bare shoulders. One lick and his entire body shuddered. But I knew he was ready. There'd never be a day I could take him by complete surprise.

He tilted his head to the side when I breathed out, as if sensing my breath changing the currents in the air. I knew he'd wait for my telltale signs of an attack. He always did. He had always been two steps ahead of me. But now I knew who I stood against. A Lycan. A natural predator. Today, I'd take my time and wait for an opening. Back to his front, I smiled, licking my lips as I eyed his groin once more. As Miguel started to smile along with me, I jabbed him once in the throat, to his disbelief. It wasn't as hard as I would have hit him had he been my enemy, but it took him by surprise, to my utter amazement. It was a rare occasion to catch him off guard. With a leg behind Miguel's, I hooked his and rode him to the floor, my hips against his. As soon as his back hit the floor, he twisted out from under me and pinned me down.

"A throat jab? Unless you're going to take a bat to my neck, it won't stop me." Miguel leaned over me, pinning my shoulders with his hands and holding my legs down with his. "Know your enemy, Lish. There are creatures out there you've yet to meet, and I'd hate to meet for a second time."

"Miguel, you're hurting me," I whispered wide-eyed. My voice came out in a quiver. "Please, you're hurting my stomach. It's not fully healed."

He pushed himself up and sat on my hips, letting go of my shoulders. Instant guilt flooded his face. I jerked under him and brought my legs up behind him, gripping under his chin with the tips of my feet, pulling him backward. In a flash, I was on him, my fingertip under his chin, mimicking a knife. I pushed my nail in just enough to warn him. One wrong move, and he'd bleed for me. My groin hovered over his, and he struggled beneath me.

"Know your enemy, Miguel. There are creatures out there, like little witches." I grinned. "I win."

"Ow, you're hurting me," he replied, mimicking the fake I had just done.

"Next time we spar, I get a bat," I teased.

His laughter filled the room and pulsed something deep inside my chest. Miguel gripped my hand and twisted my arm behind my back as he sat up. In one swift movement, he rolled me off his hips, turned me over and had me face down. He stood and brought me to my feet, twirling me with my bent arm until I was standing back where I had been when I had attacked him. It always ended this way with us — me thinking I beat him, and him reminding me I didn't even come close.

"Well done, little witch." He smiled.

He took one step toward me, and I stepped back. The look on his face made me bolt. My scream tore through his gym and echoed down the halls. I ran full speed, jumping over workout mats and gear. Miguel lunged from behind and caught me around the waist. He tossed me over his shoulder and headed for his bedroom, with me squirming and laughing in his arms.

"Put me down!" I yelled, amusement in my voice.

Miguel dumped me on the floor. "Run, little witch, *run!*"

"Catch me if you can, wolf," I teased him. I jumped to my feet and ran the rest of the way to the bedroom with him hot on my tail.

I stood on the far side of the bed, the anxiety of the chase making me laugh uncontrollably. Miguel skidded into the room, blocking off the only exit. His eyes lit up with eagerness that made me pulse deep down. I knew what would happen when he caught me, and I wanted every inch of it. Although I had no intention of running, the game of being stalked drove my pulse into my throat, and I screamed again. When he came around the bed, I scrambled across it, a sad attempt to get away. He caught my legs and dragged me toward him. He crawled up my body and pulled my arms above my head, holding me down. When my squirming did nothing for me, I screamed at the top of my lungs. His deep laugh vibrated through my body.

He put his hand over my mouth and grinned. "Screaming will do nothing, Lish. No one is brave enough to open my front door." My breath caught in my throat, and he pulled his hand away. "I like hearing you scream. But you'll scream for me, little witch, soon enough."

He gripped the waistband of my shorts, and with two rough pulls, they were off and on the floor, jerking me toward the edge of the bed. My shirt was next. His mouth was hot and sudden as his lips found my nipple. A soft groan escaped my lips, replacing my screams and fight. He latched onto my breast and ran his hand down my front to find my sweet spot, wet and swollen. He rubbed and flicked until my entire body felt flushed and needy. He kissed his way up my chest and ate my moans as I rocked against his hand, panting.

"Please," I whispered.

"Tell me what you need, Lish."

"You," I replied. "Release."

"What kind of release? Say the words," he replied.

"I need to feel your mouth and hands," I whispered, lost to need. "Please, fuck me."

"I'll fuck you when you're ready, but first, I'll enjoy bringing you to completion with my mouth." He grinned, released my arms and moved down my body, licking, flicking, kissing, nipping. When he had my thighs over his shoulders, he breathed me in and ran his tongue over me. A small scream escaped my lips. I covered my mouth until he pushed my hands away.

"I want to hear you, all of you," he said, pressing his tongue back into me again.

Not knowing what to do with my hands, I gripped his hair, pulling him into my hips. He licked me while I rocked myself into him, losing myself in the pleasure. When I climaxed, I dug my nails into his shoulders. He drank down my orgasm as I screamed his name and jerked hard enough for him to need to hold my hips down. My body roared with pleasure. I came undone, shaking and digging my nails into his flesh and calling out his name.

He pulled away until my twitches calmed, kissing my thighs. When the feeling lessened, I grabbed his hair and pushed his mouth back to me. I could have stayed in that position until time ended. The world could have burned around us, and I wouldn't have noticed a single flame. I ground myself against him, asking for more. He pushed my thighs wider and ran one finger down my wetness. When his finger entered me, it felt like time stopped while I regained my ability to think and speak again. A rush of heat coursed through my body, and I couldn't get enough. I rocked harder while he worked me with his mouth and fingers.

"Don't stop," I whispered. "That's... Yes."

"Hold on, it's about to get better."

He moved his fingers in a 'come here' motion, and my voice caught in my throat. Slowly at first, he moved his fingers until he found the perfect spot. With his mouth and hand, he kept me riding the edge of not enough pleasure and too much of it. I thrashed under his grip. When not a sound escaped my throat, he eased up and climbed up the bed to add a little pressure to my lower abdomen. My next orgasm tore out of me and soaked the bed. My back bowed, and my scream could have been heard for miles.

I jerked off the bed and shoved Miguel to his back. When my mouth found him hard and ready, he tried to pull me away, but I held on. I gripped his hips and held him against my mouth.

"I won't last," he begged. "Wait... Oh fuck...wait!"

"You're always focusing on me. It's my turn," I replied.

I grabbed his hands and placed them on my head, guiding my speed. Half sitting, he jerked against me and moaned until finally, he collapsed on the bed, shuddering under my mouth. I brought him all the way down my throat and held him there while my throat convulsed around him, only to come back up quick and rough, just how he liked it. He jerked again and grabbed my hair. I dug my nails into his thighs, just enough to break the skin. The touch of pain sent him over the edge.

"I'm going to...*fuck!*" He screamed and pulled my face down as far as it would go. His scream was lost to something resembling a growl. He pumped against my mouth until his orgasm flowed down my throat, and his growl vibrated my very bones. Pulse after pulse, I swallowed him down, pumping my mouth and hand until his body calmed.

As soon as he could move again without twitching, he pulled from me, still hard. *Lycan stamina at its finest.* Sitting up, he dragged me onto his lap and leaned his back against the headboard. I positioned my body for him to enter me. Slowly, he pushed himself inside. It was both too much and not enough. It was pleasure and pain and everything in between. I winced but wanted more at once. I stretched open and sighed as he filled me.

"So wet," he moaned. "So, fucking tight."

I pulled back, kissing him briefly. "Fuck me."

"Oh, I like that." He smiled at my curse. It wasn't often I swore without hell nipping on my ass. It was all it took for him to find his way inside to the hilt.

I clenched around him as he held my hips and pushed them down to meet his, rocking me back and forth. This position was a tease for him. It always has been. He liked being in control. He liked watching our bodies joining. He loved being in any position that gave him what he needed. He lifted me, in one movement, onto my back. He held one thigh higher to get the perfect angle. When he found my G-spot, he focused on my pleasure over and over.

I moaned into his mouth as he kissed me. I raised my hips to meet his. I gripped his hair and pulled his mouth away from mine. "Harder."

His smile filled his face. It was dark and primal, and everything I knew him to be in the bedroom. Miguel positioned both of my thighs higher and moved his arms under my back, gripping my shoulders. With each plunge, he pulled my shoulders down to meet his hips. He started slow, working my body up to take what I knew he could give. My moans became louder, and my nails dug deeper. I moved with him and ripped my nails down his back. As my pleasure built, he didn't stop. He moaned my name as I rode my orgasm to the brink. And when I didn't think I could take another drop of pleasure, he switched positions. He finished against the wall, holding me tight against his body while he worked for his second orgasm. In a scream that sounded more like a roar, his pleasure washed over him and pinned me into the drywall until it cracked. He collapsed, bringing us both to the floor, him on top of me, his bliss bringing a final moan from his hoarse throat.

With shaking arms, he helped me crawl back onto the bed. My legs and arms felt weak and useless. He got me onto the bed and inched up slowly, pausing to look down the length of my body. He kissed his way up my legs and settled in beside me. His heart hammered against my side, matching the beat of my own. Our bodies sunk into each other as though we were made to lie side by side. I tucked myself into his arms and concentrated on how his heart beat against my back and how his body temperature warmed me instantly. My hand found his, and I held on to the moment for as long as I could. He moved his hips closer to mine, and I shook my head with a laugh.

"I suppose being Lycan isn't all bad." I rolled to face him. "Your libido has always been insatiable."

"I'm glad you approve." Miguel laughed. "The urge to mate never goes away when we're with someone we are bonded with. The moment you step into a room, I have to touch you. I want my smell all over you."

With a playful shove, I pushed his hips away. "Unlike you, I'm a witch and not built for lazing in bed all day, every day."

He pulled me back against his body. "As I remember, you've never complained."

"We're out of time," I replied and glanced at the clock. With a groan, I stretched and rolled off the bed. "I'm grabbing a shower. Can you drop me off at my hotel on your way to work?"

Without saying the words, he knew why I was leaving. Tonight was the full moon. He stood as if he had all the energy in the world and pulled me into his arms. "I love you."

"Some holiday this turned out to be," I teased.

"It's not all bad." He kissed my temple. "I owe you a vacation."

"Five stars, Miguel. For this shit, I want someone rubbing my feet and hand-feeding me grapes for a week," I answered. I didn't bother adding the caveat of 'if I survived'.

"Deal," he replied. "Maybe I'll tell Caser to put on an apron while he hand-feeds you those grapes."

I huffed a laugh, imagining Caser wearing anything so tacky. I moved to walk away and paused, turning back to him. I swallowed the lump in my throat. "If I don't make it, take care of my cat. Make sure..."

"Make sure you come back to me." He pulled me back into his arms and squeezed me tight. "You're going to make it, Lish. You smell perfectly witchy and without a hint of a wolf."

"Could you smell it, if I was going to change tonight?" I asked.

"Until you shift the first time, it can be hard to smell the inner wolf. And with you, your witch smell is a potent scent. It overpowers everything else," he replied and breathed me deep into his chest. "I smell nothing but you, me and my wolf, your cat and more dead rats than I've ever smelled in one place before, pancake syrup in your hair from breakfast, but no monsters."

"Thank you," I whispered and hugged him. I couldn't bring myself to hope for anything more than this moment. There was no better way to die than with a heart full of love. "I love you."

"I love you, too," he replied. "And later, when we're back home and in bed, I'll love you until the fear of this nightmare has settled to the bottom of your soul. And tomorrow, we'll start the rest of our lives, leaving the worst of Mexico behind us."

"If I'm still here tomorrow, Miguel, I don't want another day without you. Promise me, you will still be here."

"I promise. It'll take the heavens to keep us apart now."

"If I die, I'm not going upstairs, Miguel. If I don't make it, swear to me that you won't follow me into hell," I said, pulling back. But even as he nodded, I knew he was lying. If I didn't make it, he'd give up. I didn't push him on the topic. If something were to happen to him, it would take the will of the man upstairs to keep my heart beating.

Chapter Eleven

The drive to the hotel was tense and uncomfortable. We both tried to ignore that this could be the last we'd see of each other. We made small talk until he finally asked, again, to be the one to sit with me during the full moon. I was firm in my decision. I wasn't being stubborn, as he'd accused me of several times. I simply didn't think he had it in him to do what was needed if I shifted. His love for me would risk innocent lives when he left me alive rather than kill me as I wanted. And if he could do it, I didn't want him to carry that burden on his shoulders, which is why Caser would be with me. He'd do what Miguel couldn't and shouldn't do. He'd end my life, regardless of if I changed my mind, begged, pleaded, promised or threatened. He'd do it because it had to be done. He'd be the one to take my last breath so that his friend, Miguel, didn't have to live with killing the person he loved.

"My last breath, dying at your hands, is not how I want you to remember me," I finally said. "I don't want you to live with taking my life."

"I'll feel it whether I'm there or not." He had an answer for everything, as though he had practiced this discussion over and over in his head. "My soul will know the very moment you are gone."

"You promised me, Miguel. I can't have you be the one to take my life. I can't have those memories of you when I leave." My throat felt tight, and my words came out strangled. "When I die, I'm headed to the pits. I go with all my love and memories. I can't sit down there, knowing you gave me the final push. Please don't ask that of me. Let me go with the memories of your touch being gentle and not life-ending."

He squeezed his steering wheel until it groaned but finally nodded his head. With hugs and kisses and stalling for as long as we could, we finally parted ways. The goodbye ripped my soul apart, but I kept my tears to myself until I got to my room. I don't remember my walk through the lobby or standing in the elevator. My death grip on my sadness carried me straight to my room. There, in the shower, sitting on the floor, head tucked into my knees, I cried until there was nothing but dry heaves left.

I washed from head to toe, using every drop of the expensive soap from the hotel. If I was paying for the place, dead or alive, I was using up what I could in the last hours I had. I used every towel, two toothbrushes, all the toothpaste, the complimentary brush and comb, and every drop of skin cream. Smelling like I had spent the day in a spa and feeling like silk, I packed my things and waited for destiny to knock on my door. Miguel sent text after text, reminding me of his love, his belief that my strength would carry me through to morning, and the hope he had for me to have the life he thought I deserved. I replied each time that I loved him in return. I sent him all the pictures I had taken of us touring Mexico, along with the ones of us with his Pack. In the background of almost all of them, Cisco and Sofia were arguing, and Caser was running to get the hose. If I didn't live to see the sun rise again, I wanted to make sure Miguel had those texts to look back on.

When my door knocked, I slipped my phone into my pocket, swallowed hard and opened the door. "Cisco?"

"Ready?" he asked, leaning against the jam casually.

"I thought Caser was picking me up?" I asked. "I'm not fully packed yet. I thought I still had until tonight?" I glanced out of the window to the sun still in the sky. "I still have six hours and change."

"Don't worry about packing. If you kick the bucket, I'm going through all your things for stuff I want to keep," he replied. I shook my head but still laughed. Cisco had a way of shaving off the sharp bits of life with the kind of gallows humor that scratched a lot of people the wrong way. I was *not* one of those people. I loved him all the more for it. "Don't worry, I'm dropping you off with Caser. He had a few things to take care of first. I just have to make a stop along the way."

"If it's to pick up Miguel, I'll call another ride," I replied and gave him a stern look.

"A deal is a deal. No Miguel," he replied, and I felt myself calm down. "But not all of us are on vacation like you. I need to make a stop." He stood from the frame and shook his head when I moved back to my suitcase. "Leave your things. If you don't come back, you won't care about them. If you do come back, they'll be exactly where you left them."

"Vacation." I laughed at the word. I released a long breath and stepped out of the room. Shutting the door gave the day some sort of finality I wasn't fully ready for. The click of the lock was deafening, and my stomach flopped at the sound. I handed Cisco my key card. "In case I don't come back, can you give the card to Miguel?"

"*After* me and Sofia go through your things." He winked. "I want to pick through your underwear drawer."

"Cisco." I whispered his name as if speaking any louder would make me cry. Alone in the hall, I finally asked the question that had been on the tip of my tongue since I was attacked. "Will it hurt? If I shift? Sofia didn't say if it hurt when she shifted. It sounded painful. It sounded like her skin was torn apart and fell off in a sloppy mess. Jesus, it was awful to hear, never mind how it would have felt."

"I hate to say this, but you won't shift fully, Ailis. Caser will take your life before your shift is complete before you're too hard to kill. This is supposed to be a mercy, not a full hunt for a werewolf," He pulled me into a hug that held all my brokenness together. "But to answer your question, the first time? Yeah, it hurts. If you start to shift, try not to fight it. If you try to stop it, it'll be worse."

"How will I know it's going to happen?"

"Caser will feel it coming. I doubt he'll warn you. He'll try to keep you calm and do his part when you're not expecting it," he answered. "But you'll know, unfortunately. In my experience, it starts as a feeling of alarm. An unease settles over you. Your pulse starts to speed up, you feel your heart pounding against your ribs, your ears pick up every sound around you and every smell comes into hyperfocus. You'll feel your body start to get hot — the kind of fever that makes your skin almost painfully sensitive. Your joints and muscles will feel like they've all been overextended and exhausted. The part that hurts the most is your bones. When your bones start to throb, stretch out your limbs and allow it to happen. If you ball up, it hurts even more. I've seen a few people shift while in the fetal position, and they've stabbed themselves with their own claws. It didn't look like a fun ride." Cisco kissed the top of my head. There was nothing romantic about it. It was like hugging a sibling. "For me, the part that still hurts is my eyes, for some reason. It feels like a tension headache or like I swallowed an ice cream truck in under five minutes. For Sofia, it hurts her feet the most. Miguel once said his rear hurts when he shifts, but I think it's because he's so used to sitting on his ass all day, so it's not used to the workout."

I laughed at the comment. "Thank you for not lying to me."

He pulled back and breathed me in. "I don't know why we're even wasting our time on this. You don't smell the least bit wolfy to me. You still stink like a witch and a cat with a sprinkle of hell."

I sniffed him back. "And you still smell like a wet dog."

"You wound me with your words. For the record, many people have complimented me on my smell. I'm a pretty big catch, you know, aside from the whole claws, teeth, fur and poor manners thing," he joked. "Let's roll. The day ain't getting any younger, and I still have a few things to do before dropping you off."

I followed Cisco down the hall and into the elevator. We passed all the shops I never got to spend time in, the spas, restaurants and lounges. I grumbled that even though I'd likely die tonight, the hotel would still bill my credit card, and I hadn't even enjoyed the place. Cisco gripped my shoulder and pulled me under his arm. I smiled and knew I looked as pathetic as I felt.

"Sorry you didn't get to enjoy the place," he said the same thing I had said to myself. "When you come back, you should spend a day in the spa and make Caser cover the bill."

"*If*," I replied.

"Have faith. It's all you got. Nothing else is going to pull your ass out of the flames," he said as he led me to his truck. The moment we stepped through the lobby doors, the heat hit me like a slap. Being in a climate-controlled, temperature-regulated building made the heat harder to handle. I still breathed in the humid air, sad I may not be alive tomorrow to complain about it. "Without hope, your soul starves. You and I both know what an empty soul becomes. But hope keeps us alive. You just gotta keep it going for a little longer, Ailis. Your fight for life isn't over. Faith will help you walk into that field later and stick your middle finger into the face of fate. We've all sent up our prayers. The rest is up to you and your faith."

I didn't reply. I didn't know what to say. Faith wasn't going to remove a curse from my body, since faith hadn't done a damn thing for my witch blood, and I remember praying hard enough for it to happen that my knees had carpet burns from kneeling. I could feel the anger slinking in as I buckled myself in. Being mad about this would be easier to deal with than fear or sadness. But as much as I wanted to let it overcome me,

I didn't want Cisco to remember my last hours as a hostile psychopath being driven to her death. Though, it was tempting as hell.

Cisco turned on his stereo, and we hit the highway, skidding sideways as we hit the main road. He was a chatterbox, now that Pack wasn't a secret. I tuned most of it out but picked up bits and pieces when he became more animated with his hands. The swerving of the truck made me dig my nails into the leather of his seat. If I even made it to the field in one piece, I'd be surprised. He gossiped about every single person, including Miguel. Some of the stories made me laugh, while others made my heart break a little for him. Cisco had known Miguel since joining the Pack, and the way he spoke about Miguel, if I hadn't known, I would have thought he was talking about his brother. Pack was very much the same as natural wolves, as he had called them. They were a family.

"Where are we going?" I asked Cisco when he pulled off the main highway onto a dirt road. The road was like every other side street I had been on. Unlike Miguel, Cisco didn't slow down for the bumps. It reminded me of the back roads in the mountains back home. The locals took them at breakneck speeds, knowing every pothole and turn. Dust kicked up and clouded the view of the road. My pulse jumped into my throat. "You're going to ditch us if you don't slow down."

"I know these roads like the back of my hand," he replied and kept up the speed. "We're running late. I hate being late."

"For what?" I asked.

Cisco took a sharp turn onto another road, the first hint of a smile starting. The energy in the cab started to climb. "The bloodsuckers."

"What?" My jaw fell open. "Why are we going to see vampires?"

He grinned and pulled his shades down his nose. "It's not a social call, witchy woman. I saved the best for last. They are the reason you're cut up, the reason you will look death in the eyes, and he decides whether he will take you or not."

"One of your people did this, Cisco," I said, reminding him. "A vampire wasn't there and didn't will it to happen, either."

"And Nichole died for what she did," he replied. "But it wouldn't have even happened had it not been for the vampires helping the witches. The Pack traitor was dealt with, the witches are gone, hell is back where it belongs, and now, we have one last piece of the puzzle to punish."

"I thought this was already dealt with?"

"Mostly, but it has taken time to find the last one involved," he answered. "The one you found drinking from me wasn't the only one, Ailis. There were half a dozen of them involved. The last two are in a house up the road."

"And?"

"And? We're going to pay them a visit before you have to pay the moon a visit. They will see the sun before you see the moon," he answered plainly, as if he hadn't just suggested we kill them. "You should not be the only one to look death in the eyes tonight. Those responsible for your coming to Mexico should pay for it."

"I..." I didn't know how to respond. I didn't want to make a pitstop along the way. The sun was slowly setting. I didn't want to waste the last hours I had on vampires. But I also didn't want to spend them pacing and waiting for the inevitable. Instead of arguing or trying to convince Cisco to turn around, I shrugged. "I don't know what to say, Cisco. Isn't this a Pack matter?"

"And a witch matter," he replied. "It isn't just my blood they're paying for, Ailis. They took your blood off a knife and placed it in a vial."

My eyes widened. "How'd you know about my blood being taken?"

"The last one I hunted down said one of their people was at the church. She watched a witch stab you, then collect your blood. To what end, he didn't know. The vampire in question wasn't local—or so he claimed. I don't know how much of his story to believe. I had him strung up in an open field as the sun was starting to rise," he answered. He was so calm about death that it made me uncomfortable. "So, this isn't just a Pack matter. The vamps watched you suffer rather than help you. The two I saved for today were outside while you and Anna were dying. If they would have helped you, I'd have forgiven them for taking my blood. If they would have saved you both, I'd have accepted that as payment. But they didn't. They watched and walked away. That makes them monsters, and we hunt down monsters."

I felt my anger stir. "They watched?"

"Oh yes. I got a play-by-play of everything that happened to you and Anna. They watched you crawl, bleeding out from a stab wound, toward Anna, a child tortured. And now, they can face the same fear you did. They watched a child being tortured. They beat her for hours. She wakes up screaming every night because of what was done to her. These bastards don't get to walk away from this, Ailis. There are very few rules in our world, but the number one across the board is none of us fuck with children. For that, they die."

"I'm in," I finally said.

"I thought you'd see it my way," he replied. He pulled off the road and drove through a field and into the trees. "We walk the rest of the way."

"Right, because hiking through the forest with the sun about to set to hunt vampires is a good way of keeping my ass above the dirt," I replied.

"Vampires are the least of your worries, little red. You got into a vehicle with a big, bad wolf," he replied. It got a chuckle out of me.

"Grandmother dear, what big teeth you have," I said.

"The better to eat you with," he replied and leaped over the front of the truck. I jumped back and caught my scream with my hands over my mouth. My heart pounded in my chest as he landed at my side. His laughter made me smile ear to ear. He grabbed a bag from the box of the truck and motioned for me to follow him. "Let's go find the little cabin in the woods."

Cisco didn't make a sound as he moved through the trees while I stomped around like a bull in a China shop. "You make less noise than Miguel does."

"No, he's quiet as the wind. He just makes noise around those who aren't Pack," Cisco replied. "We all do. It's unnerving to the regulars if we're too quiet."

"The regulars." I snickered.

"It was my polite way of saying, someone not part of our group. You're human," he replied and held a few branches back for me to slink under. I had once thought I was quiet in my movements, but after being around Lycan, I felt like a marching band. Cisco grinned each time I tried to tiptoe. "Ailis, it isn't the noise of your feet that give you away. You're quieter than most people. The majority of what we hunt can smell us coming from miles away or hear the very beats of our heart."

"How the hell do you snag a vampire, then?" I asked. "Miguel made it sound like you all hunt them on the regular."

"We do," he answered. "But I'm Lycan. My feet move much faster than your little size eight, witchy feet."

"How do I help you hunt one if I'm not fast enough? Won't I just be in the way?"

"Use what you have at your disposal. If you can't outrun them, outthink them. They have a one-track mind — survival. It trips them up and slows them down. It causes them to make mistakes. But you have the sun on your side. Hunt them by day when they are weaker, and you'll have better luck. If you go for them at night, you won't win. Hell, I won't even go for one at night, not without a few Pack members with me."

"Cisco, can I ask you something, and have you keep it between just you and me?" I asked. "I'd rather the others didn't know, in case it's true."

"Depends. If it brings my people harm, I can't keep a secret. If it's about anything else, my lips are sealed."

"It's about the night I called the hounds," I replied, and he nodded. I took it as he'd keep what I said between us. "When I was with Anna in the field, the hellhound I was found with, he called me a little demon. I don't think I'm as human as I want to be," I answered. I hadn't told anyone what the hellhound had said to me. I kept claiming I didn't remember, but I did. "What does the Pack know about witches? Do I smell like a demon to you?"

"Unfortunately, what I know is the same thing the hound told you. All I have are stories and lore passed down through Pack, most of which I'm sure you already know. Being a naturally born witch is a curse, spun by a devil from hell, that's bound to your line. Witches are the reason demons can come topside. You're the door to this world. Sure, they need to be summoned, but the door is there because your people are on this side of it."

My eyes widened. "And you all haven't killed us for it?"

He laughed. "Oh, it's not for lack of trying, witchy woman. It's the reason your people were hunted. The church saw your kind as a sort of half-breed demon, the reason for hell on earth," he replied. "My people, on the other hand, thought of doing it many moons ago. It was decreed that since you all had souls, we wouldn't hunt you down. A few rogue Lycan, early on, tried, though, and damn near succeeded. Three-quarters of all witches were wiped off the human map. But, like all humans, you breed like rabbits, and your population recovered. There aren't as many full-bloods left, but enough of you are kicking around to keep the witches as a formidable group to stand against."

"Witches don't pop out kids like the rest of the humans. Genetically, almost half of us are sterile."

"Part of the curse. All cursed have issues conceiving. There's always a catch to every curse. The devils wanted to walk in and out of hell and needed a doorway on the other side. Their path is the energy we all pull from, and witches are the focus. It's why every war between unnatural groups has included witches. They provided a focus for others to draw energy through," he answered and turned with a grin. "You're like my own tiny familiar."

"Huh, I've learned more from you in five minutes than five years in university," I said and took the opportunity to ask the question that has plagued witches since they stopped hiding. "Do you know if there is a way to stop the curse? Say a witch didn't want her children to be her hereditary witches."

"No. It is literally as much a part of you as my wolf is to me. It is in your genes. Take those out, and what would even be left? Plus, it isn't like you can kill the curser to end it, like you can with other curses. Demons and devils can't die, and no one knows who made the original curse to ask for them to lift it. The payment on that would likely wipe out the entire witch population," he answered, and it was what all the research I had done had suggested. Though, it was still unproven, since none of us were brave enough to knock on a devil's door to verify. "To be honest, I doubt there's a way. It's a devil's curse. Those aren't known for being reversed. But you know this better than anyone else."

I nodded. "First, we'd have to find the original to be cursed. No one knows for sure which human of our line was cursed, to track their demon involvement. We believe we know but could be wrong. Then we'd need to know what kind of curse it was. Was it a deal unpaid, or was it purely to teach a lesson? What was used to make the curse? Who twisted it and so on."

"Whatever the case, it's been passed down throughout so many generations that it would be near impossible to track it. So far, there isn't a way to stop the curse from continuing and keeping you all from popping out little half-breeds."

"Half-breeds?" I asked. "I've heard some crazy stuff before, but this is the first for the half-demon claim."

"It's not a claim. It's what lore says, that's all. I don't think you're a demon, but some of you sure do smell like one," he answered and turned to face me. "Haven't you ever noticed your smell after you twist a spell?"

"I smell like my mother did, but I've really thought of it in greater detail," I replied.

"I've met a couple of born witches, and every time they used their magic, they smelled like I was standing beside a demon," he replied. "Their magic comes from hell, not the elements or whatever gods they pray to. It's probably why naturally born witches use it so sparingly. The more you call on hell, the harder it is to stay out of hell when you die."

I groaned. I couldn't really argue with the last part. It was as true as the crow flies. You can't borrow a cup of sugar from hell and not expect them to come asking for a cup when they're out. "The hound said something similar about where the energy for our magic comes from."

"Don't get too in your head about it. It's not just witches. We all use the energy of hell. Lycan use it all day long. Our natural state is wolf, not man. We use it to keep our human side at the surface, whereas shifters use it to bring their animals out. Every unnatural out there uses the energy of hell in some way or another. It doesn't make us all demons or half-breeds and doesn't mean every unnatural will go to hell for using it, either."

"I'm going to hell," I said, cringing at the thought.

"You and me, both." He winked, trying to lighten my mood.

"You're going to guard the gate. I'm going to a cage. Not exactly the same thing," I replied. "The hound said I could earn my way out quicker. Do you know how?"

"No. I don't get the keys to those secrets until I'm down there guarding them. But if I did know, I'd tell you, Ailis. For you and Miguel, I'd hold the doors open for you to leave," he answered. "If I had to guess, I'd imagine it is by going down as pure as can be and suffering for any sins, willingly. Repent and all that jazz. Doing good in the world, sacrifice, the whole shebang—or that's what Miguel always says."

"An escape plan would be more helpful," I answered. "It was worth a shot."

"You can't escape your fate any more than I can escape my wolf. It's a part of us. But you can hope you'll find a way through it and find those who will walk your path with you. Don't worry. If there's a way out of there, rest assured that Miguel will find it," he said and paused. "How can you call yourself a witch and know so little about where your power comes from?"

I shrugged. "My parents died when I was pretty young, and my grandmother was a god-fearing woman. She never really talked about the darker side of being a witch. She was scared of me growing in power and attracting the monsters. She didn't want me to follow in my parents' footsteps. A lot of our learning is passed down through our lines, but my grandmother only taught me witch-lite, just enough to stay alive and fly under the radar. Most of what I know, I learned through trial and painful error and from a Guardian back home."

Cisco smiled. "Samuel."

"Do you know him?" I asked.

"No, but Pack knows of him. For his sacrifice to man, he has the protection of Pack."

"I thought I was the first human to receive protection?" I asked.

Cisco smiled but didn't comment. Did being a Guardian take away Samuel's human side, or had he never been human at all? I wasn't going to ask him. If he wanted me to know, I'd know.

"Huh. Does he know this?"

"I doubt he'd care. I'd run if he had my name on his naughty list. No one stands up to a Guardian, retired or not, and lives. I'd either die by his hand, or my Pack would hunt me for an attack on him," he answered and caught my grin. "I'm glad you have him at your back."

"Me, too. I wouldn't be half the witch I am today without him."

Cisco laughed. "I have the feeling you'd be dead without him."

"There's that." I grinned.

"Here's a little secret I can tell that won't get us both killed. Start giving your taint to the demons who come after you. Pulling it off your aura will hurt like ripping off a scab, but start giving it to those who deserve it."

"I can't do that." I was surprised he'd even suggest it. That was no better than cursing someone.

"Why not? Every time those creatures touch someone, they dump their taint onto them, making them susceptible to future attacks. The taint belongs to them. Just give it back."

"Isn't that dark arts?" I asked.

"No, it's returning a gift. Don't go looking for them, or you'll get yourself killed. But if they knock on your door, they're taking the risk, not you," he said. He stood in front of me and shook out his arms. "Call it my thanks for saving my hide. The rumor is, the less taint you have to heal or pay for in hell, the less time you'll spend down there. Taint is what ties you to the cages. No taint, no way to hold you."

A clue. If I could heal my aura before I died, I'd be taint-free and not bound to hell. I grinned, then groaned. If I died tonight, I wouldn't have enough time to offload the buckets I carried around. I wondered if it was a trick I could do while already in a cage. I'd tuck it away, just in case. Cisco waved his hand in my face, bringing me from my daydream of escaping hell, as we came to a stop at the tree line and pointed to a shack on the verge of falling over, aged well beyond repair, at the end of a grown-over drive. It looked like it had already been condemned several times over.

"We're here. Are you ready, little red?"

I nodded and shook out my arms and legs, limbering up for whatever the hell was coming next. Miguel opened his bag and pulled out a set of binoculars for me. He didn't have a pair for himself, but I guessed his sight was as good as a wolf's. I followed his lead and knelt down, waiting and watching. I didn't know why we watched the house or what we waited for. A mix of tension and excitement made Cisco's hands twitch. I had seen the same movements on Miguel before hunting for monsters. Cisco was scanning the field and trees we stood in. Every noise got his full attention.

I checked my watch a few times, seeing the time fade away. My stomach filled with butterflies and nerves. I shook my head, trying to calm myself, but I couldn't control my urge to leave. I knew the reasons for coming, but I wasn't a hunter. I didn't hunt down naughty little vampires. That job was filled by people with a stronger backbone than I had. I only came in after it was all said and done, the blood already dry, and only if someone suspected a demon had been involved. I was trained to hunt those who could be killed with words and phrases and a little blood. I wasn't trained to hunt those who would drink said blood straight from my throat.

"I can smell your fear, Ailis. Calm down." Cisco leaned into my ear. "I won't let anything happen to you."

"How can you be so chill about this?" I asked. "I'm literally shaking in my boots and want to vomit. I've no idea what the hell I'm doing."

"This can't be your first hunt?"

I felt my face heat. "Back home, we don't even have a full-time vampire hunter. The one we have is retired and works at the local university, Dr. May Zhang. She's scary enough that no fang steps out of line for fear she'll come out of retirement. Hell, not even I'm willing to piss her off, and I'm one of the most abrasive people I know. The very rare occasion there is a vampire issue, they handle it among themselves."

"Abrasive is putting it mildly." Cisco laughed. "I've heard of Zhang. Everyone has. She comes from a long line of hunters. She trained in China, then Germany, from the age of five, and I'd think twice about messing with her. She has come to Mexico a few times to help the locals with pests and has always hunted the bloodsuckers on her own. She once told the police chief in Tulum that he was a useless blood bag and would be her death if she allowed him and his men to help her. I laughed until she stared at me, then I cowered like everyone else."

"She came to Vancouver when her parents retired there," I replied. "We haven't had any vampire issues since then."

Cisco pulled out his cell phone and sent a text. "Time to stop stalling, Ailis. As much as I'd like to draw this out and make a night of it. We have to get you to Caser in three hours."

"I'm not stalling. I can't do this, Cisco," I whispered from my crouched position. "I can't just kill someone."

"Someone?" Cisco laughed at my comment. "They're not people. They're monsters, and you will want to when you get in there."

"Why, what are we walking into?"

"A blood den," he replied. "The one fang has a taste for the unwilling."

"Why the hell would you wait on this?" I asked. "You should have taken him out as soon as you found him, not wait for me to exact revenge I don't need. It's not going to turn back the clock."

Cisco stared at me, then frowned when he realized I was serious. "You think I'd save him for you if he was hunting innocents? I want a pound of flesh, sure. I want you to take out one last monster, one last hunt, before your time runs out. But I don't want it bad enough for someone else to pay for it. Sofia has been on the house since we found him. No one has gone in or out, and there's no one with a soul inside. If they had someone, they died before we got here."

Sofia stepped through the trees, not even crinkling a leaf as she moved. "You're both louder than my twin nephews on a sugar rush, and they sound like an airplane landing."

A small yip escaped my lips at the sight of her. She hadn't made a sound as she approached. "Jesus, Sofia, you scared the hell out of me. Wear a bell or something."

"If you were a wolf, you'd have heard me or smelled me long before I arrived." She smiled. "If I can still sneak up on you, I think you're home-free tonight."

I smiled weakly. I doubted my hearing or sense of smell was diagnostically relevant, but I smiled just the same. "Thanks, Sofia."

She motioned to the run-down house with broken and boarded-up windows. "There are two bloodsuckers in there, along with a dozen dead bodies. They smell like they've been dead for three or four days now."

"They'll be heading out soon for a meal," Cisco added. "It's rare for them to go this long without feeding. You're certain there's no one in there opening a vein for them?"

"Yes, I'm sure. And their meal run is not happening. They know Pack has been out here, circling the house," Sofia replied. "I nailed a note on their door yesterday afternoon to let them know we'd be popping in shortly."

"Why would you toy with them like that?" I asked. "Why not just kill them and get it over with?"

"You won't look so appalled when you see how young they like their blood," she replied.

I stood. "Children?"

"Mostly teens, from what I saw in there," she replied. "They likely went willingly."

"Willingly..." I scoffed.

"The movies make vampires look glamorous. Vampires regale them with stories and promises of everlasting youth. But once back in the den, it's a goddamn nightmare," she answered, her tone disgusted. "Hollywood has made blood dens an epidemic. We're losing our young to these bloodsuckers on a daily basis. I'm so tired of this shit."

My stomach dropped. "Sweet Jesus."

"I've been in far too many of these bloody shacks over the years," Sofia replied softly. "It never gets easier to see it. It brings back dark thoughts from even darker times that I'd rather not have."

"I'm sorry you have those memories, Sofia," I replied. I'd do just about anything to take the pain from her voice. I knew all too well what it felt like to have memories I couldn't shake.

"Cisco found the vampires who took me," she said, a grin on her face that told me there were no survivors. "It took him the better part of a year and a lot of broken bones, but he always comes through."

I glanced at Cisco, who was getting our supplies out of his bag. "Broken bones, good times. Not that I'm a chicken, but this sounds like something Pack should be dealing with. I'm not a hunter. I'm a teacher, for Christ's sake, and a piss-poor witch, to boot. I'm only a level one, so you know. And I only got my level-one status so I can be licensed, or I couldn't keep my job at the University."

Sofia chuckled. "Level two must be fucking terrifying, then. Does it come with a matching caldron and pan set?"

"I wish. A brand-new spelling pot is almost a grand. I'm still using the one my grandmother had," I replied. "My mother had an amazing one. It was a wedding gift from my dad. A three-gallon, cast iron, heavy SOB, with a pentagram embossed on the side. It came with a matching set of metal spoons. I looked into it. It's five grand for a tiny one, made by a fellow full-blooded witch in Chile. His family line has made them for decades."

"Why not use your mother's?" Sofia asked.

I scrunched my face and swallowed a budding memory. "When their house caught fire, it didn't make it. The house was knocked down, and everything inside was buried and salted. It's probably still in one piece, twenty feet down."

"Ah, damn. I'm sorry, Ailis." Sofia's face softened. "Sometimes, even when the monsters don't win, it feels like they did, with the lasting pain they've caused."

"Such is life," I replied.

"You're stalling again," Cisco piped up, holding his hand out for me to stand. "Full transparency here. It was Caser's idea to bring you here. So here you are."

"Why?" I asked.

"Won't you be glad you asked," Sofia added before Cisco could answer.

Cisco smiled, but it wasn't cheerful. "One of the vamps in the house is a child of your Master of Van City. Caser said the problem comes from your home, so you get to help us deal with it. If you want Pack protection, you have to pull your weight like everyone else. As he said, '*Until you're dead, you work like everyone else does.*'"

"He said that?" I asked, not knowing why I'd be surprised.

Cisco nodded. "That's a direct quote from Caser himself."

"Naturally." I rolled my eyes. "From what I understand, vampires don't vacation outside of their territory. What did this one do back home to get sent away from his Maker?"

"Drinking from the forbidden fruit," Sofia answered. "I called your local Pack. They said he was sipping from the young locals, bringing in too much attention. It was leave or see the sun. Mexico took him in. His brother belongs to the local Master. He claimed the youngsters gave consent, which they probably did, but—"

"It doesn't matter if they went of their own volition or not," I finished her sentence with my own stance on the matter. "Kids don't fully understand long-term consequences, not like this."

"I agree," Sofia said. "Which is why I knocked on their door. Living their final moments in fear is a small taste of what they did to those they killed. There are laws in place for a reason, to keep the young and foolish from meaningless deaths. When you break the laws that protect mankind, Lycan come knocking."

"Death is usually meaningless," I replied and started to stretch out my muscles from being in a crouch for too long. "I've never hunted a vampire. Any tips?"

"Don't get bitten," Cisco replied. "I'd hate for you to survive the moon only to die by the sun."

I shook my head. "Gee, thanks, Cisco. Why didn't I think of that?"

"I don't know if their gaze will work with you since you're a witch, but just in case, don't look them in the eyes. Don't let one grab you. They'll rip your limbs off before you can put up a fight." Sofia shoved Cisco out of her way, glaring at his joke. "You know what? Treat them like you would a demon. They're as deadly and as fast."

"Aside from the usual, holy water, wood stake in the heart, fire and beheading, is there any other way to kill one?" I asked.

"A blessed silver bullet to the heart," Cisco answered. "If you were an elemental witch, a holy circle would work. But because you're not an elemental, I don't know if it would work."

"Do you have a cross?" Sofia asked, and I shook my head. "How the hell do you not have a cross? You deal in demons, for crying out loud." She paused, and her face flushed. "Sorry, Ailis. I forgot about your curse. We can leave ours under our shirts if they bother you."

It took me a moment to realize she wasn't joking. She actually thought they bothered me. "I can wear a cross, Sofia. I just don't have one. I wear my necklace from Miguel. But I'll take one if you have a spare."

"Nice, Sofia. Insult the witch by calling her a demon." Cisco pulled one from his bag. "It's new. Keep it and wear it, please. By aligning yourself with Pack, I have a feeling you'll attract a few vampires when they smell us on you."

"You just finished calling me a half-breed demon, Cisco, and Sofia is the jerk?" I said, making him blush.

He shrugged. "And I also told you I have no manners."

"So, what's the plan?" I asked, pulling the silver chain over my head and resting it beside the pendant from Miguel. I picked them both up and kissed them, sending a silent prayer to anyone listening that I would make it out of this new mess alive. The peanut gallery must have been on the edge of their seats. Out of one fire and into the next should be my middle name.

"Same as usual," Cisco said. "We kick down the door, kill a fang or two and head home for drinks. You stick behind us, and when it comes time to do the deed, we'll hold him down for you."

"What if I chicken out?" I asked. "I've never actually killed someone before. Well, I mean, I've never directly done the deed with my own two hands."

"Then you don't do it," Sofia replied. "If you can't, just stay back, and we'll handle it."

"And if things go south?" I asked. "What do I do if they kill you both?"

"Run," she answered. "I'm not kidding. If we go down, get the hell out of Dodge. If you can't get back to Cisco's truck, the field you're meeting Caser in is a few klicks to the east. Scream for help. He'll hear you."

"Here's to hoping I slide into my grave, battered, bruised, covered in vampire blood, with one hell of a good story," I said. "No other death would feel nearly as epic."

"Let's go take out the trash," Cisco said, and we followed behind him toward my first and likely last vampire hunt. If I lived through this, I doubted I'd sign up to do it again. Once was enough.

Chapter Twelve

I had always wondered how freeing it would be to be a bird — to graze the clouds and kiss the stars without worry or demand from the world below. And for a few brief seconds, I got to feel the wind soar through my hair and carry me to the stars, where nothing hurt. It was the landing that skinned off a new layer from my arms. I hit the ground, full force, on my back, the air bursting from my lungs from the impact. It took longer for me to realize what had happened than it had for me to soar through the air and land. With my chest burning and ears ringing, I tried to relearn how to breathe again. With a few small breaths in, I rolled to my side in a dizzy scramble. I told myself to get up and get to safety, but my arms dragged on the rocks like wet noodles.

In the distance, over the roar inside my head, I could hear flashes of screaming and what sounded like the house losing its final fight to remain standing. Wood splintered, glass broke and a mixture of what sounded like a horror movie filled the field around us. I shook my head, but the ringing lingered, eating up pieces of the world around me. Wetness trickled down the side of my neck. Either my ears were bleeding, or I had another head wound. I lifted my shirt and cleaned the dust from my eyes and blood from my nose. Aside from skipping across the ground like a stone on water, I wasn't in that bad of shape, considering. But too many near misses took a toll on me, and every inch of my body screamed out in protest.

"Kicking down the door, smart plan," I grumbled to myself.

Cisco hadn't joked when he said we'd be kicking our way into the house. Within minutes of the door hitting the floor, the sun tucked its beauty behind the hills, and the cavalry showed up. My pendant from Miguel had heated when we stepped inside and burned my skin a few moments later. I didn't have to tell Sofia or Cisco that more trouble was on the way. They had smelled them coming. The fight broke out before my brain could wrap around what was going on. Cisco pulled me into his chest, away from the grasp of a vampire, while Sofia cleared a path and threw me from the house as it filled up. Her toss wasn't gentle. It had been enough force to send me twenty feet from the front porch. Her screams were cut short when I hit the ground.

"Get up!" Miguel's scream carried over the field. I glanced toward his voice and saw nothing, but I could feel him close by. I shook my head. He wasn't supposed to be here. "Get up and fight! Fight like you want to live!"

I knew that the last comment meant more than just my current situation. "I hate vampires." I groaned and pulled myself back to my feet.

I stood outside of the blood den, eyeballing the house. I glanced to the east and thought about running. Sofia had told me to run when she'd thrown me. My brain told me to get the hell out of there. I should have bolted to the tree line and out of harm's way, screaming for help as I ran. But when I heard Miguel's, I wasn't as scared as I had been when I'd landed. I grabbed the first branch I found and snapped it in half. If I was going to die tonight, I'd do it my way. I'd sooner go down in a blaze of glory, my death meaning something, than walk to my grave, depressed, with not a story to tell. Rarely do we have a choice on how we leave this world. But tonight, I could choose, and I could take as many nasty fangs with me on my way out.

I shook out my arms and ran back into the house. Cisco and Sofia were in the rear of the long living room, vampires inching their way toward them. I counted six left standing. The closest one to me was injured, his arm hanging by strips of skin. I shoved the branch into his back, and he went up like a decade-old Christmas tree in a bonfire. He fell to ash, leaving the branch in my hand. I'd count him as mine, even if he didn't really have an arm. No one had to know my first vampire kill had been a nearly armless vampire. When I told the story later, I'd say there were a dozen, and they all had working arms.

"Don't just stand there," I called out to Cisco and Sofia. "Eat them! Bite them!"

I pulled out my cross and pendant, both of them cooking my skin. The vampires cowered from the holy symbols, and I took the opportunity to move forward. My vision was blotchy from the brilliant light that had blazed from the cross, ruining my line of sight. I now understood why I had never seen May, the hunter back home, wearing a cross. It screwed with a person's ability to see a damn thing. When hands grabbed me, I stabbed forward with my stake and a war cry, bringing my other arm around with the twin branch. It was all or nothing, and I wasn't going out without taking someone with me. I couldn't see what I was doing, but I kept swinging until I hit something.

"Whoa, calm down, little red." Cisco pulled the branches from my hands. "It's just me. It's over. They're dead."

I stepped back, blinking away the tears and blurred vision. There were only three people left standing, and all of us had souls and pulses. The room was ash and torn-apart bodies. Sofia snapped her fingers in front of my face, pulling my mind out of the horror of the room we'd painted red. It had been a blood den before we got there, and now it was a roomy coffin.

"Ailis!" Sofia called my name as though she had said it more than once. "Let's get you outside."

"Did we get the two we came here for?" I asked, looking back to the house. If they were still alive, I was willing to go back in.

"You stabbed the one when you came back in," Cisco said from behind me as we walked out. He pulled a glass jar from the bag outside, stuffed a rag inside the top, lit it, and tossed it in the front door we had kicked down.

"Wait!" I screamed, holding out my hand as if I could stop the fire in midair. "My blood. Did you find the vial of my blood?"

"It's going up with the rest of the house if it's in there. Don't worry. No one will track you back to this place," he answered. "The fire will cook away the evidence."

"I'm not worried about that. If my blood wasn't in there, it means someone else has it. If they've stored it properly, a lot of bad things could happen with my blood," I replied and turned to Sofia. "Did you see a vial of blood in there?"

She shook her head, cleaning the blood from her arms. "Sorry, Ailis. There was a lot of blood in there. Bags and vials of it. A lot of times, vampires will steal from donation banks before it's processed. Fast food for fangs."

"Hopefully, it goes up in flames," I answered, groaning at the thought of my blood out there in the world for anyone to twist a curse with.

"If the vamps have it, the worst they can do is track you with it," she added. "Rest assured, back home, they already know where you live and where you work. They do their homework on everyone worth notice."

"So far, they've left me alone," I replied and kept my worries to myself. Finding me wasn't the worst thing that could happen, but if I lived beyond the full moon, I'd worry about it then. If I died, my blood would be useless.

"So far, you haven't been tied to the only thing they fear—Pack. When you get home, vampire-proof your house," Cisco chimed in, making a good point. "You should have run, witch. Now I have to drop you off all bloody and broken. You're making me look bad."

"*You* should have had a better plan," I replied. "You make yourself look bad. So far, all of your plans have gone tits up. Perhaps strategizing isn't your thing? You seem like more of a roll-the-dice kind of guy."

"I get the job done," he replied. Cisco's phone buzzed, and he frowned. "Playtime is over. It's time to go, little red."

"Damn," I mumbled.

Sofia pulled me into her arms. "You've got this, Ailis. I have faith."

"Thank you. If this was my last hunt, it was terrifying and so bloody cool," I said, swallowing a rock in the back of my throat. "If I don't make it, watch over Miguel. Don't let him go off the deep end, and don't let anyone hurt him while he's wounded. I don't know how challenges work in Pack, but please do your best to keep everyone back until he doesn't willingly want to die."

"I give you my word. We'll have his back until he's well again," she answered. "Get going before Caser comes asking questions."

We left Sofia to make sure the fire didn't spread and burn down the neighboring fields. I limped, picking rocks out of my hands, and Cisco shuffled a little louder than he had before. We were both bleeding and smiling. We walked through the trees toward the truck, making a whole world of noise. Cisco whistled, and I hummed. Whatever the end of the night brought, I'd got one more adventure, and it was a hell of a rush.

"Thanks for this, Cisco. It was horrible but fun," I said as we cleared the trees. "I don't want to ever do that again."

"Eat them?" Cisco laughed as we got back into the truck. "Do you know how gross that would taste? Vampires are essentially dead. It would be like eating a rotten body you found at the dump."

I shrugged. "It's the first thing that came to mind."

He started the truck and turned us around. "Are you sure about this?"

"About what? Meeting Caser?"

"I know that if you shift, it's law to put you down as humanely as possible, but say the word, and we can leave," he said. "We can hide you until we can figure something out. We have cages that can hold you if you shift. You won't hurt anyone, I swear."

"Who is this 'we' you're talking about? You and Miguel?" I asked.

"And Sofia," he answered. "She's ready to rock. Just say the word."

"I heard Miguel when I was tossed out of the house. He knew you were bringing me here, didn't he?"

"Just in case you wanted an out, that's all."

I reached over our hunting bag with a soft smile. "This is what I want. I mean, I don't want to die, I don't want this to be my last day, but I won't spend a single day as a beast that needs to be caged and hunted. I don't want to kill innocent people because I was too scared to face the music. If ever I got out, Cisco, I'd hurt people. I'd rather die."

"Fuck, I hate this shit," he finally said and cleared his eyes with the back of his hand. I ignored the tears. "If you change your mind, call, and we'll come."

"Thank you," I replied.

"I'm sorry this happened to you," he said, grabbing my hand. "I wish I could take that night back."

"I know, but it's okay," I whispered, wanting to take away his guilt more than I wanted to fix my own self. "It's not your fault. It's not anyone's fault. No one meant for this to happen."

"Just the same. I'm so sorry."

The drive to Caser was short. He had been a few fields over, waiting in the middle, in the box of his truck. I was relieved to finally be here, finally see what fate had in store for me, but sad the trip hadn't felt like an eternity the way waiting for Christmas morning always felt like forever. I unbuckled and blinked away the prickles starting. I chewed my bottom lip and worked up the courage to get out of the truck.

"Thank you for bringing me and for the final hurrah," I squeaked out. The dam finally broke, and I covered my face while I cried into my hands. "I'm scared. I don't want to die."

Cisco jumped from the truck and came around to the passenger side. He pulled me into his arms and hugged me as I sobbed. He didn't need to say anything for me to feel how brokenhearted he was for me. His chest shook against mine, his misery mixing with my own. I could hear him whisper a prayer and finally step back. Caser stood at my front and took over.

"Goodbye, Cisco," I whispered and walked from him into the arms of Caser. I looked up at Caser, whose eyes were as glittery as my own. "What happens now? Do I get tied up or something?"

"No, nothing like that. Now, we have a drink, toast to those who were foolish enough to stand against us, curse those who will try again and give thanks to those who are waiting for us on the other side."

From the corner of my eye, my cat darted through the field. Seeing him settled something broken and scared inside of me. If I left the world tonight, I wouldn't go into the pits alone. Somehow, that felt less scary. I watched my cat chase what I assumed to be a rat as I followed Caser to the box of his truck. In the back, pillows and blankets, a cooler and two fresh beers were waiting for us.

"You look like you've already been to hell and back," Caser said as he jumped onto his tailgate. "You stink like vampires, housefires and cooked skin."

"I burned myself with my cross and charm necklace," I answered, pulling down the neck of my shirt to show a freshly blistering wound.

Caser laughed. "Rookie mistake."

"How was I supposed to know? That was my first time. Cisco's only advice was not to get bitten, and I think Sofia thought I could actually fight my way out of a wet paper bag." I climbed into the box of the truck beside him, wincing when I took my seat. "Sofia chucked me out of the house. The landing wasn't a pleasant one."

"I didn't hear you scream for help, and I was close by, listening," he replied.

"You could have come to help us, you know, if you were close enough to hear me," I said and took a long swallow of a frosted beer. I moaned when the coolness hit my throat. "Oh, that's good."

"You didn't need my help. Sofia and Cisco rarely need a rescue. They work well together," he replied.

"No, they don't," I laughed. "I saw you having to hose them down and break them apart a half dozen times in one day."

"That's love for you."

"Oh, *ohhh*, I didn't know they were an item," I answered.

Caser laughed. "You humans and your understanding of love is so basic. Love is a spectrum. It holds many meanings. They aren't an item, to my knowledge, but they do deeply love each other. When Sofia returned to us, after she was…wounded, we'll call it, Cisco took on every challenge that came her way. He cleaned up her messes and helped her heal the best he could. You remind me a lot of her, when she came back from her own version of hell. Cisco cared for her in ways the rest of us couldn't reach her."

"Bloody vampires," I said, my voice holding the heat of a thousand suns. I didn't know exactly what happened to Sofia, but I knew enough stories of what they did to their victims to know she took a trip to hell.

"Not a single blood den stays standing in our territory because of Sofia and Cisco."

I leaned back and winced again. "I think I have road rash on my back."

"You do. Half of your shirt is missing," he laughed and clinked his bottle against mine. "Here's to hoping you can complain about your bruises tomorrow."

After a few minutes of silence, I finally broke the tension. "I lied to you, Caser."

"About?"

"I remember almost everything the night I called the hounds," I replied. "Bits and pieces are still missing, but the important parts were always there."

"Why the lie?"

"I think because I was ashamed. I called them to kill people. I felt good about the way they died, and I didn't want anyone to know," I answered and felt my face flush at my admission. "I didn't want to answer any questions in case everyone found out."

"And why the sudden truth now?" he asked.

"Like everyone else, I felt the need to absolve myself before I kick the bucket," I answered. "I figure, if I'm going to die tonight, I might as well give you a chance to ask those questions. It's not like there's anyone else alive to answer them for you."

"I only had one question," he replied. "I've never come face to face with a hound. What was it like? I mean, I'm sure it was terrifying, but what did they feel like? How did your soul feel, not your brain and its fear, but your soul?"

"Terrifying doesn't cover it, Caser. My brain and my soul were scared shitless. This wasn't my first time seeing them. I had the pleasure before…in hell. They used to pace the halls, smelling each cage. Sounds weird, but I think they were constantly checking to make sure those in the cages were supposed to be there. Every now and again, they'd double back on a new soul. Sometimes they'd howl at each other, and the soul would be gone in a matter of minutes. Other times, the soul would stay. The one I met the other night, I had met before," I explained. "He'd walked by my cage and found me on my hands and knees. I never stopped praying, not once. But I never prayed for my release. I always prayed to the man upstairs to forgive the next person who made the same mistake as I had. I offered myself to take whatever punishment they had coming, if they got sent down here. I mean, I'm already there, I'm already suffering. What's a little more, ya know?

"The day I met the hound, I was on my knees praying. He stopped in front of my cage and poked his nose in. Weirdly, down there, they never scared me like they did up here. I reached forward and touched his muzzle, kind of like what you would do with a dog. The moment my hand rested on him, my entire body relaxed. All the pain was gone. The screaming around me ended. It was peaceful and finally quiet. It felt like everything had frozen in time. I leaned forward and rested my forehead on his snout. And when he pulled away, I thanked him for that tiny sliver of sanity.

"That was the last time I was tortured or even saw a demon. When he came back, my cage was lowered to the floor and opened. He was the one who sensed two souls in my body, and the moment he had, he made sure I was protected. I was released from hell. Well, technically, I was chased out. I woke up in the hospital, stinking of hell and cooked skin. I met Miguel soon after. The demons weren't too fond of letting me go and kept coming back to take it out on my hide."

"Miguel told me about your first few years out of hell," Caser replied.

"The other night, when the hound touched me, I had the same peaceful feeling all over again—like hell could open up, and we'd be okay. I was scared, but I was calm in knowing that the hound would save Anna if I died."

"Those are mighty big shoes to fill when it is my time to guard the gate," Caser said, clearly proud of his people.

"Don't forget who you are, Caser, when you are walking the halls down there. Not all who enter are evil. Some were foolish, some were broken, some didn't mean it," I said and rubbed the center of my chest as it tightened. "Although I went to hell and still smell of the cursed place, I don't think I'm evil. And when I go back, I don't think I'll be evil then, either."

He nodded. "We can smell evil, Ailis, and I've never once smelled it on you."

"The hound told me something interesting," I said, and Caser's face lit up as though I was about to tell him a secret. "He said magical users are pulling their energy from hell. Cisco said something similar earlier today. Do you believe that?"

"Yes. Where else are you getting that kind of power from?"

"Huh, looks like I was the last to know," I replied, and he laughed. I looked out over the field. "In case I don't get to say thank you. If I shift, thank you for taking my life."

"You're welcome."

"I have a gift for you," I said.

He laughed. "No one has ever given me a gift for taking their life."

"It's information," I said. "Anna will become Lycan. The hellhound said he could smell it on her. I don't know when, but I thought it would be easier to prepare if you knew for sure."

He sighed. "I figured as much. It has never skipped a soul in my line, but I had hoped it would skip her. Thank you."

I had thought about whether I should tell him or not and had decided at the last minute that the information wasn't mine to keep. I didn't want her to be out with her friends and shift. It's hard enough being a teenage girl in high school. She didn't need to add that to her list of unexpected reasons no one liked her. He looked saddened by the news. I could understand why and didn't blame him in the least. The world of a Lycan was a hard one, so it seemed – a constant fight for survival. Her life would be harder for who Caser is, the Lycaon of the Los Luna Pack. I didn't envy him or Anna.

"You're welcome."

"Thank you for what you did for my people, Ailis. There were many others who could have fallen prey had you not put yourself at risk. My daughter would have died if it wasn't for you," he said, squeezing my hand. "I'm sorry the payment you've received is this."

"You know what they say, 'a witch in time saves nine'. I wish I was number nine in this case," I answered with a smile. I'm pretty sure that isn't how the saying goes, but it was mine now. I glanced up at the sky, waiting on the moon to hit its fullness. "Have you done this before? Sat with someone while they waited?"

"Unfortunately, I have," he replied. "Before you ask, none of them survived."

"You're the first one not to shovel hope and faith down my throat," I replied.

"I have hope, I have faith, but I'm also pragmatic."

I nodded slowly, suddenly uncomfortable. I rechecked my watch and fiddled with my beer bottle. Caser opened the cooler and passed me a small white box with a bakery emblem on the top. I opened it up and grinned. Red velvet cupcakes with more icing than I had ever seen before.

"Miguel had these made for you," Caser said. When I pulled one out, he huffed a laugh. "It looks like you'll die of diabetes before anything else can kill you."

"Rolling into hell on a sugar rush," I said as I took a giant bite of cupcake. I groaned as I chewed. "Dear God, this is good."

I sat with Caser in the box of his truck, eating cupcakes, and waited. Time stood still for some moments and sped by in others. Time was weird like that. The bad moments seem to come faster and stay longer than the good. He told me stories of his childhood, Mexico and things that were pretty. Anna was his favorite thing to talk about. His face lit up every time he said her name. Her mother had died during delivery. When I asked about Evette, he shrugged and said not every choice had been a good one in his grief. He and I had more in common than I thought. I had made some bad choices during my heartache over Miguel. Sure, none of them resulted in a psychopathic serial killer, but who was I to throw stones?

Caser spoke about those who had died like they would be at Pack tomorrow. He talked about them like they were still alive. In a way, they always would be, through memories and stories they told. He told me things about Miguel that made me understand a little more of why Miguel was who he is. Caser loved Miguel like a brother. They all did. They were Pack. They were family. They weren't as horrible as I thought. Though, I'd keep one eye open when I was around them, if I lived to see more days. I was accepting, not stupid.

"I'm scared," I said, staring up at the sky, watching the moon make its way to its peak in the center.

"It's okay to be scared, Ailis. But I'm right here. You're not alone, and if this is your end, you will not face it on your own," Caser replied.

He held my hand and changed the subject each time I got too scared or wanted to make a break for it. As the time neared, he broke out the expensive champagne. We drank it out of the bottle until I puked twice, and the full moon came. He walked me into the middle of the field, and we braced for it. Caser wore shorts and an old shirt, in case he had to shift, in case he had to kill me. I held his hand and told him I forgave him as my watch vibrated.

"It's okay, Caser. I forgive you. When this is over, forgive yourself." My words came out in a rush. "Please tell Miguel I love him. I always have, and I always will. Tell him I'll see him on the other side."

"Sofia was right. You don't like to deliver your own messages." Caser smiled and pulled me into his chest. "Tell him yourself."

I jerked back and quickly ran my hands down my body. "I didn't...but...I'm still me."

"All you, all witch," he replied.

I hadn't shifted. I hadn't changed, not even a tickle. I cried with relief. His Pack streamed from the tree line. Miguel was the first to reach me. His smile, the one I had learned to love and trust, made me cry a little harder. He held me as we both laughed and let the fear and happiness fill the night sky. I dug my fingers into him, making sure I wasn't dreaming. He was real. The moment was real.

"Oh, God, you're real. I'm not... I'm alive." I breathed him in, filling my lungs with the smell of home.

"I'm real, Lish. It's okay. You're okay," he answered.

"Why are you here? You're not supposed to be here," I finally asked, realizing Miguel was in a field he wasn't supposed to know about. I looked to Caser. "You all swore you wouldn't tell Miguel. He was at the blood den, too."

Caser grinned. "You should know by now, Ailis, you can't trust monsters. They lie."

Cisco grabbed me from behind and spun me around, picking me up into his arms. "Trapping you and caging you would have been a real bitch. You're a crafty little witch."

"What?" I laughed.

"It's why we're all here. If you shifted, we were going to trap you and cage you on the nights of a full moon until we could figure out how to cure you. There might not be a cure today, but Miguel is stubborn enough. He would have found it," Cisco answered. "And before you point out the flaws to my ideas, this one is on Miguel. I tried to get you to agree, but his plan was to kidnap you."

I hugged Cisco. He felt like family. I hadn't had one of those in a very long time, and it felt like how I remembered. Secure. Loved. Like any monster could come knocking, and my family would stand between me and the beast who had my ticket. It felt right, standing in a field on a full moon with a group of mythological creatures, having staved off another dance with death. In the distance, snarls and wails from shifters who couldn't fight the pull of the moon. Sofia's smile told me she recognized a few of those howls.

"What would you have done if you couldn't find a cure?" I took a seat beside Miguel in the box of Cisco's truck.

"I wouldn't have given up," he answered, wrapping his arm around my shoulder. "I planned on keeping you in one of the cells we use for new shifters whenever the moon is full."

"That doesn't sound like a good way to live," I countered.

"Neither is death and hell, but you sign up for that every chance you get," he replied. "I watched you at the blood den. You went back in for more, knowing full well you might not come back out, and you're going to complain about spending a night in a metal room?"

"Every time we get together, somehow I end up in a prison," I teased. "I could get used to it. I suppose."

"A lot of Lycan, when they first learn how to control their wolf, are caged until they're no longer a risk to others. Rather than call it a prison, think of it as ethical captivity," he answered. "I've spent plenty of nights in there, myself, unable to control my wolf after I returned to Mexico."

I tucked myself into Miguel's shoulder and listened to Cisco tell the story of us kicking down the door of a blood den. He left out the parts where I was terrified and screaming. When he got to the part where I told them to eat the vampires, everyone cringed, and I blushed. Cisco had this way of telling a story that made you want to lean into it. He spoke with his hands, and his face held every emotion possible. I had seen it drain of everything a few times before, but tonight, it made me grin ear to ear and laugh along with him.

"Don't worry, Lish. Damon over there puked the first time he killed a bloodsucker," Miguel joked.

My body stiffened. *Damon.* Without losing the smile on my face, my eyes tracked the wolf in question. He stood on the edge of the group. He wasn't outside of the Pack, but he didn't move any closer than he needed to. He was a wolf with a tightly held secret. He was to be Evette's number two, the man who helped kill the weakest members of Pack.

"Damon, I don't think we've met," I said, sliding from Miguel. I kept my breathing steady but could feel my aura shifting. I wondered if Pack could tell. Cisco coming to a stand as I walked by him told me that perhaps they could. The Pack opened for me to walk through. Damon took a step back, and I shook my head. "There's nowhere you can run, traitor. You helped Evette sell out your people for power and status. You helped her take us all. I'll see you in hell."

"I did no such thing," he replied and did what guilty people always do. He tried to run. Damon turned only to find Sofia and Miguel standing behind him. He turned back to me, glaring.

Caser tapped me on the shoulder. "I think it's time for you to go, little witch, unless you want to see how a wolf really loses his head?"

"You knew?"

Caser smiled. "By the time I found out, Anna was already missing. I couldn't risk making a move and having them kill her. We were going to wait for you to return home before dealing with our little rat problem."

I contemplated staying to watch. Did I need another nightmare? No. But would this even give me so much as a bad thought? Likely not. Before I made the decision to pull up a chair for the show, Miguel stepped to my side and grabbed my hand, pulling me away from the group.

"Let's not ruin the night with death. You've escaped your own. Let us leave the night with that being our last thoughts."

I snarled. "Fine. But next time I'm tortured because of a traitor, I'm watching them get their just desserts."

"Next time?" he asked.

"Every time you need help, I end up bleeding for it. I'm simply planning ahead," I replied.

Miguel led me to his Jeep, the Pack howling at our backs. From learning I can't fly to keeping my skin out of hell to a traitor losing a head, the night was more than I had risked hoping for. The drive back to Miguel's house was what he had promised it would be. All my worries slipped out the open window, replaced by excited laughter. I survived an absolute nightmare. When we pulled into his rocky driveway, I stared out through the window and finally let the night pour from me. The adrenaline had worn off, leaving me with bitter truths that were hard to swallow.

"It's okay, Lish. It's over. You're okay." Miguel pulled me from the Jeep into his warmth and walked me to the front door.

I shook my head. "It's not just tonight. I feel like two years just came crashing down on me. The feeling of relief that I'm not alone anymore... I have people now.

It feels like I have a family again, and it terrifies me. I'm scared I'll wake up tomorrow, and I'll be alone."

Miguel opened my door and scooped me into his arms. "You were never alone. I've been over your shoulder every single day. There is not a corner in your world where I wasn't standing, watching, protecting you from any who came."

"I love you," I whispered as I tucked myself into his arms. Every fiber of my being knew, in the time it took to breathe him in, he was always *the one*, the only one. From the first time I saw him, kneeling at the foot of my hospital bed, praying for my soul all those years ago, my soul knew he'd always be there. "You don't just smell like home, you—"

"*Feel* like home," Miguel finished my sentence. "It's been that way for me since the day my wolf met you." His grip tightened as he spoke, and I quickly brought my face to meet his as he leaned down. He kissed me deeply, with an edge of hunger. "I've always loved you."

Carrying me, Miguel made it ten feet through the front door of his house before his hands roamed my body, and his mouth ate the passion from mine. The heat from his body rose with each step as I grabbed for his neck, squirming under his touch. Even with my body pressed against his, it wasn't close enough. I twisted around in his arms until my legs were wrapped around his hips. I pulled my lips from his for just a moment and pulled at his shirt, jerking it out of his pants and over his head. His mouth followed mine closely, reluctant to break the kiss. I tossed his shirt to the floor and sighed at the waves of heat that poured from him. When I pulled back to meet his eyes, I understood why. The browns of his eyes had turned orange and yellow. I could feel his energy shifting from passion to wolf. My breath caught in my throat, and my pulse raced in my throat. The instinct to run twitched my thighs to the ready.

"You're safe with me," he said, his voice deep and penetrating.

Rather than pull away, I kissed him. I trusted Miguel with my body and soul. Even as the room filled with energy, prickling up my arms, and the same smell I had experienced with Sofia, I knew I was safe. I was always safe with Miguel. "You don't have to hide from me anymore."

Miguel dropped to his knees, cradling my body from the fall, and placed me on my back. With a grin I knew all too well, he inched my pants down, hissing as my thighs were exposed. A small groan slipped from his lips when he gripped my panties. Slowly, as if torturing himself, he pulled them off, one leg at a time, letting my legs fall open. Leaning back, digging his fingers into my thighs, he moaned.

"You're already wet," he muttered, licking his lips. He ran his hand down my front and dragged his fingers across my slit, pulling me open. I twitched at the sensation. "Oh fuck, I need to taste you."

I opened my legs wider, inviting him to touch and taste as we both needed. His hands shook as he positioned himself onto his stomach, holding my legs open. I had expected to be devoured. Instead, his touches were soft, slow and deliberate. Miguel inched forward, breathing me in, filling his chest with the scent of my excitement and need. He kissed my thighs. Small licks slowly made their way to my core while his middle finger ran over my center, slowly bringing my pleasure to the surface. Little by little, he coaxed my orgasm to the surface. I closed my eyes, gripped his hair, and pulled him into my body.

"You're mine." Miguel growled his words. His energy pulsed out of him, filling the room with static and heat and a familiar smell that said just that. I was his. He was mine. Hell or high water, we'd go down together.

"Mig…" I whispered, the words getting lost in the pleasure. Grinding my hips and groaning out his name, my orgasm washed over me in a flood of relief and emotion. The world went quiet, and all I could hear was his voice and encouragement.

"Come for me, Lish," he commanded, around his licks. The energy pouring off of him was tangible. It rolled over my skin, bringing every inch of my body to life. It felt like a small current coursing through my middle.

My back arched as the final waves washed out, and my body slowly floated back down. Still riding the high of release, I pulled myself to my knees beside him, pushing him onto his back. Like Miguel, I needed to taste his pleasure. I pulled his pants open and jerked them down enough for me to free him. I swallowed him down and moaned around his cock, as he tried to wiggle free of his clothes. Twitching under me, he gripped me by the hair and moved against my mouth, growls filling the room and vibrating into my bones. He inched two fingers inside of me and pulled out the last of my pleasure with force. I screamed my orgasm around his pumping hips, and as my body turned to jelly, he moved me to the back of the couch, leaning me against it. Gripping the sofa, Miguel pumped himself down my throat, ripping the fabric and pulling it hard enough to break it away from the frame. I wouldn't be surprised if the world didn't hear him scream my name through the night.

He pulled my head from his hips up to his mouth. I reached between us and positioned myself over him. With a groan shared, I pushed myself down, grinding back and forth. I gripped him by the hand and yanked his head back, licking his throat while I rode him. I listened to his breathing pick up and felt his pulse race under my lips. I sank my teeth into the side of his throat, and he screamed my name. He held on to my hips and rode from beneath me until his orgasm rolled through his body and washed out in thrusts that echoed into the night. The energy poured out of his very soul, covering me in the smell of wolf and Miguel. It clung to me like sweat. For the briefest of moments, I could feel the warmth of fur, hear nails on hardwood and feel the vibration of a growl against my bones.

Miguel collapsed under me, pulling me to his chest. His heart hammering, his body on fire. "Lish…"

"Jesus," I whispered back, my breathing rapid and my heartbeat matching his.

"Are you okay?" he asked once he was calm enough to speak again. "Did I hurt you?"

"No, I'm good. That was amazing," I replied, pulling myself off his hips and to his side. "I could feel your wolf, his energy. It was incredible. Were you always holding that back, or did I just not notice?"

"Holding back," he replied. "He's always been here, but now, I don't have to hide him. Now, I can share all of my aura with yours."

"When you said I was yours, it felt different."

"You've always carried my smell, but now, you carry his and the smell of my Pack. His marking is a sign of protection. You are mine, but you are also his. You, little witch, are ours. Pack."

I turned to face him and smiled. "Ours. I like that."

He kissed my nose and helped me to my feet and into his arms, my legs around his waist. Miguel carried me toward his bed, kissing me along the way. His fingertips brushed across my nipples, sending me arching into his back. My mind raced, my need unquenched. I could do this with Miguel forever. My mouth was insistent, motivated and greedy. I ground my core into his waist, silently begging for pressure. Miguel reached under my thighs, finding me wet and wanting. The moment his fingers brushed my bundle of excitement, I moaned into his mouth. My back hit the door while he fumbled for the knob, pressing my back into the chilled hardwood. I let him go and braced myself on the jamb. I positioned myself for Miguel to penetrate me but got a shake of his head.

He pressed his mouth to my ear. "Patience, Lish."

"Please," I whispered back.

"Let me love you as I said I would," he replied. "Let me touch you as I used to. Let me taste you, tease your pleasure to the surface. Let me have tonight."

"You can have them all, Miguel, all of my tonights and tomorrows."

Miguel's body shuddered at my words, sending his fingers back to exploring my core, where I was soaked and quivering. My moan ricocheted between us as he slid two fingers inside. His touch was gentle but firm, but it wasn't enough. I needed more, so much more. I loved how his hands and mouth felt on my body, but I needed to feel him. My eyes watered with desperation. I moved my hips back and forth against his hand but felt empty.

"Please." My voice came out in a long groan. I grabbed his hair, forceful, making my point known. "Miguel, fuck me."

"You're so fucking greedy. I've always loved that about you," he replied behind a grin.

The movement below me was the only indication I had before he pressed the swollen head of his cock against my aching core. Although he knew from my begging and whines how badly I wanted him, the groan that escaped my lips the moment he pushed himself inside me was answer enough. Inch by inch, he filled me, and my nails down his back said it was exactly what my body and soul craved.

Deep, insistent thrusts brought his name to my lips in between heated breaths while my back bumped the door until he was fully sheathed inside. I whimpered as he tightened his hands around my hips, his pace matching my hunger for more, as I became lost in a delicious haze of ecstasy.

"Close," I moaned. "Don't stop."

Miguel rocked deep inside, and I closed my eyes, disappearing into every sensation, memorizing every breath he took as he navigated my body and need with expert precision. Days and nights, years together filled with passion, made us experts in touch, in knowing exactly what the other needed without a word exchanged. Goosebumps covered my skin, and small twitches began as my pleasure built. His speed and force shifted as I grew closer, and it wasn't long before I detonated around him. I screamed his name, my voice cracking and my nails claiming flesh. He sank his teeth into the crook of my neck, biting down and drawing out my orgasm, claiming me, marking me as his.

With his teeth firmly in place and my orgasm gripping him tight, he pulled me into his chest and set a pace that cracked the door jamb. Long and hard thrusts echoed down the hall, coupled with the hunger that poured from our throats. My moans were joined by his. I wrapped my arms around his shoulders and held on while Miguel searched for his own orgasm. A delicious symphony played — of love, need, greed, hunger and absolute pleasure, ending with the sound of our bodies joining as he slammed into me. His body tightened around me, holding me firmly in place. I knew he was close. He had always been the type to orgasm multiple times, whether he came or not.

"Fuck...Lish...close," he groaned between labored breaths.

I grabbed his hair, holding on to the force of his need. "Come for me, Miguel."

His scream, which I felt deep in my bones, shook the paintings on his wall. Pushing himself as deep as he could go, Miguel's orgasm shook us both to our cores. His entire body shuddered as he pressed me into the door, holding me firmly in place. His orgasm kept his knees locked, and his face pressed into my neck. His heart hammered against my chest while I ran my hands through his hair, slowly bringing him down from his pleasure high. Rather than setting me down, Miguel staggered back, found the doorknob, and carried me to the shower. On his lap, on a bench, hot water pouring down my back, we relearned how to breathe again. Our hearts pounded against each other as the rush of the night washed down the drain. The hot water stung my back. I had almost forgotten about the road rash and hunt with Sofia and Cisco. Wrapped in Miguel's arms, it was easy to forget about what haunted us in the night. I didn't care what lurked in the shadows, I had a wolf standing at my side, and he was fucking vicious.

True to his word, Miguel loved me until the horror of facing fate had washed to the bottom of my soul and didn't needle me into a panic. We spent the rest of the night on his front porch, watching as the sun climbed into the morning sky. We filled the darkness with stories and the important parts of life we had each missed out on. Cat lounged on his lap, to Miguel's surprise and absolute love. He had never owned a cat. Apparently, they weren't a fan of wolves. The blasted creature could love a Lycan but won't cuddle a witch unless her life was falling apart.

Miguel told me stories of the original Lycan and how each territory guarded mankind. Miguel and Caser would spread the word to the other Packs around the world that holy water may help to clean the virus from the system if gotten to the wounds in time. I wasn't able to say holy water was the cure, but a little hope went a long way. When I suggested they come out of the doghouse for the world to see, it would save more lives, Miguel thought my head injury wasn't yet healed, and I was speaking nonsense. Who was I to argue? We all had secrets we lived and died for. Some just had more bystanders who would die for those secrets than others. If he had suggested I tell the world just how deep my magic was, I'd say he had too much wine. I wasn't willing to bring the wood to my own witch burning any more than he was ready to explain his people to the world.

Chapter Thirteen

I got the vacation I went to Mexico for without a clock ticking in the background, signaling my coming doom. The Pack paid for me to stay at my resort for another week, and I spent it side by side with my cat and Miguel. It didn't come close to an adequate payment for my troubles or the near-death experiences. I sent Caser a bill for my consultation fees. He sent me a photo of his middle finger and the invoice for Nichole's funeral. *Touché*.

The night before I left Mexico, I went to the Pale House with Miguel and Cisco. The walk down the stairs didn't feel as intimidating, but I still stopped and checked to make sure each level had an ax and a way out. I may not have been on their hitlist, but things change in the blink of an eye, and people die even faster. Tonight, we attended an official service for those who had died at the hands of evil. Being the one who killed the people responsible for their deaths had helped keep me from another round with a Lycan.

Although I wasn't on the menu for the night, I stood on the outside of the group, my eyes scanning and my hand in my pocket, where my knife sat. They were all thankful, polite even, but it was awkward and uncomfortable. I'm alive and well, but I didn't feel like I came out winning. I'd be leaving a part of my soul on the hills of Mexico, chunks I'd cut off to survive.

When I had said I didn't need a victory parade, I meant it. I didn't like the attention or the hugs or lifting my glass to those who were dead. The stories they shared would keep each of the fallen alive, but all it did for me was remind me that I couldn't save everyone. It was harder knowing that the victims died because they wouldn't give up any of the good guys. They willingly went to their deaths to protect innocent people. Watching Pack mourn for those who met senseless deaths, it was hard to still call a Lycan a monster when they were better than the rest of us, who killed each other over inches of land. When it became too much, I slinked out of the door and cried in the stairwell. Sofia joined me, and we cried together. Our emotions came from different places, for different reasons, but the pain in our souls was the same. Both of us mourned for what was taken from us all, what we'd never get back and what we gave away to live another day. Sure, we weren't best friends, but I added her to the list of people I'd always go back for. And really, in a world like ours, having someone who would challenge a beast from hell to keep you alive was pretty damn good.

* * * *

Climbing onto the plane to leave left me feeling torn between two lives. My life back in Van was waiting, and I wanted to feel home again, but I was leaving the life I wanted and the person I had always considered to be my home. With promises and tears, I left Miguel at the airport. Leaving him for a second time hurt something deep inside me. Like the first time, I didn't want to go. Fear needled me and followed me all the way back home. I was scared I wouldn't see him again, and it had been all for nothing. But if I knew one thing about Miguel, he always followed through with his word. He said I'd see him again, and I had to trust that I would.

When I got home, I missed the heat but welcomed the rain. The drive from the airport was cold and gray and everything I had remembered it to be. The first pothole the taxi hit reminded me of taking the backroads with Cisco and Miguel, and I settled into my seat with my cat on my lap, sounding like he was being dragged under the car. He wasn't a fan of being in a cage. I didn't blame the beast. Neither was I. The cab pulled into my drive, dumped my luggage and sped away. Almost an hour of listening to a hissing cat had worn on his very short nerves.

My lights were on, likely by Samuel, who knew I wouldn't want to come home to the darkness. Sitting neatly at the top of my front stairs sat a basket. I paced at the foot of my stairs, debating if I should look at it or not. Finally, holding Cat under my arm, I inched up the stairs and took the card from the cellophane. It was a welcome home card. It was signed *Noire Lune Pack.* I dropped the card and jumped off the stairs. With my cat tucked under my arm, from the safety of my shed, I called Miguel. I thought the basket might symbolize my last meal. He calmed me down, laughed at me and said it was customary to welcome a friend of Pack. I didn't want to be their friend, but it was better than the alternative — being an enemy. It was an invite to meet the Pack, I was informed. Miguel told me not to worry. The local Pack would wait for him to arrive before forcing a meeting. *Great.* I hoped that meeting would go better than the first time I had been invited to meet Pack in Mexico. Someone had lost a heart at that one.

Within an hour of walking in my front door, with a basket from a group I couldn't mention and keep my head, Samuel called. My conversation with him went as I thought and ended as I knew it would, with his reminder that I was loved deeply, me crying and a promise of a hug I had been looking forward to. We would get together once I was settled. My aversion to learning real magic had come to an end. I couldn't keep skinning my soul off every time something powerful came my way. If I wanted to play with the monsters, it was time to learn how to put them down when they got too rough.

"I can't lose you, Ailis," Samuel had said, and that's all it took for me to agree. I felt his love all the way to my soul and couldn't thank him enough for loving and helping me in the only ways he could and I'd allow. After his stern talk and his prompts to bond closer to my cat, I turned my attention to the little spitfire. It was time to train my little trash goblin. When I had tried before, Cat had ignored me hard enough for me to doubt my own existence and worthiness. Every book I've read told me one thing. I don't own a cat. The cat owns me. I've never read anything that's been closer to the truth.

After a bloody showdown, my blood and the veterinarian's, I learned Cat is a girl. She still has no immunizations and, now, no veterinarian. The vet couldn't get near her and suggested I put her down. In the opinion of the doctor, Cat is feral, and there's no hope of domestication. I took Cat home and won't be going back. Of course, she isn't a domesticated cat. She's mine, after all, and I'm far from domesticated myself. She has a tattered ear and a tail that's been broken twice. When she eats meat, she drags it into whatever room I'm in and eats in front of me, staring me in the eyes. *Evil little thing.* We're cut from the same cloth.

I've done as Samuel has suggested. I now talk to my cat as if she's a person. I tell her my problems, and she leaves the room like I've bored her with troubles she cares nothing for. *Yep, we're the same.* If anyone ever walked in while I spilled my beans to my cat, they'd think I was crazy. Then again, if anyone ever walked into my house, they'd be too dead to tell anyone about my conversation. One of us would get them before they made it out of the door. But that's the price of crossing a little witch and her familiar.

A week after I got home, a package from Mexico arrived. The return address was Sofia's. The box was heavy enough that the delivery driver needed a trolley to get it out of his van and into my living room. Inside the box was the cast iron spelling pot I had told her about, with a little note.

The monsters don't get to win this time, not when you have people who have your back.

Although this pot wasn't your mother's, I hope this brings you the same joy it brought her. You deserve to have happiness. You deserve to have good memories.

Cisco sends his love. He wants me to tell you that he chipped in twenty bucks, and that you're welcome. What an ass.

Much love,
Sofia.

I laughed at the note and taped it to my fridge. The caldron went onto my kitchen table, right in the middle, where I could look at it every day and remember I had people who cared, people who wanted me to find joy in the world. That was worth more than the spelling pot. Immediately, my cat took up residence in the pot.

On nights when the darkness became too much, Miguel was a quick call away, and I made that call every night and a few times during the day. Some scars wouldn't heal without the gentle touch of someone who loves you. And some nightmares didn't go away until someone reminded you of that love. I had forgotten how Miguel could settle my soul in ways no one else could. Whether it was because he was Lycan and guarded souls or because he loved mine, broken pieces and all, I didn't care about the reasons anymore. He loved me, and I love him, and for once, I didn't have a desire to pick at something good just to see if it would break.

Of all the things I've learned, suffering has been the biggest lesson. We all suffer in life. Not because we are bad but because we don't realize when and where we need to stop being good. As they say, the road to hell is paved. But if you were lucky enough, you'd find someone who would put the pieces back together and didn't care about the taint on your soul. We all carried stains. The trick was finding someone who loved the imperfections as much as the perfect parts.

Want to see more from this author? Here's a taster for you to enjoy!

The Cursed: Payback's a Witch
L.A. Kennedy

Excerpt

I fumbled in the dark, my hand clearing off the edge of my nightstand as I searched for my phone. The shrill ringtone made me hate the cursed thing even more than usual. It was becoming increasingly difficult to ignore the world when it sat in the palm of our hands. I inched my eyes open and had to blink several times before they'd focus on my clock. Three in the morning was not a favorable hour to call me, especially not when I had been awake until well after midnight, pacing, scared of my nightmares. I usually slept with the ringer off on my landline and cell phone, but lately, I had kept them on. I didn't like missing a call from Miguel. He and I talked every night, me when I was going to bed and him when he was getting up for the day. The time difference worked for us. It was the distance that killed me. Mexico was a five-hour flight from home, but it felt like a world away.

Thinking it could be Miguel on the other end of the line, I reached for my phone with a smile. The call display showed an unprogrammed number. The only people who called in the middle of the night were people who wanted help moving a body and strangers who needed worse things than an alibi. In my world, it was a coin toss. Would I be digging holes for a friend or finding myself in one? That was the question of the night. Hell, that was the question of my life on a daily basis.

"Who is dead or dying?" I asked, my voice still half-asleep. I envied people who could sound pleasant and professional no matter the day or time. My assistant, Philip, was like that. But, to the chagrin of everyone lucky enough to call in the middle of the night, I wasn't that person. I was a goblin when I woke up and sounded every bit the part.

"Dr. Kyteler?" a man asked.

"This is she," I replied. "And who am I speaking to?"

"This is Father Michael from the Holy Rosary Cathedral."

"What can I do for you, Father Michael?" I asked and sat up with a groan. Churches didn't ring anyone's bell in the wee hours without a hellish reason. My money was on a loose demon or a possessed person that the church had tried and failed to exorcise. I knew the route to most churches by heart for both reasons.

"We need you to come down here," he answered.

"Right now? Do you know what time it is?" I yawned around my words. "Unless someone is dying, call my office during business hours and schedule an appointment with my assistant, Philip. If it is demon-related, there are plenty of agencies with people on shift right now, just waiting for calls like this. Hell, call the cops. They have licensed witch practitioners currently on the clock and only five minutes from you."

"Ah, yes, your assistant, Philip. He is already here," he replied. "One of your students, Ruby, I believe her name is, is at our church. She called Philip when her circle was damaged. He told her to get onto holy ground. He's mentioned a demon may be near."

"Come again?" I jerked, a jolt of panic starting and pulled back my covers. "Where is Philip?"

"Talking to the police," Father Michael replied. "We contacted them when Philip became hostile."

"Hostile?" I questioned. Philip was the last person to become aggressive. He might be built like a brick house and could probably bench press one, but *hostile*? That would be the last word I would use to describe him. "What exactly did he say to you that made you feel like you needed police assistance?"

"He began yelling at us and manhandled several of my staff, attempting to pull people into the church," Father Michael replied. "He is locking people inside."

"Shit. He wasn't being hostile, Father. He's trying to save your life." I got out of bed, swallowing my urge to yell at the poor man. "I'm getting dressed. Tell me what happened and what's going on so I know how to prepare." I put my phone on speaker and changed out of my pajamas. I pulled on my usual black outfit. It hid the blood better. I didn't own a lot of color for that reason. Between my pitiful idea of fashion and being covered in blood at the end of most days, black was my go-to.

"Ruby summoned a demon and, from what I've overheard from your assistant, the demon was too strong for her. She contacted Philip for help. He told her to get to holy ground, and Holy Rosary was the nearest church. That is all I know."

"Fuck," I whispered, checking my phone and seeing three missed texts from Philip, telling me about Ruby. He'd call me if things went south. This had gone so far south that it scraped the gates of hell.

"Do you know where she summoned the demon?" I asked.

"Cathedral Square, across the road," he replied.

"Is that ground not consecrated?" I asked.

"We try, but no, not all of it," he answered. "The kids today make it difficult for us to maintain."

"Is the demon still there?" I asked as I put on my shoes.

"Excuse me?"

"Father Michael, is the demon loose, still held in the circle, or on the part of Cathedral Square that's blessed?" I sighed through my nose, trying to calm down. When he didn't answer, my temper flared. "Do you see the goddamn demon or not? He won't be hard to miss."

"Um, I don't know," he replied. "I can go find out."

"No, don't go looking for it," I replied and shook my head. Who in their right mind would go poking around with a demon potentially running around? "Did you listen to Philip? Are you inside the church or outside?"

"Outside."

"Idiot," I muttered. A man of the cloth should know better, but they rarely did. Until they came face-to-face with a demon, they never truly believed. But by then, it would be too late, and now his ignorance would make him a tasty snack for the cursed. "Get back inside and tell the others to do the same, including the police you called. You need to ask Philip if the demon is secure or…" I was cut off by screaming in the background. The sound raised goosebumps over my entire body and answered my question. The demon wasn't contained. "Get into the church. Get back on holy ground! Run, Father Michael!"

I bolted for my front door, grabbing my black duffle bag along the way. Inside was my usual gear for exorcisms, demon cleanup and witch gear. It was nothing more than a bag of hope and prayers that I wasn't too late. From the screaming on the phone, I'd be later than I'd want to be. When it came to demons and devils, I was always too late. People were always dead before I was called.

I jumped in my car and fired it to life. The moment it started, my Bluetooth connected. The screaming played from all speakers as I drove downtown. It would be a twenty-minute drive with my hazard lights on. Aside from emergency vehicles and the odd car from shift change, the roads were dead at this hour. It being the witching hour was the only saving grace. Fewer people on the sidewalks would mean fewer people would kiss death's lips this morning when the demon did as demons do — kill everything with a soul.

I hit the Number One and gunned it. I knew the highway like the back of my hand, having traveled it daily for years. I kept eyeballing my GPS to route around any overnight road construction and emergencies. When the phone disconnected, I called Philip. I hit redial twice before he picked up. Screaming ate up the start of the conversation, not his, but everyone else's. Philip was in the middle of chaos but maintained his cool. Not much scared the guy, which is probably why he was the only assistant I've had who hadn't quit within weeks. My last assistant had put in their notice before they'd even been in the system. She had said it was uncomfortable to be alone in the same room as me. My soul made her feel sick to her stomach. *Judgmental much?* To be fair, my soul made me sick, as well. Slicing it to bits in hell had left a few scars and tainted the air with the smell of brimstone and matchsticks.

"What the hell is going on, Philip?"

"Ailis!" Philip yelled into the phone and didn't bother with niceties. "There's a demon loose. I don't know where it is. There are people dead in the streets and screaming coming from everywhere. Dear God, it's bad. Father Michael is dead. He wouldn't come inside." More screams filled my ears. "Oh, Jesus. Where are you?"

I liked that he didn't bother with a long explanation. "Ten minutes out. What am I walking into?"

"I don't know. I'm in the church, and I'm not sticking my head outside to find out," he answered. "When I got the call, I came straight into the church. I only went outside to get everyone else to come in. They wouldn't believe me when I told them all hell was about to break loose. The church wouldn't send anyone to check the circle. They didn't believe me. They called the cops, thinking I was a nut job. Most of them are still outside, Ailis, along with a few squad cars of cops. They don't have a witch practitioner with them." Philip paused, screaming for someone to step away from the door and finally cursed when they left the church.

"No one will listen to me, Doc. People are coming and going as if they won't die out there. They think they can run faster than a fucking demon." Philip yelled again at someone else about it being their funeral. The phone rustled, screaming about lawyers and lawsuits, and a door slammed shut. "Get the fuck in the corner, you idiot. You can't sue me if you don't have a head in the morning. You can't outrun a demon, for Christ's sake. If you open that door again, I'll let you go." Philip pulled the phone back to his mouth. "I left Mannix a voicemail, hoping he was on duty and could help, but he hasn't called me back."

"Jesus. If they want to dig their own graves, it's on them. It's your job to keep yourself out of hell, not to make sure everyone else sees tomorrow," I replied and tried to think through the problem. "I'm almost there, Philip. I can see the police lights. Stay inside. Get to the head of the church and hunker down. Do not step outside until it's over. I don't care what you hear, if someone tries to leave or if the demon makes promises, do not inch a single toe out of that church."

"Same drill, different monster," he replied. "I'm sorry I didn't call you sooner. I didn't know Ruby actually summoned anything until I was already here."

"It's okay, Philip. Who would have known this would happen?" I replied. I would have known the minute she called me, but I assume the worst in people. People make bad decisions every day, including myself. But telling him he missed something wasn't going to help the situation. "Did Ruby tell you who she summoned? Higher level or lower? We may need backup."

"Yes, a lower-level demon, some murderer from a couple decades ago. She said she called him to ask questions for a paper she's writing for her sociology class."

"What?" I couldn't keep the surprise from my voice.

"She wanted a better grade, she said," he replied. "She thought if she had a few quotes from the main man, in his words, it would increase her grade percentage. She was showing off, and now we all get to hear and see the psycho firsthand."

"I hope it was worth it."

"She's dead, Ailis. The thing came up the church steps and took her. She thought she'd be safe as long as she was on the property. I tried to pull her inside, but the thing yanked her right out of my hands," Philip answered. "So, no, it wasn't worth it."

"She knew the rules, Philip. All my students do. This isn't your fault. She called on hell, and hell answered as it always does," I replied and slammed my brakes, squealing to a halt. "Do you have his name?"

"Theodor Black," Philip replied. "That is the name on the top of her notes."

"Fingers crossed, that's his real name. *Hey you*, doesn't have the same quelling power," I replied. "I'm here."

"I'm sorry, Doc. Be careful. I'll clean you off the road when it's over," he said, and I disconnected the call.

I parked a block from the church and grabbed my duffle from the backseat. I pulled out my bible, holy water and bags of herbs to have in my pocket for quick reach. I hung a hex bag around my neck and climbed out of my car on wobbly legs. Even if the demon was lower-level, I didn't like touching hell in any way. When you dipped your fingers into the pits, they always reached back. I cursed out loud. My aura had just fully healed from Mexico, and I was about to skin off a chunk because someone wanted a better grade. I once said mankind would be the doom of us all, and tonight was an excellent example of how quickly we were nose-diving into the end of days.

Up the road from my car bodies were sprawled on the ground, staining the slushy end of winter. The blood was brilliant under the street lights. It looked like the church had just gotten out with the number of people in the streets. People were strewn like trash, dead and twisted. I blinked away fresh tears and said a quick prayer for their souls. I scanned the area and cursed at how wide of an impact the demon had made so far. Demons were like bombs, killing everything for blocks wherever they first landed.

I pulled my bag on like a backpack and jogged up the road, feet already wet from melting snow, while I sliced the palm of my hand. It wouldn't take a lot of blood, just enough to drip a circle. At the intersection between the church and their small park, I stopped in my tracks. Ahead, in front of the church, stood the demon in question. I swallowed my scream. I might have the ability to send him back, but I was terrified.

The demon in question, Theodor Black, was somewhat clothed. Bits of old and stained fabric hung from his burned body. When he died, he had been burned, going into hell blistered and melted. He turned his scarred face to me and smiled. His nose was gone, leaving behind a raw hole. His lips, what remained of them, were thin and scorched. A shiver ran from my head to my toes. I swallowed my gag.

A thunder in the clouds rolled down the corridor, followed by a deafening silence. The nauseating stench of cooked flesh, decay and sin hung in the air like smog. The scent of burnt meat soured my stomach. With twenty feet between us, I was the only soul standing between his heaven and hell. His massive pupilless eyes stared at me with agonizing spite that made my throat flex, trapping a scream before it could break loose. I whispered a prayer that if I died in an intersection of downtown Vancouver, I'd take this beast of hatred and hell with me.

I dripped my circle of protection. *Tutela*, I thought, feeling my magic take root and flare my circle to life. I breathed in through my nose and out my mouth, clearing myself of the nausea that rolled through my gut when I pulled energy from my aura. My vision pulsed with my newfound headache. I wiped my sweaty palms on my pants, cleaning away the stickiness of blood and power that coated my hands.

The air in my circle carried the smell of my mother, ozone and matchsticks. The scent grounded me. I opened my bible to a random page and began to read out loud. It didn't really matter what I read as long as it came from the one book they hated the most. When I read from the bible, it caused the demon pain. When Miguel read from his worn bible, his absolute and unwavering faith could send a lower-level demon back to hell without the need for all the blood and pain I was soon to experience. I was a work in progress when it came to faith. Miguel was born into the arms of grace and had never once faltered from his beliefs.

My words carried on the breeze like whisps of a flame, starling the demon. A shriek escaped from his scarred mouth in unfathomable agony. Holy words were another fire for the creature to burn in. He turned his body fully toward me. His jerking steps gave me enough warning to know I'd be leaving pieces of my skin on the concrete. He wasn't just contained violence. He was hurried energy and death, waiting to pounce. He was on a clock, and he knew it. The demon became more and more menacing with every tick on that clock. He gave me his back and took two more steps toward me.

"Stop!" I screamed at the top of my lungs and held out my hand toward him.

The demon tried to move again and failed. I frowned. I should not have been able to control him without using his name unless I had been the one to summon it. I released tendrils of my aura, tasting the world around me. I could sense an imprint of myself in the air, following it back to a ruined blood circle in Cathedral Square. Someone had used something of mine to help invoke the summoning circle. I pulled my aura back in, along with the whisps of power rolling off the demon. Why borrow energy from hell when it was free for the taking?

I would have one chance at this, and it would be painful. I dripped more blood into the circle around me as the demon walked toward me. His hairless head jerked and twitched as if the movements had caused him pain. The skin on his neck stretched until even I winced at the strain. He tilted his head to the side as if surprised I wasn't running like the others had. My feet shuffled as I forced myself to remain in one place.

"Ailis Petronilla Kyteler." His words hurt my ears. It was like nails on a chalkboard and raked down my nerves. "There is a clock on your back. Tick-tock, bitch. We will never stop coming for you. You have something of ours, and we want it back."

"But *your* time is up today. Mine is not," I replied. "If you all didn't want me to learn the secrets of hell, you shouldn't have spoken them so loudly near a witch not fated to be caged just yet."

"Your time will come, and next time, you won't walk out," he answered.

"Same song you all sing," I answered. "Now, we can do this the easy way or the painful way. You can leave willingly or with force. You've had your fun, got your pound of flesh, and now it's time to go."

His laughter was all the answer I'd need.

"Theodor Black," I called his name, and the first flicker of fear flashed across his melted face. I braced myself for what would come next. "*Propello*, Theodor Black. I command you back to hell, to never return again."

Energy burst from my soul, and I was thrown across the pavement on my back. I was thankful I had left my duffle on, or I'd have left chunks of flesh on the road. The demon was on me before I had even seen him move. He was ready for the fight, but I was prepared for the attack. Demons did nothing the easy way, and the lower-level ones always kicked up a storm on their way home. His nails dug into my arms as we struggled. He sat up and raised both hands, bloody claws waiting to come back down, slashed through the air. I smashed the bottle of holy water into his side, the glass cutting us both. I flipped him off and watched him twist on the ground like an eel in a pan. The smell filled my nose, and I vomited on top of him. Burned flesh, demon or not, smelled the same to me—absolutely disgusting. With fresh blood dripping down my arms, I rolled to my feet and stepped around the screaming demon, dripping my blood on the ground. With a final drop of blood, I closed the circle, holding him inside.

"*Dominus reget me*," I started my prayer in Latin. "The Lord is my shepherd."

"I will see you soon," he said, getting to his knees. "You're cursed, just like the rest of us."

"Until then, go to hell," I replied. I gave him the middle finger while I sent him back to hell. "Don't forget your party bag on your way out." I held a ball of taint in my hand and blew it over him, sending him away. "*Discedite!*"

"You bitch!" The demon screamed as my taint coated him.

"Just returning a gift," I said and closed my eyes for what was yet to come. I loved and hated this moment. Sending him home would kick my ass all over again.

The energy of sending a demon back to the pits hit me in the chest like an invisible punch. Blurring my vision, seeing through my aura, I watched the ground open up and dozens of hands pulling the demon back down to where he belonged. The earth closed up as if all was right in the world, with a burst of energy that sent me flying. I was tossed a few feet away as the circle holding him came down, and the air filled with the stench of hell. The moment my body hit the ground, I was thankful I couldn't breathe. I stared up at the morning sky with little sparkles dancing in my vision. The sounds of the surrounding screams finally faded, replaced with ringing.

Philip was the first to lean over me. "Relax, take a few breaths, and you'll be right as rain."

I closed my eyes and calmed my body. This wasn't my first rodeo, but I still fought the panic as if it were. Slowly, I breathed in a few gulps of air and rolled onto my side, groaning. Around me, paramedics were checking on the dead. The only wounded person was me. Anyone else stupid enough to be outside the church was meat for the critters. Philip helped me to my feet and to the first ambulance. I tried to wave them off when they began cleaning my wounds.

"Don't bother closing them up," I said to the woman looking over my hand. "I'm going to have to open the wounds to clean them with holy water when I get home."

"Holy water?" she asked.

"Demon blood mixed with mine," I answered. "Between his cursed scratches and the wound on my hand, I'm in for a special bath this morning."

"Does it work?"

I crossed my fingers. "Most times, yes. The odd time, the victim waits too long, and the curse takes hold. It opens a door between the victim and the demon who infected them. After that, they need a full exorcism and a few weeks living on holy ground, drinking holy water like Gatorade."

"I got you, Doc," Philip said, helping me off the rear bumper. "I'll give you a ride home for your special bath."

I took his arm, but before we were inside my car, my skin crawled like ants dancing across my flesh. I turned and scanned the crowd of onlookers who had arrived just in time to see the bodies but not become one of them. Most people were wearing work clothes and holding briefcases and handbags. Others were hitting the gym or heading to the seawall for their morning jog. But in the back, there were three people who stood out like sore thumbs. Two men and one woman, and they had my full attention. For one, their outfits said they didn't walk to work. For two, they didn't care about the bodies on the ground, like everyone else. Their eyes were on me and not the excitement of the morning. Before I could point them out to Philip, they walked to the black town car at the end of the block and pulled away. Something told me I'd hear from them again. They would either try to hire me or would ship me Bibles for my damned soul. I had received enough holy books in the mail that I could set up my own shop. Philip had used them to make a throne in the front room of my office and propped plants up with the rest. It gave our demon wing the kind of flare it needed.

Philip sat me in the passenger side while he took the driver's seat. He cranked my seat all the way back and pulled away from the nightmare that had been our early morning. Philip rambled about Ruby while I tuned him out. I cared about the reasons, but not while my body throbbed because of them. It bothered me that Ruby was dead, along with two dozen other people, but I wouldn't allow myself to think too long about it. This is what happened when inexperienced people dabbled in dark arts. Rule number one, when summoning demons, never call something you cannot put down on your own. If it takes more than you to call it, leave the cursed thing alone. And it was clear Ruby hadn't been able to summon on her own, given the carnage left on the streets. I was sad and angry. Ruby had paid for that lesson with her life and caused the deaths of innocents while making that choice. She would wake up in a cage for that. And as angry as I was with her, my heart hurt knowing exactly where she'd end up. I pushed the image of hell, the cages and the intersection on Richards Street from my mind and stared at my hands instead. The cuts weren't severe or life-threatening, but they did leave me with the risk of demon blood in my veins.

About the Author

L.A. Kennedy, beyond the story…

L.A. Kennedy is a Canadian born writer, living in the ever-growing city of Vancouver, Canada. Here, she spends her days getting lost in the beauty of reading and writing. L.A. Kennedy mainly writes fictional books. And can be found researching myth, folklore, and everything in between, with a special interest in edge-of-your-seat paranormal romance. L.A. Kennedy can be found behind a mountain of books, on any given Sunday.

L.A. Kennedy's writing credits include two hit series that mix mystery, horror, paranormal romance, fantasy, and intrigue.

L.A. Kennedy loves to hear from readers. You can find her contact information, website details and author profile page at https://www.firstforromance.com

Home of Erotic Romance

Sign up for our newsletter and find out about all our romance book releases, eBook sales and promotions, sneak peeks and FREE romance books!